MW01125506

Jonathan R. Miller
Copyright © 2017

www.JonathanRMiller.com

contents

FLORIDA

If it were possible, I would gather the race in my arms and fly away with them.

-Ida B. Wells

the city of fort mose

"I tore the trees out by their roots," I say to the woman. "It was the only way I could make room to build."

The woman's name is Harmony, a misnomer if there ever was one. I know this because we used to know each other. We are strangers now, but there was a time in our lives—back when we were just a couple of lost children living homeless next to a creek in Northern California—when we would have called each other friends. Best friends, even. But so much has happened since then. Honestly, I'm not even sure how we ended up in this situation—standing together under a dim orange streetlamp in the parking lot of my apartment building in the city of Fort Mose. The last time we were together before tonight was fifteen years ago. I'd hurt her that night; I hadn't injured her permanently, but I'd caused her immeasurable pain. I was seventeen at the time.

Seeing Harmony the way she is now, as an adult—the pale, blonde, lanky thing in front of me—is a stark reminder of just how many years have passed me by, and how blindingly fast. I suddenly feel as though I just woke up on a train and discovered that I missed my stop, that I slept all the way to the end of the line.

"It wasn't just some trees, Tallah," Harmony says. "It was a forest—a national forest. Don't trivialize the damage you did."

"I'm not trivializing anything."

"You are," she says. "Your words are. And your attitude speaks volumes."

"I'm just stating facts."

Harmony snorts. "I've got some hard facts for you, Tallah. You single-handedly ruined a thousand square miles of old-growth longleaf sandhills and flatwoods that had gone untouched by mankind for over a century. You changed the landscape of the country itself. For the worse."

"How about unembellished facts."

"You think I'm embellishing now?" Harmony asks. "All right. Tell me, then. What are the hard facts?"

"Look around you for a second," I say, gesturing toward the vegetation surrounding the parking lot. Even in the darkness I can see the limbs of countless trees bending lithely in the wind; I hear their leaves rasping against each other and it sounds almost like rainfall. "There's still life here. I only took what I had to take, and we built Fort Mose in the empty space. As the city went up, we replanted as much as we could."

"That's bullshit," Harmony says. "Be honest—what you did was plunder a piece of land that didn't belong to you. It was basically a lesser form of rape."

I pause for a moment.

This hippie bitch is unbelievable.

She has the same smattering of freckles that I remember, the same Pippi Longstocking pigtails, the same wide-eyed expression, the same penchant for self-serving exaggeration. Other than the expensive-looking peasant blouse (undoubtedly made from the finest hemp) and the crow's feet at the corners of her eyes, she hasn't changed a single bit.

"So you think I'm a rapist because I uprooted some trees?" I ask. "I violated your Mother Earth—that's what you think?"

"You clear-cut a fucking forest," Harmony says. "You single-handedly changed an entire ecosystem. And you managed to set back race relations by at least a hundred years while you did it."

I laughed out loud. "So I ruined race relations, too? Okay, Harm. Sorry for rocking the boat."

"You think this is funny?"

"No. I don't, actually. I think it's tragic," I say. "What I did, and what drove me to do it—both are tragedies in my mind."

Harmony shakes her head. "But no regrets, right? It sounds to me like you'd do it all over again."

"For my people?" I suddenly smile a little bit—I'm not really sure why. "For my people, I'd level every one of your precious forests.

I wouldn't give it a second thought."

Harmony's mouth drops open half an inch—apparently my uppity attitude has finally rendered her speechless. With that empty expression on her face, she reminds me even more of the child I remember from more than a decade ago, the child who would get high at any opportunity and then sit outside on the bank of a stream, staring vacantly into the running water as though she couldn't comprehend how it moved so sinuously, how it filled up the hollows, how it carved out its own space.

"They're right about you, Tallah," she says. "I have no idea how you can be so laid-back about the chaos you've caused. All the wrong you've done."

"And I have no idea how you can care more about the lives of plants than the lives of people."

"People?" she almost spits the word. "People are the ones—look, you name a problem anywhere on the planet, any problem at all, and ninety-nine times out of a hundred, there's a human being behind it. The way I see it, people aren't the ones who need protection in this relationship."

"My people do."

"Your people?"

"Yes."

"Well, that's always been your problem, Tallah—one of the biggest ones, anyway," she says. "You've never been able to embrace a one-tribe, one-love perspective on life. You're always turning everything into you against the world."

"The world is against me."

"Come on, Tallah. You want to talk about embellishment. That's really what you think?"

"No. That's not what I think, because that would imply it's a theory or an abstract idea," I tell her. "I'm talking about what I know through experience. What I've lived through."

Harmony says something that I don't quite catch, shakes her head in obvious disgust, and turns her back on me. She shoves her hands into her pants pockets and starts walking toward her car, parked at the far end of the lot.

By all appearances, the smug bitch is leaving—leaving my apartment complex, leaving the city of Fort Mose itself and, hopefully, leaving my life for good—and while I'm relieved to see her go, I can't keep quiet as she makes her exit.

"Don't ever come back here," I call out to her. "I don't want to see your face in Mose again, Harm."

She doesn't respond.

As I watch her unlock the door to her car and climb into the driver's seat, I notice something protruding from the back pocket of her jeans.

It looks like the polished wooden handle of a sheath knife.

It looks familiar.

• • •

Most of what I know about survival, I learned young.

Too young, maybe—I'm not really sure anymore. The older I get, the more I wonder which is better: to learn the art of survival when you're still a child (which means you lose a part of your childhood in the process), or to grow up blissfully unaware of the dangers all around you, and run the risk of never growing up at all. I don't know what the right answer is. But I do know one thing—my father would most definitely advocate for the former if he were still alive.

It's been twenty years now. Twenty years since Mr. Isaac Williams was shot between the shoulder blades by a San Jose police officer as he lay face-down on the floor. Twenty years that I have been, for all intents and purposes, alone in the world, left to fend for myself. Even after all this time, I can still hear my dad's voice inside my head telling me that I shouldn't complain about my past, that I should be thankful for all the hard lessons, for the opportunities to grow stronger (because that's what pain really is, isn't it: an opportunity to grow stronger?), and that *I've learned exactly what I need to know to keep myself alive, nothing more or less.*

Even to this day, I miss that bullheaded man, but I have to admit: I don't always miss the hard-nosed brand of wisdom he used to dish out.

In any case, for better or worse, I learned how to take care of myself when I was still young. In fact, I would say that my education in survival really started with the children's books about nature that I used to read in elementary school—books that told wild stories about the primitive dynamics of the hunt. Most of the stories showed the world through the keen, glittering eyes of the hunter (which was instructional in itself), but a few of the books shined a light on the miraculous survival adaptations of the hunted. I could relate to both perspectives, to be honest with you. Even when I was young, I understood that I had both the hunter and the hunted inside of me. But even so, I always seemed to gravitate a little bit more toward the stories of the hunted—the stories of lives lived under constant duress, lives filled with near misses and great escapes, lives that would most likely come to an end between a set of powerful jaws, among rows of ivory teeth.

So, as a child, I would read and read and read. Like a girl possessed. And as I got a little bit older, I learned that there are certain animals that manage to keep themselves alive out in the wild, against all odds, by doing something called *advertising unprofitability*. Basically, these animals put up a damn convincing front. They might mimic the sounds of more dangerous creatures like rattlesnakes; or they may wear markings on their backs that look like wide, haunted eyes; or their entire bodies may be colored misleadingly—*wrongly*—so as to appear distasteful or poisonous; or they may make their bodies appear much larger than they actually are. These animals stay alive, not necessarily by being the baddest of the bad, but by giving the impression that they're more trouble than they're worth—which may actually be true in some cases, of course, but the point is that it doesn't *have* to be true.

All that matters is that the predator is convinced to turn his hunger elsewhere, to move along to the next unfortunate soul in line. And this is exactly what "advertising unprofitability" really means for these animals: *to be so convincing in your lack of appeal that you are passed over by those who would do you harm.* Which leads me to the single most important lesson I've ever learned about survival—to survive out in the world, you often need to become one of these animals.

• • •

I'm about to leave the city of Fort Mose for a little while. It isn't what I want to do, but the decision has already been made, and now I'm packing a carry-on bag to catch a flight out of Tallahassee. I'm not planning on taking much along with me. The thought of packing light is comforting for some reason. I think it helps me to believe in my heart that I won't be gone for very long.

It's difficult for me to put into words, the particular brand of *push and pull* that a place like Fort Mose can exert over a person. Mose takes hold of you by the shoulders and draws you in close like someone who loves you might do, and for a while everything feels good—just as you'd always imagined it might—but at the moment that you start to get good and comfortable with the proximity, to settle into that familiar fantasy, the city violently shoves you away. And here's the craziest part: *you know it's coming.* It's happened so many times before, but somehow you're still unprepared, still genuinely surprised when it does. The city repeats the same cycle over and over, back and forth, push and pull, almost as though the place is trying to shake some damn sense into you, to convince you once and for all that there's no such thing as the home you always used to dream of.

The morning after Harmony's unscheduled visit, I finally get around to packing for the trip, which is a good thing considering my flight is scheduled to leave out of Tallahassee in a few hours.

I start by tossing a pair of worn-out running shoes, a pair of socks, and a pair of jeans into the black duffel bag on the fold-out cot in my living quarters, which is essentially a small standard-issue dormitory room similar to what you might find on a university campus. (Everyone in Mose has the same basic no-frills setup, but the point is *everyone has it.*) I grab my toiletry kit—a zip-top plastic bag containing a toothbrush, a tube of toothpaste, a bottle of lotion, and some makeup—and wrap it in a long-sleeved black t-shirt, which I place on top of the jeans, followed by a grey hooded sweatshirt and a navy windbreaker because, as the saying goes, I'm headed to San Francisco in the summertime. Once I arrive at SFO, I'll get my hands on a car and drive a few miles north of the city until I reach Marin County, which is the location of my actual destination—San Quentin State Prison. A sprawling 275-acre correctional facility built on a peninsula jutting out into the north side of San Francisco Bay.

Getting to San Quentin will be the easy part of the plan.

The difficult part will be breaking into the fortified prison building, making my way past countless layers of security, finding my particular prisoner of interest, and getting us both out of the complex and back to Fort Mose alive.

I zip up the duffel bag, throw it over my shoulder, go to the entryway, and open the door, pausing as the heavy heat of Fort Mose nearly knocks me flat on my back. I catch sight of my face (rather, the face I've chosen to wear this morning) reflected in the mirror on the wall by the doorway, and I take a moment to check the position of my cheekbones, the smoothness of my brow, the angle at which my eyes are set, the fullness of my lips—all of which I've altered to the point that I no longer look anything like Miss Tallah K. Williams. I crafted the appearance I'm wearing—not surgically, but *gravitationally.* Using my God-given (?) ability to influence the flow of gravity, I modified everything from the width of my nose to the firmness of my jawline, all in an attempt to construct an alternate identity for myself—in this case, that of an undergraduate student at Florida State University named Gabriela Wyse (but "just Gabby" is fine). Gabby is one of several personas I've invented, each of which comes complete with a detailed backstory, elaborate mannerisms and speech patterns ("Remember who said it" is one of Gabby's favorite catchphrases), as well as an official driver's license and Social Security card.

The original idea of using gravity to alter a person's appearance came from my dad, but my particular execution of the idea—namely, the exquisite attention to even the smallest detail—is all me. I'd go so far as to say that I've mastered this part of the game; in fact, the only reason I even bothered to double-check my face in the mirror at all is that I don't feel so well today. I'm just plain *off*.

Some of it is that fool Harmony's fault—seeing her again after all this time has brought up memories that I'd just as soon forget—but I'm also suffering from a case of good old-fashioned shakes. This San Quentin plan of mine? It's got my insides twisted. Even with the considerable skills I bring to the table, I'm not sure that I can pull off a jailbreak at a maximum-security prison completely alone. But I'm committed to the idea at this point; I've made up my mind, and I have no intention of turning back now.

I take one last look at the contents of my simple room—the wooden chair, the halogen floor lamp, a stack of plain white note paper on the desk, the wall clock, the metal wastebasket, the air-conditioning unit wedged into an open window—before I head outside, locking the door behind me.

Wilting in the summer heat, I walk for about a mile up a road called Tallah K. Williams Drive, although most people in Mose call it *the TW* or, rarely, just *T-Dub*.

I don't want to come off as narcissistic, so let me be clear on something: I didn't choose this particular route to bolster my self-esteem or massage my fragile ego (any illusions I ever had about my so-called "celebrity" ended pretty quickly after the street signs went up).

No, I chose the TW for a much more practical reason: It's the closest thing we have to a "main street" in the city of Mose. Some people might even call it the *main drag*, in fact. Which is pretty funny, considering that some people also consider *me* to be the "main drag" of Mose, the one thing pulling the city and all its residents down like a heavy weight.

Speaking of which, I should mention a little bit about the history of the city.

My city.

We chose the name Fort Mose because it was the name of the first legally sanctioned free-Black settlement in what would eventually become the United States of America. The original Fort Mose was founded in 1738 and only housed around a hundred escaped slaves inside of its walls. The modern version of Mose—my version—is a proper city in terms of size, although in terms of organization, it would be better described as the largest communal living situation ever conceived in modern times, if not in all of recorded history. I founded the city only twenty years ago, but since then the population has ballooned to more than a million residents, roughly the same population as San Jose, California, which my father and I used to call home. When I first got the city of Mose off the ground, folks traveled here from almost every state in the Union, wide-eyed and bewildered, almost like foreign refugees. A stream of asylum-seekers. I took in almost everyone who applied, regardless of income, politics, religion, or education level. The only non-negotiable requirement for admission was this: you had to be Black. Period. I didn't care *how* Black you were or weren't. You just had to *be it*.

• • •

Duffel bag by my side, I sit on the bus stop bench and wait in the steaming heat for the 326, the only outside bus line that runs through Fort Mose.

It's not our only form of public transportation—we have a small fleet of shuttle vans that take folks around the city for a modest fare—but if you want to grab a cheap ride to somewhere outside the borders, somewhere like Tallahassee, this is your only option other than paying for a ride-service like Uber (taxis still won't come to Mose, and even if they did, they wouldn't come cheap). It may not seem like much, but it was pretty revolutionary when the deal was first made with StarMetro to provide us with an outside bus line. More than just a way to get from here to there, the 326 was one of the first tangible signs of the world's willingness to reach out and connect with us, the First Rebel City of North Florida. Prior to that, we provided pretty much every basic service to the population of Mose ourselves, with no outside government intervention. I'm talking about water, electric, garbage collection, septic service—almost everything a person considers a necessity in the United States of America, other than an internet connection. So when the 326 line finally came to fruition, it represented something monumentally important to the city: it was our first meaningful taste of acceptance. A reluctant, begrudging acceptance, maybe, but acceptance nonetheless. And maybe that's all acceptance really is anyway—an acknowledgement that something you hate ain't going anywhere any time soon, so why keep fighting it?

As expected, the people of Mose were happy about the 326 in the beginning. Matter of fact, I remember cutting a yellow ceremonial ribbon on this very bench in front of a crowd of a few thousand people when I was only sixteen years old. But once the bus service had been operational for a month or two, the hype wore off and folks started asking the type of questions that no one in leadership ever wants to hear: *What else is there? What is the next good thing coming?*

I check the time on my phone.
Shit.

The 326 is running behind schedule by around fifteen minutes, which wouldn't be a problem ordinarily, but my agenda at the moment—catching a flight to the Bay Area so I can break into a Class-A prison facility, stop an execution from happening before the clock hits 12:01 a.m., and escape with the (formerly) condemned—is anything but ordinary. I don't exactly have the luxury of wasting time.

I need to get moving.

The best transportation option—the one that I should have chosen in the first place—is to schedule a damn pickup from a ride-on-demand service. Normal people (rich, white) do this kind of thing all the time: They try to find the easiest way, the path of least resistance, and they often pay more than they ought to for the privilege. Right or wrong, I need to give myself permission to be normal for a few moments. Which means I need to find somewhere with air-conditioning so I can schedule a car to come pick me up while I sip a cool beverage at a table by a window.

I climb to my feet, shoulder the duffel bag, and make my way toward a coffee shop halfway down the block, passing by a few of my "constituents" along the way—a middle-aged man wearing a bright orange construction vest and concrete-spattered work boots; a group of girls who look like they could be in middle school; and an elderly woman with a severe stoop in her posture, shuffling along with the help of an aluminum cane. None of these folks show any signs of recognizing me, and I would be surprised if they did, because I'm not even *me* right now. I'm "Just Gabby" Wyse, a college student studying journalism at FSU. Young, gifted, and Black. Remember who said it.

When I'm a few yards from the coffee shop, I see someone else walking down the sidewalk toward me: a wispy white chick wearing a conservative blue frock and a wide-brimmed hat, like what a church-goer might wear to Sunday services. Even though Mose has been around awhile, the sight of a white person out on the sidewalks is still notable—it's not like white folks are forbidden from entering the city limits or anything, but they don't often elect to visit our fine community unless (a.) they are friends with a Black person who lives here, (b.) they are liberal and want to eat at one of our restaurants so they can seem super progressive, (c.) they are dangerous bigots trolling for Black folks to harass, or (d.) they are artists, writers, or singers looking to be "inspired" by some "real-life culture." For some reason, this particular white lady doesn't strike me as falling into any of these categories.

The woman looks up at me.

Shit.

It's Harmony.

I stop short. I can't believe what I'm seeing right now. I can't *believe* that this ninny has got the nerve to show her mousy face in my town again after what I told her last night. I thought I'd made it crystal goddamn clear that she was to stay the hell away from me and mine.

"Dammit, Harm," I say as she approaches. "What the hell are you trying to do? You shouldn't be here."

Without a word, Harmony lunges toward me with her teeth bared, and before I have a chance to react or to even think, she plunges a six-inch hunting knife into my stomach, burying it all the way to the hilt.

san jose part one: where (and when) it all started

When I was just an eleven-year-old brat with a head full of Havana-twist braids and a mouthful of crooked teeth, I took the life of a police officer only moments after he'd put a bullet into my father's back.

This is not me bragging. Believe me.

I'm not claiming that what I did to the officer was justified, and I'm not trying to gain anybody's sympathy (or respect) by bringing up the incident. It happened. Nobody else has ever found out—the blame fell squarely onto the blood-soaked shoulders of my dead father, which is what he would have wanted. But the fact that my involvement is a secret doesn't make it less true, less *real*, any more than keeping your actual age a secret will suddenly make you twenty-one again. It won't. You'll still carry the weight of all the years you've lived, same as you always have. The only difference will be that you'll carry the additional weight of a lie along with it.

I've never figured out why, but for some reason, a lot of folks seem to believe that draping a veil of secrecy over a bad deed is the same as draping a bandage over a wound—that it will provide some form of relief, speed up the healing process, and help prevent a permanent scar from forming—but there's no truth to those beliefs. None at all. A veil of secrecy is less like a bandage and more like a plastic bag over your head, tied closed at the throat. Both will keep out light and air, but only one will help you stay alive.

• • •

I had no known family besides my father, so after he passed away (and after I spent about a year confined to a group home), I started living on the streets of San Jose at the age of twelve.

I set up camp in the middle of a stand of cottonwood trees

near Story Road with a shallow brook called Coyote Creek to the west of me, a Walmart store to the east, a small amusement park called Children's Play Land to the south, and the I-280 interstate to the north, forming an almost perfect hollowed-out rectangle of urban desolation. At any given time, you could hear a rollercoaster car rattling along a set of old wooden tracks, a steady stream of customers pushing shopping carts across the sprawling Walmart parking lot, the endless droning of vehicles on the 280 South, and a quiet burbling sound coming from the creek waters, which was the only aspect of my new home that made it even remotely tolerable. Other than that, I was basically squatting in filth, surrounded by a collection of garbage, used drug paraphernalia, random household junk (including, literally, a kitchen sink), countless tattered blue tarps, and a few piles of clothing scattered across the ground near the sagging chain-link boundary fence. In short, it was a dump. A dump in the middle of a grove of cottonwoods with a gorgeous little stream running through it. But still a dump.

Dozens of homeless people used to camp in that spot (once upon a time, the locals called it *the Jungle*) until the police came in and started sweeping the area twice a month, rousting the inhabitants out of their sleep, passing out business cards printed with phone numbers for Social Services, and then razing the makeshift shelters with heavy machinery. By the time I started calling the Jungle my home, it was an abandoned wasteland. For better or worse, the place belonged to me.

It wasn't an easy life.

Not only did I have to meet my own existential needs as far as food, clothing, and shelter were concerned, but I also had to adjust to living every single minute of every single hour of every single day without companionship. Without anybody to crack jokes with, to argue (and make up) with, to listen to my stories, to run my thoughts by. I was never the type of person who needed somebody by my side around the clock, but after spending a few weeks living completely alone in the Jungle, I realized how deeply I missed having *somebody* in my life—a family member, a friend, or even an acquaintance from school. I didn't need a confidante as much as I needed a witness.

Someone to confirm through simple observation that I was alive. That *I was here.*

I could have easily left the Jungle and gone somewhere else, somewhere more populated. There were a dozen other places where I could have lived with random strangers, from homeless shelters to foster homes, and I could have tried to enroll in school, at a minimum. But I chose to stay where I was. At the time, I didn't know why (nor did I give it much thought, honestly), but in retrospect, I think there were a few potential reasons.

(a.) My recent mistakes—the lies I'd told, the bad decisions I'd made, the people I'd injured (or worse)—were weighing heavily on my conscience, and my "living situation" was an unconscious attempt to punish myself for everything I'd done wrong;

(b.) I was depressed, probably clinically, so the décor was a perfect match for my general state of mind;

(c.) I was testing myself—testing my ability to survive on my own, with nothing but the clothes on my back and the abilities I'd discovered only months earlier;

(d.) All of the above.

The answer was almost definitely "All of the above," but perhaps because I was searching for something positive I could use to distract myself from my own misery, I chose to focus as much of my energy as possible on the third option. Testing myself. Experimenting. Pushing my limits, just like my father used to do.

• • •

In the beginning, I spent most of my downtime sitting cross-legged in the opening of a dome-shaped camping tent I'd managed to salvage from the wreckage of the Jungle. I sat between the zippered flaps and stared vacantly at the creek water winding its way through the remains of the grove, a tangle of bristly reeds growing from its banks on either side, and I tried my best not to think about my past, present, or future. Sometimes I imagined myself as a silt-polished river stone, grey and shiny and smooth as marble. Or I wished that I could transform into the splintered trunk of a felled tree, with shards sharp enough to pierce through skin. I didn't want to entertain any real memories, apply my focus to my immediate surroundings, or make actual plans for what might come next. My only desire was *to be*—and even that desire was faint, like a light bulb on the verge of burning out.

• • •

To keep from starving, I stole whatever I could from Walmart shoppers as they slogged across the parking lot near closing time. It was wrong of me—even in the moment, I knew that. But if life in the Jungle taught me one thing, it's that hunger can change a person. Make them do unimaginable things. I once read about a wild rat snake that was found dead after swallowing around two-thirds of its own body. Becoming an infinite loop of consumption. If hunger could drive an animal to such an extreme, what chance did I have against it?

When I stole from folks, at least I was humane about it. What I mean is that I didn't hurt anybody physically or scar them emotionally. I was subtle—closer to a pickpocket or shoplifter than an armed robber. It worked like this: under cover of darkness, I would press myself against the chain-link fence on the other side of the creek and watch as a steady stream of exhausted-looking women (they were almost always women) trudged across the asphalt to their waiting minivans and SUVs. I would watch and bide my time. And once the crowd had thinned out enough to limit the number of possible eyewitnesses, I would search for the fullest shopping cart I could find, with brown paper bags piled high over the lip of the basket, and wait until the woman had turned her back to open the rear tailgate of the vehicle, and then—in the ultimate act of long-distance burglary—I would *reach out with my mind*, snatch one of the bags from the cart, and float it silently across the parking lot around an inch above the surface, lift it over the fence, and drop it into my waiting arms. Slicker than grease.

Of course, I had no way of knowing what was actually inside the bags until they'd reached me, and there were times when all I ended up getting was a bunch of baby clothing or gardening supplies or cans of spray-paint or a box of lubricated condoms, but most of the time there was at least something with caloric value in every haul: candy bars, mints, Doritos, a cold plastic bottle of Dr. Pepper, *something* that was edible. Sometimes I thought it would be simpler to try my father's old trick with the ATM machine—he'd mastered the art of forcing the cash dispenser to push out an extra handful of twenty-dollar bills—but I'd never practiced the effect myself, and in any case, that would have been *his way* of getting by. This was my way. And my way included its own bag of tricks, its own signature stamp at the bottom of every page. That was important to me for some reason—distinguishing my choices from his, drawing that line between us, and telling myself over and over that what happened to him was never going to happen to me.

But even I could see that there was a problem with my way, at least in this case.

I realized pretty quickly that—even at night—a parade of brown paper bags floating across a parking lot was bound to be seen by someone or something eventually, either by the people I'd stolen the bags from, other shoppers, or an employee who happened to check the video footage from one of the security cameras outside the building. Yes, I always waited until the parking lot was as empty as possible before moving forward, but I knew I still had a problem, and I needed to solve it as soon as I possibly could.

• • •

I woke one night inside the tent with something heavy pressing down on my chest. Cold, rigid, and coarse, like a cinderblock.

For a moment I thought it was something left over from a dream, but when I opened my eyes I saw that it wasn't; it was someone's hand groping my body. I couldn't see clearly in the darkness, but I knew the person was a man—his shape was a man's shape, his weight was a man's weight, his sounds were a man's sounds, his smell was a man's smell. Somehow, even at twelve, I knew about all of these things. Was this my instinct? A kind of predator recognition?

I tried to scream.

Almost instantly, I felt another, heavier hand pressing down against my face, covering my mouth and nose. I couldn't take a breath. The back of my head sank a few inches into the soft earth from the pressure; it felt like the beginning of a burial.

The man leaned in close, hovering a few inches above me. He said a few words that I couldn't understand because of the blood rushing in my ears.

And then he was gone.

Or, rather, I sent him away—with force. The man's body rocketed backward through the tent opening as though he'd been yanked by an invisible cord. He disappeared so quickly, with such force and finality, that I felt the wind of his departure against my damp skin. For a moment I felt as though I was lying inside of a space capsule with a breach in the hull, and someone had been suctioned out through the opening into an almost perfect vacuum, the coldest void anyone has ever known, and unless I held onto something immovable, I would be taken along with.

I spent the rest of the night huddled in a far corner of the tent, watching the zippered flap, terrified. The red nylon fabric drifted and ballooned outward like a ghost whenever the wind picked up. But the man on the other side of it never came back.

• • •

At the first sign of light the next morning, I wrapped one of the frayed blankets around my shoulders and crouch-walked slowly to the tent's opening. I cautiously peered out at the landscape of the Jungle, scanning the barrier fence (nearly buckled-over, as it always was); the scattered heaps of debris; the grove of cottonwoods with their long limbs bobbing up and down in rhythm with the ebb and flow of the wind; the twisting path of the creek through dense clumps of brittle reeds. I saw no sign of the man. If it weren't for the ache in my chest, I might have wondered if I'd dreamt the entire thing.

I stepped outside.

It was summertime still, but the weather was cold enough at that hour that I could see my breath spilling out in front of me like a string of devils leaving one by one. I pulled the blanket tighter, holding the ends together at my throat with a closed fist, and moved slowly to the edge of the creek, shivering.

I looked down.

There was a deep depression—a trench I'd never seen before—in the soft sand of the stream bed beneath the water, like a grave that was only partially filled in. It was roughly the size and shape of a sarcophagus—the size and shape of a man with his feet pinned together and his hands folded neatly over his breastbone. The sloped edges of the depression were slowly crumbling inward as the currents swirled wildly through the center of the pool.

It was a hole shaped like a man.

Staring into the water, I could only think of one thing—that the body of my attacker had created that shape in the sand. The man had landed there, in that exact spot in the creek. The only question in my mind was: had he gotten up again? Had he managed to scramble to his feet, sputtering, gasping and heaving water out of his air-starved lungs, and walk away?

Or was he still there?

Had the man's body been driven underwater, then forced even more deeply into the cold earth? Had his open mouth been flooded with heavy silt, like wet concrete poured into a post hole? Even now, were his eyelids still open, the sockets packed to capacity with deposits of thick black mud? And had he felt it?

I almost burst into tears.

Letting the blanket fall to the ground, I turned away from the creek, trudged a few yards into the thicket beside the tent, and picked my way through the underbrush until I found a long-enough branch among the leaf litter, at which point I dragged it—etching strange, jagged tracks into the earth behind me—to the riverbank. I hoisted the branch over the water, dropped the jagged tip through the surface, and started jabbing at the edges of the outline in the sand. Frantically breaking the boundaries, destroying the human shape. Blending everything together. As I worked, I considered stopping what I was doing and instead using the branch to probe the depths of the depression itself, to poke around in the riverbed to see if I could feel anything that resembled flesh and bone or maybe snag a piece of clothing, but I quickly pushed the thought out of my mind. I didn't want to know. With tears streaming down my face, I stabbed feverishly at the edges of the crater, muddying the waters with clouds of sediment until the form was unrecognizable. Every visible trace of the man had disappeared.

• • •

That day changed me.

I hadn't even had time to reconcile myself to the first life I'd taken more than a year ago, and now I suddenly had to come to terms with the possibility that I'd taken a second. I couldn't do it. I wasn't able. Instead of accepting the truth, I took both of these deaths—one confirmed, one highly probable—and buried them in a compartment of my mind, far away from my heart, where I hoped that I could safely experience them as dreams, as two horrific events that an abstract version of myself had gone through, but not the real me. I dropped both of these two deaths one by one into the coiled folds of my brain like grains of sand in a mollusk shell. And once they'd been embedded there, my grey matter began to do what I'd hoped it would: protect itself—protect *me*—by covering over these terrible events with successive layers of color, sound, light, warmth, *anything* to cordon off the contamination, to keep it away from the healthier parts of myself.

Over time, it seemed to work.

After a few weeks, the memories of the two men—old and new—became more and more distant, more removed from my day-to-day reality, as my mind continued to cover them with additional layers, smoothing, lacquering, polishing, and repeating the process. Over and over and over. It worked so well—this fledgling strategy to save my fragile sanity—that I ended up using it again. And again. And again. All through my life, in fact, whenever I was confronted with something that I simply couldn't bear, like coming to terms with my father's murder, the relationships that I'd destroyed, the lies I'd told, the crimes I'd committed, the abuse I'd suffered at the hands of so many others. I took all of those things and covered them, burnished them, and started over again.

I sometimes wonder: When I die and an autopsy is performed on my body—when my skull is sawed open and my brain is peeled into an untold number of plump, pinkish sections—will those two deaths come spilling out like two luminescent black pearls, clatter onto the stainless-steel dissection table, and roll slowly toward the center drain? Would a thousand other dark pearls soon follow?

The truth is that I've never forgotten those two deaths entirely. From time to time, I can still hear the final labored breath of the first man, his wide eyes just inches away from mine. And sometimes at night, I see the second man inside my dreams, rising slowly from the water in the darkness. Moonlight on his dripping bones.

san jose part two: harmony

One afternoon toward the end of my first summer living in the Jungle, I was sitting in the opening of the tent, killing time. Nothing special on my mind. Just chewing on a peanut-butter protein bar and staring at the asphalt surface of the Walmart parking lot through the chain-link fence, watching as the heat rose up from the blacktop in a swirling haze.

I suddenly realized something that I'd never understood before.

The air coming off the parking lot was blistering; I knew that. But it was so blistering that it was actually affecting the light that passed through it, causing the light to ripple and waver in front of my eyes—literally bending light. Creating a field of what I could only describe as *interference*. The heat was causing the light to quaver so wildly that every object on the other side of it was distorted, masked, nearly beyond recognition. The wheels of parked cars, yellow concrete dividers, the legs and feet of shoppers walking by—everything had been blurred almost to oblivion, like the faces of innocent people in photographs or videos shown on the news.

It gave me an idea.

• • •

I spent the next few weeks trying to figure out how to bend waves of light.

More specifically, to curve light around my body.

To make myself invisible.

I'd read somewhere once that *seeing an object* just means that the light coming from the object—whatever amount of light it reflects—makes its way into your eye. This would mean that to make an object (like myself) invisible, all I would need to do was make sure that no light could touch me—nothing ricocheting off of me, and nothing being absorbed. If I could make light bend around my body, then no one would be able to see a single trace of me, not even my shadow.

Unfortunately, becoming invisible was a lot harder than I'd thought it would be.

The main problem was my basic ignorance of physics: all I knew about waves of light was what I'd learned in the fifth grade—light waves are made up of particles called photons. And in my twelve-year-old mind, *particles* were just like any other objects (smaller, but otherwise the same, right?), which left me convinced that manipulating photons would be the same as manipulating any other physical body. Pebbles lining the creek bed. Ants streaming from a dirt mound. Tufted seeds drifting in the wind. As far as I was concerned, these everyday objects—the objects all around me in the Jungle, all of which I could successfully influence with my unusual abilities—were no different than particles of light in the heavens. The magical and the mundane: they were all the same. If it was made out of matter, it was controllable; that's how I saw things. I just needed to figure out how to apply my will effectively.

Thinking I had everything figured out, I stared up at the sky and tried my best to pick out individual photons from the atmosphere and bind them together into something useable—something I could guide, something I could *wield*. Sitting cross-legged in the mouth of the tent, gazing upward, with little more than rags covering my wasted frame, I must have looked like an absentminded daydreamer, a meditative philosopher-in-training, or a raging drug addict, depending on who was watching (if anyone even was). I didn't care. I sat and I sat, and I tried and I tried, but I didn't get a damn thing for my trouble other than a horrible twinge in my neck from staring upward for hours on end.

Eventually, I gave up.

I didn't abandon the idea of bending light, but I quit fooling myself into believing that I could wrangle photons out of the sky like a self-styled Cowgirl of the Stars.

Instead, since I didn't have a phone to my name, I decided to take a trip to the public library to figure out what I was doing wrong.

• • •

"What can I help you find?" the white lady asked me with her puckered, thin-lipped mouth. The nametag pinned to her blouse read "Anne."

Anne had been watching me from the moment I set foot in the King Library downtown, and she'd been following me like a bloodhound ever since I started browsing the nonfiction shelves about ten minutes ago. While she may have been concerned about me because of the ratty clothes I was wearing—I'm sure they looked (and smelled) like something that the walking dead might wear—I couldn't help but feel as though I was getting a little "extra attention" because of the skin I was in, not the rags.

"Excuse me?" I said.

"Can I help you find something?" she asked flatly. It sounded like a challenge, not a question.

I stared at the woman. Her dry, frizzy, grey curls piled up high on top of her head. Her watery, yellowish eyes.

"No," I replied. "Thank you."

"Are you sure?"

Am I sure you can't help me?

"Uh, yeah, Anne. I'm pretty sure."

"Because this isn't a hangout place," she said. "You know that, right?"

That settled it.

"Actually, I changed my mind," I replied. "You can help me find something. I'm trying to find myself a library—actually, any place, anywhere in the city, or anywhere in the country for that matter—with no busybody, gap-toothed, prejudicial white ladies walking around, trying to act like they want to help me 'find something' when all they're really trying to do is keep tabs on somebody."

The woman's eyes widened. For a brief (and painful) moment, she reminded me of Dr. Beedie, the head of the group home I'd left behind only a few months earlier. For all her many annoying traits, Dr. Beedie had been good to me—a royal pain in the ass, but still good somehow.

"Hello?" I said. "Can you help me find a place like that or not? An annoying-white-lady-free zone. That's what I need right now." I stared at her and grinned. It was my finest *fuck you* grin.

"Wow," the lady mumbled, shaking her head. "You sure are a little shit—you know that? You need to learn some respect."

"And you need to get out of my face, Anne. Nobody's asking you for your help. So scat. Be gone."

"Fine," the lady said. "That's absolutely fine. But you're wrong about me, just so you know. I'm not racial-minded. Not toward anything or anyone. Never have been in my life."

I laughed out loud. "Then why are you following me around?"

"Because—hello, welcome to the real world!—you're dressed like a homeless person, girlfriend. Just look at yourself," she said, wrinkling her nose. "And I wasn't following you, by the way."

"Yeah, okay. You weren't following me."

"I wasn't. All I was doing was *checking*. I do it with everybody—making sure they're in the library for the right reason, that's all."

"And what's the right reason, Anne?" I asked. "For example: I'm here to learn about how light works—is that the right reason for being in a library? Is that okay with you?"

Anne didn't answer.

I noticed that a crowd of six or seven people had gathered at the far end of the aisle to watch the conflict unfold, to be entertained, but I didn't give a shit about spectators or what they thought. Wearing my nastiest expression, I stared down every single one of them, moving from person to person, until I came to the final face in the group: a white girl around my age, a little bit older—fifteen or sixteen, maybe. Blonde hair in pigtails (dyed purple, natch), two nose rings, too much dark makeup. She was wearing what looked like a private-school uniform: a navy blue polo shirt, plaid skirt, and white knee socks.

The girl met my stare without even blinking. Her eyes looked like a doll's: long-lashed, bright blue, and glassy.

I felt my anger flare up like a grease fire. I couldn't help it.

"Bitch, can I help you with something?" I asked. The words came rushing out of my mouth before I had a chance to think.

I've always been that way—quick to plant my feet on the ground and assert myself—but not about every little issue that comes up. I don't usually flip out on a dime. Only when somebody tries to put themselves above me or use me as a stepping stone. I've never been able to put up with that, not even for a single second. And for some reason—in spite of the fact that I'd only been in her presence for all of thirty seconds—I felt like this chick genuinely thought she was better than me.

This was unacceptable.

"Hello?" I said, taking a step forward. "Do we have a problem?"

The girl didn't respond. She kept right on staring and even smiled a little—her own version of a *fuck you* grin—which only served to fan the flames in my chest, making them burn even hotter.

I didn't want this to turn into a situation in which I'd be forced to lay hands on another female, but I was prepared for it. I wasn't about to shy away. Even before I realized what I could do with my abilities—how I could use gravity to do almost anything, including to inflict pain—I was willing to engage physically with somebody if it was called for. You couldn't live at the places I'd lived, around the kinds of people that I had, without knowing how to apply a degree of force when absolutely necessary.

I took another step forward. Out of the corner of my eye, I saw Anne take two steps back.

"Bitch, are you registering me?" I said.

"Loud and clear, love," the girl said. "A bit too loud, actually. If I'm being honest."

She had a heavy British accent; it caught me off guard for some reason.

"Well then you need to move on," I said. "Keep stepping. This isn't your business."

"Now that's just not true," the girl said. "I think I can help you with something."

"I doubt that."

"Well, let's give it a go anyway, shall we?" she said, turning her attention to the old lady. "Anne, right? I need to speak with you, Miss Anne."

Surprised by this bizarre turn of events (and more than a little curious about what might happen next), I glanced at Anne—she looked terrified. I wasn't sure which scared her more: the British girl sporting two nose rings and two purple ponytails, or the American girl sporting brown skin and braids. (Actually, I was pretty sure.)

"All right, Miss Anne," the girl continued. "I'm fairly certain I know what's got you on the end of your tether. You don't want some dodgy little *chav* to waltz into your library, sneak into the Visual Media section, and nick a bunch of your precious DVDs, yeah? Be honest now—is that what you're all in a paddy about?"

Anne stared, wide-eyed. If I hadn't known better, I would have said she'd just aged by about ten years. "How do you know about that?" she asked quietly.

The girl smiled—it looked friendly this time, not like a snide insult plastered across her face. "You want to know how I know what I know?" she asked. "Because it was I, Miss Anne. I am the *chancer* who's been pinching your fancy DVDs all along."

Anne gasped. "You little shit," she growled.

"Mm hm. I've been selling them down at the music store for cash, yeah? But you've run out of the good ones, haven't you. So, here we are."

"You little shit."

"I understand," the girl said. "It's upsetting isn't it—when you've pointed a finger at the wrong person and everybody sees that you've dropped a proper clanger. But no one fancies a sad *arse* who lets their guilt get the best of them, right? So *grasp the nettle*, Anne. Chin up, okay?"

Anne looked completely lost.

The girl ignored her, took a few steps toward me, and extended her hand as though expecting me to take hold of it. I noticed that her nails had perfect, squared-off tips. Her skin was as white as polished teeth.

"Shall we run off together, then?" she asked. "I promise you— it'll be blinding."

• • •

The girl's full name was Harmonic Arris Windswept Mackenzie-Jones, but she told me I could call her Harmony if I wanted to.

These are some of the things I learned within the first few hours of knowing Harmony:

a.) She was sixteen years old.

b.) She had no place to live. Unless you counted the fact that her parents owned a five-bedroom Victorian in a bourgeois neighborhood called Willow Glen, about three miles from where we were standing. But Harmony couldn't (or wouldn't) stay there for some reason.

c.) One of her favorite sayings was, "It's fun. You should really try it sometime." She used that phrase a lot—a whole lot. And every time she said it, I had the feeling that she truly *meant it*.

d.) The uniform she was wearing? It was real. But she didn't go to private school (or any school, actually). She'd stolen the uniform from the Lost and Found bin at Allenton Academy down the street from the library—"just for the fuck of it," apparently.

e.) The British accent? It was fake. Harmony was from Beverly Hills, of all places. She just liked to put on different accents when she was out in public, especially among adults. ("It's fun. You should really try it sometime.")

f.) She cared a lot (a *lot*) about the environment—animals and plants and *chakras* and light and oxygen and any body of water except for one particular kind, called an "impoundment," which she actively despised. An impoundment is a lake created by damming a river, she told me later. And according to Harmony, you should never, ever dam a river unless you're a proper beaver.

g.) That child *loved* herself some drugs—particularly weed, MDMA, and her momma's prescription painkillers: oxycodone, tramadol, and codeine. She offered to share her "splash" (as she called it), but I decided to pass. First, I was deathly afraid of being seen by the police (we were standing in a public parking lot at the time); second, I hadn't known Harmony long enough to put my health and well-being into her well-manicured hands; and third, I was worried that I might use my powers while intoxicated (PWI?) and accidentally do something unpleasant to myself or somebody else. All in all, abstaining seemed like the right call to make.

Even without chemical enhancement, our first afternoon together felt almost dreamlike.

Harmony's spirit was like a whirlwind; I was nearly lifted off my feet by the intensity of her energy, her wild ideas, her ever-shifting wants and needs, her magazine-cover beauty, her crystal-clear perspective on life, so different from my own—every single thing about that child left me spinning. Over the course of what felt like minutes, we wandered all over downtown San Jose, arm in arm—from Interstate 280 to the Guadalupe Parkway to Route 101, all the way back to Coyote Creek—committing spontaneous acts of kindness, criminal mischief, artistic expression, and wanton destruction along the way, all in the name of good, clean fun. We hailed taxis and took off running as they swung to the curb, we collected breadcrumbs to feed a huddle of scraggly-looking pigeons, and we splashed in the fountains at Cesar Chavez Plaza like we were five again. We washed dishes at Konjoe for thirty minutes in exchange for two Shiitake Jack burgers, we threw rocks at a line of green beer bottles pulled from a back-alley dumpster, and we staged a fake karate battle in the middle of a busy crosswalk, eliciting smiles and eye-rolls and disapproving frowns in almost equal measure. We sang the theme songs to our favorite TV shows in front of Peet's to hustle a bit of spare change from passersby, we tagged the wall of a Walgreens with green spray paint (actually, she tagged; I just watched), and we picked flowers from a planter box in front of the Marriott hotel and passed them out to random strangers on the street, telling everyone to *Have a Blessed Day* using whatever foreign accent we felt like using in the moment.

All in all, it was exhilarating. Crazy and reckless, restorative and freeing, it was the kind of afternoon you could never replicate; it would feel phony if you ever tried. But there was something else also, something about Harmony herself, this wild child of Mother Earth, that scared me half to death. The way she moved through the world— a world I saw as threatening and treacherous—with such carelessness and indifference, the way she took ownership of her surroundings almost instinctively, the way her eyes seemed to drink in everything while focusing on nothing at all. It was like she existed somewhere between this world and another one, a faraway place that I would never see or understand. Maybe it was because she was high as high could be, riding on cloud nine for most of the afternoon, but at times I felt like I was in the company of someone who knew they only had a few moments left to live.

• • •

"Why light?" Harmony asked.
She and I were sitting side by side on the banks of Coyote

Creek in the Jungle, pitching handfuls of coarse sand into the water as it snaked through the sun-broken shade of the cottonwoods. It was late morning—I wasn't really sure of the exact time of day anymore—but it was already sweltering; I could feel the fabric of my t-shirt plastered against my lower back.

About a month had passed since the day Harmony and I first met—she had been staying with me in the Jungle ever since. It was overwhelming, the sudden thrill of companionship; the running-through-the-veins rush of a new friend in my life. She still scared the shit out of me on a regular basis with her volatility, her odd flights of fancy, and her seeming insistence on doing everything *different* than everyone else did—brushing her teeth with a finger wrapped in a scrap of paper towel, singing when she should have been whispering, muttering when she should have been speaking up, watching almost lovingly as a mosquito touched down on the underside of her wrist and began to drink—but there was no doubt that her presence in the Jungle, jarring as it was, gave me a much-needed release from the cage of seclusion that my life had become. We'd been almost inseparable since that incandescent afternoon we spent crashing through downtown like a pair of wobble-kneed foals. She still didn't know about my past or my powers (and I had no plans to reveal either one), but otherwise our day-to-day lives were intertwined.

"What did you say?" I asked.

"Light," Harmony said. "The bright, shiny stuff in the air. I heard you talking about it at the library but I never asked why."

"Why what?"

"Why you wanted to learn about it."

It was a pretty good question.

Ever since Harmony had come into my life, I'd completely forgotten about my plan to become invisible, to *bend light* so that it could never touch me unless I allowed it. The plan had seemed so important at the time, so necessary, but now that I had a best friend (Harmony could be counted as my best friend, couldn't she?), invisibility no longer seemed as important any more. The fact that

Harmony had made me feel visible had caused me to feel less inclined to disappear.

"I guess I just wanted to know about light," I said, shrugging.

"Really?"

"What—I'm not allowed to be interested in gaining knowledge?" I said, straightening up. "Because I'm Black, right? It's unimaginable that I could be in a library to actually learn some shit, I suppose. Unless it's basketball. Or the history of Kool-Aid or banjos made out of gourds or something like that. Is that what you're trying to say?"

"Actually, I thought you'd wandered into the library by accident. Thinking it was the National Tupac Museum."

I smiled.

Every once in a while, I liked to jab at Harmony a little bit about our racial differences, to remind her gently that, yes, I am Black and you are white, and this seemingly innocuous fact actually matters in this world. I've always found that, at least when it comes to dealing with your white friends, you need to make Blackness a routine part of the conversation, the everyday flow—not because it's enjoyable to talk about (it isn't), but because otherwise these friends start to fancy themselves as colorblind, and then one day they'll look at you and say something like, "You know what? I don't even think of you as Black! I just think of you, as you!" as though it's some kind of major compliment (both to you and to themselves). In my experience, you need to head that shit off at the pass. I've always chosen to do it with humor, but there's a price you pay for that approach—when *you* joke about it, they think that *they* should be able to joke about it *with* you, as though it's a tit-for-tat *human right of free speech*, and, well, let's just say that white folks usually aren't very artful with their ethnic humor. Maybe nobody really is, though.

But to Harmony's credit, she never took our "racial banter" too far. She kept it pretty clean: never using words she shouldn't use (girlfriend, the n-word); never bringing in the lowest possible stereotypes in the hopes of getting an easy laugh; never trying to "act

Black" using the kind of tired, pre-packaged mannerisms you find in most Hollywood movies (read: a lot of head-waving and finger-snapping). I honestly had to hand it to Harmony—of all the white folks I'd known, she was the most adept at acknowledging the Blackness between us without turning it into a fetish, an insult, or a cheap punch line. That's not to say that she gave two shits about so-called "Black issues" (she didn't) or understood even on a surface level what it meant to be Black in the United States (she didn't), but she "got it" much more than most white folks did. The bar couldn't possibly get any lower, of course, but as far as I was concerned, it was as good as it was going to get.

I scraped together another small mound of sand with the edge of my palm, scooped it up, and side-armed it into the current. When the sand hit the surface, it hissed like a Coke bottle opening for the first time.

"Seriously, though," Harmony said. "I mean, out of all the things to learn about. Why light?"

I shrugged. "I just wanted to know about it."

"What about it?"

"I don't know. How it works, how it moves through the air. What it's made of."

"Easy. Photons."

"I know that," I snapped.

"Oookay. So. What don't you know, then?"

I thought about it.

"I guess I want to know what affects light," I said.

"What affects it?"

"Yeah. I'm thinking about forces. Are there forces strong enough to make light *do* things?"

"Like what?" Harmony asked.

"Changing direction, that kind of thing. Are there forces that can make light go a different way? Like heat—I've seen heat change what light does, or at least, the way it looks."

"You're talking about seeing heat waves on the street?"

"Exactly."

She smiled. "If you want to affect light so much, why don't you go get a mirror? That would be a lot easier."

"Come on. I'm serious."

"All right, fine," Harmony said. "But there are different ways to answer the question. If we're talking about heat waves, you're right: what's really happening is that the light curves a little bit as it passes through the hot air because it's denser. And the reason the light vibrates or shimmers or whatever is because the air isn't heated the same all the way through. Voila."

"How do you even know all this?"

She shrugged. "I know what I know," she said. "Heat is one thing that affects light, but there are other things, too. They're all small, though. Like dust. Dust can affect light as it passes through—that's why stars seem like they're twinkling when you look up at them. Interstellar dust."

"Okay."

Harmony paused.

"But you don't really give a shit about the small stuff," she said. "Am I right?"

"Kind of. Yeah," I said.

"You want to know if there are forces—*big* forces—that can affect light."

"Right."

Harmony stared at me with an expression that I'd never seen on her face before: She looked impressed. Which should have made me feel happy, I suppose, but it didn't—instead, it made me realize how disinterested she normally looked whenever I spoke my mind about anything remotely serious. It reminded me of times when I'd be sitting alone in my room in our old apartment, writing or reading something for hours on end, completely lost in thought, and my father would suddenly switch on the overhead light. I would always be surprised, not by the arrival of the light itself, but by how dark it had been without it, and how I hadn't even noticed the extent of the darkness until that moment. Only when the light finally arrived had I understood that I'd been living almost completely in the shadows the entire time.

"Black holes," Harmony said. "I know that light can be affected by black holes. As in, it can't escape them. They pull light in."

"How?"

"With gravity. Insane amounts of it."

· · ·

Over the next few days, I thought a lot about what Harmony had told me.

As I saw it, I had only two options—to bend light by gathering and controlling a cloud of dust particles in the air, or to bend light *by organically generating a region of space-time that exhibits such strong gravitational forces that nothing—not stars, not planets, not even other, smaller black holes—can escape its influence.*

The choice seemed pretty obvious.

I needed to collect some dust.

Making the decision was the easy part. The difficult part, as with most decisions, was figuring out how to execute it. How was I going to pick out individual dust particles from the sky, bring them together into a single mass, and then—arguably the most ridiculous step in the plan—shape this mass of *dust* into a geometry that would bend light around my body perfectly, rendering me invisible to the naked eye?

It sounded improbable, to say the least.

But one thing I had going for me was this: I knew how to solve big problems by considering the world on a very small scale.

· · ·

Harmony and I often spent the daylight hours apart from each other. Doing our own thing, in our own way.

Wearing combat boots and some kind of flowing peasant dress, Harmony would leave the Jungle in the early afternoon, pick her way across Coyote Creek using a row of jagged stones, climb the chain-link fence, and rejoin civilization via the Walmart parking lot. From there, I wasn't sure where she went off to; the only thing I knew was that she occasionally made a pit stop at her parents' house in Willow Glen. I could tell by the prescription drugs she'd be carrying in her knapsack when she returned home.

Home.

I was starting to think of this place—this broken place—as home.

• • •

Whenever Harmony was gone, I spent my time conducting experiments with dust particles.

Which sounds incredibly boring, I know.

But it wasn't.

I would spend hours and hours sitting in the mouth of the tent and staring up at the sky, much like I had when I was trying (futilely) to corral particles of light from the atmosphere. But this time I had a much larger target in mind: atmospheric dust.

Dust particles weren't exactly what anybody would call colossal, but compared to photons they were practically boulders, and this size difference—while seemingly insignificant—made all the difference in the world when it came to gravity's influence. Within moments, I was able to perceive the unseen volumes of dust that saturated the air all around me at any given time, which allowed me to take command of these particles and gather them together into a visible, tangible cloud— a nebulous, three-dimensional haze that billowed and undulated like the bell of a dark jellyfish. With only minimal effort, I could change any characteristic of the dust bell that I wanted to change: its size, shape, texture, or density. This entity—this creation—was mine to control.

Over time, I learned to direct the bell's movements in exquisite ways: sending it careening and twisting through the sky like a dragon kite, launching it like a pointed javelin, letting it weave sinuously through the cottonwoods like an eel through a kelp forest. I used the bell to spontaneously capture sparrows in mid-flight, enveloping them harmlessly in a hollow orb of dust. I flattened the bell, reduced its density so that it appeared wispy and diffuse, and spread it above me to use as a sunshade. I sculpted the bell into the shapes of objects, animals, *people*—my father, sitting beside me in the tent's opening. My mother, whose face I couldn't even remember.

No matter what I did to the bell, no matter how I transformed its appearance or directed its movements, it never made a single sound. It was silent, steady, and always there.

But honestly, what I enjoyed most about the bell was simply watching it hang in the air above my head. Its gentle, quiet undulation. The unspoken power that lay underneath. I could easily fool myself into believing that this collection of dust particles—a collection that I'd assembled myself—had somehow taken on a life of its own. And I often did believe it. I really did.

It may seem bizarre or childish, and I'm reluctant to admit it, but the bell became a kind of companion to me, a protector of sorts. Almost like a guardian angel. Even though I could have easily harvested another volume of dust from anywhere I happened to be at any given moment, I kept the original mass of particles (from the first time I'd ever successfully worked with the medium) on my person at all times, compressed into a graphite-black sphere the size of a large marble. Tucked inside a pocket, inside a bag, inside my sock: it was always with me.

I even gave it—*her*—a name.

I called her Bel.

"The fuck is wrong with you?" Harmony slurred. "Help me, bitch."

It was late—the sun had been dead and buried for at least a few hours. To nobody's surprise, Harmony was high out of her mind. She had stumbled back to the Jungle by cutting through the back of the Walmart parking lot, as usual, but on this particular night she couldn't get her stupid self over the chain-link fence.

I was on the Jungle side; she was on the Walmart side.

There wasn't much I could do to help her get past the barrier between us. I couldn't climb the damn thing for her.

Unless I used my abilities.

"Try one more time," I said.

"What? Fuck you." She was swaying on her feet.

"Harmony. Look at me. Try one more time—just try. You can do this."

Rolling her eyes, Harmony dropped a limp hand onto the fence, her fingers curling loosely through the metal links, and started kicking the base of the barrier with the toe of her boot, trying to get a toehold (I think).

The attempt didn't look very convincing, but it wasn't going to get any better than this.

I looked around, and once I was reasonably sure we weren't being watched, I reached out with my mind and quietly boosted Harmony up and over the boundary fence, trying to make it look at least halfway plausible that she could be doing the work herself, but in reality, dragging her stupid ass like a limp dummy from a weekend CPR course. I let her hit the ground with a little more force than I probably should have, and then I helped her to her feet, threw her arm over my shoulder, and walked her across the creek and back to the tent, using my abilities to assist us (subtly, I hoped) the entire way.

"Eat shit," Harmony murmured, her eyes half-lidded. Her lipstick was smeared across her cheek, almost to the earlobe. "I love you, you dumb fuck you bitch stupid little." Her voice trailed off.

I laid her down on the bed of blankets. I unlaced her heavy black boots, pulled them off, and set them just outside the tent's opening while she continued hurling profanities at me, at herself.

Harmony passed out soon after that, thankfully.

I sat on the ground outside the tent with my knees to my chest and my arms wrapped around my shins, listening to the sounds of the freeway, the river currents, the wind in the cottonwoods. After a while, I called Bel from my pocket and let her fly, watching her small spherical shape buzz around and around my head like an idea too beautiful or whimsical—or too dangerous—to be spoken aloud.

I smiled, in spite of myself.

• • •

After playing with Bel for a few minutes, I felt my stomach growl—I couldn't remember the last time I'd eaten anything real. We didn't have any more food in camp that I was aware of, which meant that I would need to do a little shopping at my friendly neighborhood Walmart superstore.

It was time to see what my new little partner-in-crime could really do.

With Bel in tow, I got to my feet, crossed the creek using the stepping stones, and bellied-up to the chain-link fence, scanning the parking lot for potential targets. I saw a handful of shoppers trundling to their cars underneath the blue-white glow of the streetlamps overhead, but none of them seemed especially promising (not enough cargo) until I spotted a hulking white man pushing two overloaded carts simultaneously, one with each hand, on his way to an electric blue pickup truck parked about as far from the store's entrance as it could get, and at least twenty spaces away from any other vehicle on every side. The man stopped at the bed of the truck, disabled the alarm with a key fob, and lowered the rear tailgate, nodding his head to an inaudible beat (he was wearing a set of headphones over a backward baseball cap).

I glanced up at Bel, hovering near my shoulder. She slowly rose and fell as though drifting on an invisible body of water.

"You got this," I whispered. "Easy."

I returned my attention to the man, waiting until he began unloading shopping bags from the first cart, at which point Bel was off like a shot, zipping through a link in the fence, dropping to the asphalt, and rolling soundlessly across the parking lot toward the truck. Weaving around an empty plastic soda bottle, a styrofoam fast-food takeout container, an empty plastic grocery sack. Steering clear of the pools of light cast by the streetlamps. Once she was about halfway to the man, I reached out with my mind and targeted a brown paper bag piled high on the second cart, lifted it from the basket, and lowered it quickly to the blacktop, bringing the bag to rest beside the left-rear wheel, outside of the man's view (at least, I hoped). At the same time, Bel popped up into the air and unfurled herself like a swath of black netting, fluttered to the bag on the ground, and enveloped it, amoeba-like, just as she'd done a hundred times before with a hundred different sparrows. As she lifted off and began her flight back to camp, I worked in real time to modify her shape, her density, her geometry, her patterning, her overall size—any characteristic I could change in order to make her (and the cargo inside of her) more difficult to detect.

It wasn't perfect.

Bel still cast a shadow on the asphalt, and her form itself was still visible—a cloud of distortion flitting through the air—but she was traveling so quickly that her presence was difficult to detect; in fact, she probably would have been nearly impossible to spot unless you knew exactly what you were looking for. And who could have possibly known to look for something like this?

Still, the whole process definitely needed improvement.

Gyrating and twirling wildly, Bel hurdled the fence, zipped past my head fast enough to whip my braids into a tangle, touched down on the ground outside the tent and instantly dissipated like a dark vapor, leaving the brown paper bag sitting in the dirt next to Harmony's combat boots like a magician's final trick.

About an hour later I was eating a strip of turkey jerky and sipping a beer in front of the tent when I saw the beam of a flashlight—a cold bluish shaft—cutting through the blackness down-creek. Sweeping back and forth across the trees, through the groundcover. Along the riverbank, the fence line. I heard slow and heavy footfalls in the leaf litter.

Shit.

I tossed the beer can into a clump of brush, dropped the jerky, and scrambled into the tent on my hands and knees.

"Harm," I hissed, grabbing her arm and shaking it. "Harm."

She didn't move. Her mouth was slightly open.

"Dammit, Harmony. Somebody's coming."

"Mmf." Harmony's brow furrowed. She rolled over onto her side.

Shit.

I crawled to the opening of the tent and pushed the flap aside. A blinding light shone directly into my face; it was like staring at a supernova up close.

"Do not move," a man's voice said. "Do not goddamn move—do you understand me? Do not move."

I didn't move a single muscle; I didn't even take a breath.

"Stand up," the voice said. "Be slow. And show me your hands."

I got to my feet, raising my hands above my head.

The flashlight beam traveled the length of my body—from my two empty hands, to my underarms, to my throat, to my waist, down my legs to my feet, and back up to my chest. With the light out of my eyes, I could see the man now—a tall, thin Latino officer in uniform, his gun raised—standing about twenty feet away.

Oh, shit.

I was about to be arrested for theft, underage drinking, murder, or all three.

The officer lowered the weapon to his side, but kept the flashlight trained on my heart.

"Sweetheart. Listen to me," he said. His voice sounded kinder than it had only seconds ago—maybe he realized I was a kid? "I want you to stay as still as you can for me. Don't move at all. Can you do that?"

I nodded.

"Please use your words, sweetheart."

"Yes," I said.

"All right."

Staying where he was, the officer shined the flashlight all around me—on the ground near my shoes, on the front panel of the tent, on the brown shopping bag, on Harmony's boots, on the dense foliage surrounding me. Finally, he shined the light directly on my face again; I had to concentrate to keep from lowering my hand to shield my eyes.

"I need you to be truthful with me, okay?" he said.

"Okay."

The flashlight suddenly lowered, and I could see again. The officer was staring at me with an expression that looked serious but gentle, an expression that a nice-but-strict teacher might wear on his face.

"I'm not joking about this," the man said. "I want you to be real with me."

"I will."

"Good. Now, here's what I think: Somebody else is out here with you, somewhere—a boyfriend, mother, kids, somebody. Maybe multiple somebodies. Am I correct? "

"No," I said. "I mean, yeah. Yes, officer—someone is here,

but not my mom or boyfriend. Not multiple somebodies. Just one friend."

"You and one other individual. That's all?"

"Yes."

"And where's your friend right now?" the officer asked, his eyes scanning left, right. Up, down. "Is he inside?"

"She."

"Is she inside?"

"Yes."

I looked down at the officer's feet—he was standing only yards away from where my attacker was buried, moldering, under the creek bed. I felt the tears building up in my eyes; I blinked them back.

"I'm going to ask you to sit down now," the officer said gently. "I want you to sit down and put your hands tight under your legs. Can you do that for me?"

I nodded. "Yes."

"Okay. Do it now, please."

I did as I was told—I sat cross-legged in the dirt and tucked my hands flat underneath my thighs.

"Good girl," the officer said. "I want you to stay right there for me, please."

The officer raised his pistol, approached the tent opening cautiously, and used the head of his black metal flashlight to push aside one of the two zippered flaps.

"San Jose Police," he said, scanning the interior. "Miss? I need you to come outside. Now, please."

"She can't hear you," I said.

"Miss? Police. Come on out."

"She's asleep."

The officer looked down at me, keeping the flashlight focused on Harmony.

"How old are you, sweetheart?" he asked.

"Twelve."

"For the love of God. Twelve?" He shook his head.

"I'm almost thirteen."

The officer sighed. "Look—what's your name?"

"Eris."

"Look, Eris. You're not allowed to be out here camping in a tent—this isn't a safe situation," he said. "Do you have somewhere else you can go? Family somewhere? Friends?"

"No."

He sighed again. "All right. I'm sorry, Eris, but you can't stay out here—even if you weren't twelve, it wouldn't be right. I'll swing back tomorrow with Social Services, and maybe they can help you figure something else out. But either way, this is your last night out here. I'm sorry."

I nodded. "Okay."

• • •

The next morning, I tried to explain the situation—the deep pile of shit we were in—to dumbass Harmony as we lay together on the bed of blankets, but she wasn't interested in hearing about anything negative, which meant anything connected to reality.

"I don't care," she said. "Get ready—we're going."

She wasn't talking about "going," as in packing up and leaving the Jungle, like the officer told us to do. She was talking about heading off to—of all the ridiculous places in the world—Children's Play Land, the nearby amusement park.

"Are you serious?" I asked.

"Why wouldn't I be?"

"Um. Because we need to get out of here by tonight?"

"Says who?"

"Says the police. I just told you that."

Harmony snorted. "Bullshit. Watch. Even if that cop does come back here, which he won't, he isn't going to tell us to do shit."

"And why not?"

"Because you'll show him your tits," Harmony said. "What

little you've got. That's why."

My eyes widened.

"I'm kidding," she said. "I'll show him mine, if I have to. But trust me, it won't be necessary. I know how cops are. Just watch."

I was speechless.

"So are you in?" she asked.

"Am I in what?"

"In on my excursion, bitch. Let's go ride some rides. Come on. It'll be fun."

I looked around at the inside of the tent, terrified by the possibility of even *seeing* the police officer again, much less ignoring his demands.

"Hey. Tally-girl," Harmony said quietly. "Listen. I'm sorry about yesterday." Her tone had softened. It happened sometimes—she dropped the casually arrogant, flippant façade, and for a few gorgeous moments, seemed completely vulnerable—but I could never be sure if the vulnerability was real or whether it was a trick of contrast, only noticeable for what it wasn't.

"Sorry for what?"

"I don't remember much about last night, honestly," she said, grinning. "Clearly, I was properly laced. But I do remember that you helped me get back home. Thank you for that." She leaned over and kissed me on the forehead.

I didn't respond; I just looked at her.

Home.

She'd called this place—the place we shared—her home.

• • •

In the end, I gave in. We went to the stupid amusement park like Harmony wanted to. And as was usually the case when we were out on the town together, we had an otherworldly time.

It wasn't only about *what* we did. It was also about *how* we got it done.

For the entire day, Harmony was the most lighthearted, easygoing version of herself: putting on a number of fake accents (French, Italian, Australian); cracking good-natured jokes about the people waiting in line around us; playing every single carnival game in Arcade Alley, from target shooting to ring toss, with no complaints, win or lose; riding in the front car of the rollercoaster with her hands raised high, even though it scared her half to death; eating two cups of Dippin Dots and a bag of caramel corn, even though her normal diet consisted of little more than energy drinks and her mom's Xanax pills. She never lost her temper even once, stayed sober for every minute as far as I knew, and paid for the entire experience with money I didn't even know she had (or how she'd managed to earn it).

The day was magical. Not like stage magic, performed at a safe distance. This was street magic—the kind that happens right in front of your face, out in the open. The kind of sun-soaked magic that makes you wonder how the hell it could have possibly been pulled off; the kind that makes you search the air for invisible wires, the sidewalk for hidden trap doors; the kind that can turn a bitter skeptic into a bona fide believer.

"What are you really about?" Harmony asked sharply.

We were back in the Jungle, sitting in our usual spot in front of the tent's opening—just sitting together, eating leftovers from last night's Walmart raid.

I looked at her. "What am I about?"

"Exactly," she snapped. "What are you actually about?"

I kept staring. At first I thought she was joking, but Harmony was clearly pissed-off all of a sudden, and I had no idea why. If I hadn't known better, I would have guessed that she was drunk again.

"Did I do something?" I asked, immediately regretting how pathetic it sounded.

"I don't know—did you? Do you do anything? That's the question I've been asking myself."

I didn't know how to respond, and to make matters even worse, I absolutely hated myself in that moment because of it. The old me—the unattached (read: strong) me—would have known exactly how to mount a defense, how to put this chick in her place, but the proximity between the two of us made it impossible for me to see my target clearly, to take aim, to fire back.

"For real," Harmony continued. "What are you about, Tallah? You can't just live your life following other people around, you know. Responding. Reacting. You need to be about something. Offer something up. Be organic."

"Organic?" I snorted. This nitwit was either high, in a mood, or a little too in love with herself. "You sound so fucking stupid right now, Harm."

"I'm serious, Tallah. You need to stop acting like a slave and stand on your own feet. All you're doing right now is hanging on. Leeching. It's embarrassing."

Did this bitch just say slave?

"Hanging on? To what—you?"

"What else would you call it?"

"Look," I said. "If you don't want to be here, then be out. Nobody's holding you back."

"I might do that."

"Don't talk about it. Do it. Trying to act like you're so damn necessary to somebody. You came to me, remember? I didn't come to you."

"Maybe," Harmony said. "But you should be honest with yourself. At this point, you need me a lot more than I need you."

"Are you serious with this?"

"I'm just saying you need to step it up. You know I love you, Tally, but you have to admit. You're pretty weak sometimes."

"So I'm weak now?"

Harmony shrugged. "I'm sorry. That's just what I see."

"That's how you see me? As a weak slave?"

She shrugged again by way of a response.

At that point, my anger truly caught fire. I climbed to my feet and stood over Harmony, wanting nothing more than to grab those two purple pigtails, one in each hand, and drive my knee into her stupid face again and again until it was flat as a wall, but before I could do anything else, she scrambled to her feet, rose to her full height, and stepped in close, towering over me.

"Sit back down," she said quietly. I could smell her breath, a mixture of turkey jerky and warm beer.

"No," I replied.

"Tallah, I will put you on the ground if you make me. Sit the fuck down."

"No."

I was coming dangerously close to crying, but I wasn't about to give this bitch the satisfaction of bearing witness. I backhanded my eyes, squared my shoulders, and straightened my posture.

"You sit down," I said.

Harmony laughed in my face. Literally. She was only inches away from me. I felt the heat of her breath—the specks of her saliva—against my skin.

And that's when I acted without thinking.

Lashing out with my mind, I targeted the internal structures of Harmony's knee joints, pulling both kneecaps away from the underlying thigh bones with a quick and subtle tug, creating just enough separation between them to make that witch's legs buckle, using just enough force to make her collapse, screaming, into the dirt.

Standing over her body, I watched impassively as she continued to writhe back and forth.

"I told you to sit," I said. "But you didn't want to listen. Now look at you."

I didn't let go.

I held the effect in place until I was finished.

• • •

Harmony and I had a lot to talk about after that.

First came her apology—long, drawn-out, and very well-deserved, as far as I was concerned. She wasn't actually sorry for how she'd treated me; I knew that. It wasn't because she was incapable of genuine remorse—I think she was—but in my experience, she usually needed days' worth of processing before she could allow herself to express anything resembling regret (she was one of those people who prided themselves on "living life with no regrets at all"). I knew that I'd only received an apology so quickly because I had, for all intents and purposes, tortured it out of her. I had revealed myself, my abilities, in the most terrifying way possible. That poor child would have told me whatever she thought I wanted to hear.

Once the (non-)apology was out of the way, I had another problem.

How to deal with the fact that Harmony had learned about my secret.

At first I considered trying to undo the damage, either by providing an alternate explanation for the pain in her joints (dehydration?), or by flat-out denying that I'd been involved (after all, how could she have proven otherwise?). But in the end, I didn't lie. The honest truth was that I wanted to share my abilities with her. In my heart, I was desperate to tell. Yes, there was a part of me (the isolated part) that hoped it would bring us closer together, but the real reason I revealed my secret was because of her verbal attack, the way it had made me feel: worthless, weak, and enslaved. I couldn't bear it. And what better way to prove that bitch wrong than to throw my superpowers right in her perfect, porcelain face?

So, once the pain in her knees subsided (she wasn't injured; just hurt), she dried the tears from her eyes, dusted off her (formerly) pretty peasant dress, and sat down next to me in front of the tent, where we had a long chat about the laws of gravity—how they might be bent or even broken.

I started my confession with a simple demonstration. I released Bel from my back pocket and let her bustle and whir around Harmony's head a few times like a muted hummingbird, before bringing her to rest in my open palm.

"Oh my God," Harmony whispered, her eyes wide.

That was good enough. Instead of showing her additional wonders of my world, I told her about my latest boring project—working to perfect the art of stealing shopping bags from the Walmart parking lot. I revealed just enough information about my capabilities to gain some of the respect I'd craved, without making myself look too knowledgeable or experienced—which were two descriptors that could quickly metamorphose into "too threatening" or "too dangerous." In short, I chose to drastically undersell myself. But it was the right decision—I didn't need to go into any more detail. The little I'd shown was impressive enough as it was.

"I know who you are," Harmony said out of nowhere. Her eyes were still swollen and red, and her cheek was smudged with dirt; she looked like a living, breathing police mugshot. "I recognized you from the news—the stories about your dad and the things they say he did. I knew who you were right away."

I couldn't believe it.

Harmony had known who I was this entire time, but had never mentioned it.

"About your dad," Harmony said. "I mean, could he really do those things they showed online? I'm sorry, but that shit looked so fake to me—I assumed that none of it was real."

"It happened," I said. "He was real."

"So you're telling me that this power you have, it basically runs in the fucking family? Daaamn. I'm telling you, girl, we need to get you pregnant, like, right now."

I stared at her.

"I'm kidding," she said. "But seriously, can you imagine the babies you'd have? I mean, come on. The magic little motherfuckers would be off the chains."

"This is my life, Harmony. It's not a joke."

"Fine. I'm sorry, okay? But you know I'm right about this. You know I am."

"Actually, I don't."

"Come on. Are you sure you don't want me to go out and find a cute boy for you to play with?"

"Thanks. But I'm good."

Harmony let out a deep sigh and crossed her arms. She looked genuinely disappointed that I wasn't busy reproducing at that very moment.

The old me (read: thirty minutes ago) would have tried to cheer Harmony up, to give her a sweet song to drown out those blues of hers, but things were different now—I'd already noticed that the power dynamics between us were shifting, although I wouldn't have used those words to describe it at the time. On one hand, by showing Harmony my abilities, I'd proven myself powerful, intriguing, and above all else, useful, which had clearly elevated my status in her eyes; it was written all over her face whenever she looked at me. I expected that. It seemed like a normal response to someone revealing a hidden strength, something of obvious value. But on the other hand, I also sensed that my status—while higher than before—wasn't as high as it damn well should have been, given the magnitude of what I'd just revealed. I mean, honestly. This child should have been down on her knees praising my name as her new Mother Goddess of Earth. But instead, it felt as though I'd finally clawed my way up to Harmony's exact same level, as though I'd finally passed a test I hadn't known that I was required to take. Apparently, only when I'd shown myself to be truly extraordinary—a superhuman in the flesh—could I be considered an equal.

• • •

It was getting late. The rollercoaster had long since gone silent and the Walmart parking lot was nearly empty. It was dark enough in the glade that the trees all around me seemed to blend into a single shapeless mass, their leaves reflecting moonlight like a thousand eyes. The creek water had turned a sinuous black—a thick, winding snake ready to turn back on its tail and consume itself.

Harmony was already inside the tent. She was sleeping or smoking weed or masturbating or some half-delirious combination of the three. Meanwhile, I sat alone in the dirt, thinking about what to do next.

The highs and lows of the day had left me whiplashed: the amusement park (high), the argument with Harmony (low), sharing my secret and getting some damn respect (high), realizing that none of it really made a difference, that I was still penniless, homeless, and directionless—and possibly even friendless (way, way, way low). Don't get me wrong, Harmony and I had technically reconciled, but that only meant an apology had been made. It didn't mean we were all right. We weren't. And normally that would have been okay with me, because I would have felt confident that we would reconnect after heads had cooled and emotions had settled. But now? After revealing what I'd revealed?

I was nobody's fool—I had already accepted the fact that things would never be the same between us, but I had honestly hoped that our relationship could still be close. Different, but close. I wasn't so sure anymore. It was very possible that I'd just lost the only real friend I'd made in over a year's time.

If it weren't for my abilities—the sublime fact of their existence—I'm not sure that I could have kept going. Yes Lord, I was penniless, homeless, directionless, and maybe even friendless (with the exception of my imaginary Bel), but at least I wasn't the sorriest thing a person could be in this country half-filled with raging madmen: I wasn't powerless. Not even close. It made a world of difference, knowing that I could protect myself from the worst forms of savagery, that I could take—by force, if necessary—whatever I needed to ensure my own survival. My abilities didn't make me immune to the terrors of the world, but I was more resistant than I'd ever been to brutality, to cruelty, to poverty—to *want*. And this feeling of resistance saturated every part of my body, every cell of every tissue, like a second, parallel bloodstream. Yes Lord, I had next to nothing. But I had the only thing that mattered: I had some semblance of control.

The problem was this:

In spite of the fact that I had the power to (literally) move mountains, I was too terrified to use it. To really use it.

My father had. And look what happened to him.

I suddenly remembered the police officer from the night before.

Shit.

I scrambled to my feet and scanned the rough-beaten path that cut through the cottonwood grove, the main connection between our ramshackle campsite and the outside world. There was no sign of anyone—police or otherwise. Maybe Harmony was right, maybe the officer wouldn't actually return to evict us from the Jungle. But I couldn't take that chance. Even though this was far from paradise, I didn't want to risk losing the only place I thought of as home.

I turned to the dome tent. It was barely visible in the darkness, tucked into a small clearing, flanked by a thicket of dense brushwood.

It gave me an idea.

The officer had told me that we needed to leave the Jungle by tonight.

So, what if I could make it appear as though we'd already left?

I summoned Bel from my back pocket.

She unfurled, flag-like, and fluttered almost proudly above my head. I brought her to the face of the dome tent and quickly got to work: spreading her body out like a windscreen, carefully aligning her with the contours of the fiberglass frame, applying her to the surface of the nylon structure like a protective coating. Resizing, reshaping. Over time, she became what looked like a hazy shadow-shell around the tent.

That was the easy part.

From there, I began to address the individual dust particles that composed Bel's body, adjusting their angles, their spacing, their groupings, their subtle color array. Holding the overall shape together, but changing its constituent patterns and textures. Gradually, small areas of the shadow-shell began to blend seamlessly into the background foliage as the ambient light was directed (as if by an array of microscopic mirrors) *around* the configuration. Larger areas soon followed suit, and then entire swaths, until—after what felt like an hour's worth of work arranging pin-prick-sized particles—the tent seemed to disappear in front of my eyes. All I could see when I looked toward our shelter was the copse of trees that lay on the opposite side.

· · ·

With Harmony lying asleep beside me, I waited inside the (invisible) tent near the entryway and stared through the opening. Everything in my world—the cottonwoods, the creek water, the sagging fence, the empty parking lot—appeared dim and hazy when viewed through the dark prism of Bel's skin. For a moment it felt as though my vision itself was fading to black, as though I'd stood up too quickly and was on the verge of passing out.

Nothing happened for a long time. No one appeared, and nothing moved. Cocooned in grey, I kept watch as best I could, concentrating as hard as I could, but my efforts felt futile. It reminded me of a time when I'd been walking to school and found the body of a raccoon lying in a gutter near the storm drain, its side caved-in by a passing car. The animal couldn't have been dead for very long—other than the obvious injury, the corpse looked completely whole. Untouched by decay. Its lolling pink tongue, still glistening; its jagged needle-pointed teeth, white as the road's center stripe. I remember staring at the body for a while, wondering if I would be able to witness it starting to decompose, but nothing changed—at least nothing noticeable. Still, I felt like something was happening that I couldn't perceive, something roiling underneath the surface, but I could never truly understand what it was until everything collapsed all at once in front of my eyes, caving in on itself, exposing the inner workings to the light.

I was starting to nod off, chin falling to my chest, when I noticed movement outside—a beam of light traveling across the ground—to the left of the tent opening. I snapped awake, leaning further into the entryway. Soon I saw a police officer, the same one, slowly sweeping his flashlight from side to side as he entered the clearing.

Heart hammering, I watched him approach.

The officer shone his light along the length of the riverbank and then along the base of the boundary fence, after which he turned around and surveyed the treeline—going low to high, from the groundcover all the way up to the canopy. When he was finished, he shifted his focus to the ground and began exploring the patch of dirt where I usually sat with Harmony, using the toe of his boot to dredge through the assortment of trash we'd left there: discarded candy wrappers, empty aluminum cans, tattered magazines. Eventually the officer stood at the center of the glade, tucked the still-lit flashlight underneath his arm, and hitched up his pants, adjusting his heavy service belt.

He took out his cell phone and turned it on, the bluish-white glow of the display lighting up his face. After a few seconds of staring at the screen, the officer pocketed the phone, took the flashlight in his hand, raised it, and turned toward the tent—or at least, where the tent *would have been* if he could have seen it.

I held my breath.

The officer seemed to be staring directly at me. Right into my eyes.

He squinted, cocked his head, and took a few steps forward,

raising the flashlight higher, as though he'd heard a faint sound coming from somewhere deep in the trees. He'd spotted me; I was sure of it. Bel's illusion hadn't fooled him, and he was seconds away from drawing his weapon and ordering me to come out of the tent with my hands raised, at which point he would put me on the ground, drive a knee into my lower back, and bind my hands behind me with biting metal cuffs.

I didn't move.

The officer swept the flashlight beam slowly across the face of the tent.

Across *my* face.

I closed my eyes and waited.

The light, filtered through the delicate skin of my eyelids, glowed a phosphorescent orange. It was like watching a wildfire raging on the other side of a lace curtain.

Suddenly, everything went dark.

When I opened my eyes, the light had disappeared. The officer was nowhere in sight.

• • •

The next morning, I showed Harmony what Bel and I had accomplished together. Even in broad daylight, the tent was practically invisible.

"Oh my God," Harmony whispered, slowly reaching out with her hand. Wide-eyed, she ran two fingers almost reverently through the dust shell surrounding the tent, breaking the surface as though it were made of standing water. Her touch sent a series of ripples coursing across the façade like tiny swells on a pond, disrupting the illusion as they traveled, causing the tent on the other side to flicker in and out of view. As I watched the structure rhythmically disappearing and reappearing before my eyes, I felt like I was catching a fleeting glimpse of a parallel existence, another universe in which most things were the same but certain details had changed, and I wondered for a moment whether there could be another Tallah Williams living in that universe, and whether she was living almost completely alone and homeless in the Jungle like I was, or whether she had a real home and parents who were still alive and friends who were made of something other than dust. Before long, the waves subsided, the surface became smooth again, and the illusion settled back into place; there was no sign of the tent anymore. We saw exactly what we'd seen before Harmony's gentle touch: a copse of trees in an otherwise empty clearing.

The two of us went our separate ways after that. (Just for the day—not permanently.) Harmony told me that she had some business to handle. As for me, I decided to take Bel over the boundary fence to Walmart so I could practice my new (badass) skill—invisibility cloaking—in front of a full-length mirror in the Young Miss department's fitting rooms.

But I had a few chores to do before I left.

First, I undid all of the work I'd done last night: I dispersed the shadow-shell that covered the tent, whipped the dust into a dark cloud overhead, pulled the cloud down to chest level, and reshaped it into a sprightly little sphere—my Bel. I dropped her into my back pocket for safe keeping.

Then came the difficult part: recreating last night's illusion using a different batch of atmospheric dust, one that I didn't consider to be a close friend. I know it was bizarre—my attachment to little Bel, this particular collection of fine, dry powder made from microscopic particles of earth—but I didn't give a shit if my love of Bel made me a misfit. All dust wasn't equal, as far as I was concerned. Bel was my dust, my earth. I was able to feel the individual motes that composed her body as readily as I could feel a handful of warm, smooth pebbles placed inside my palm. Say what you will about me, but Bel wasn't replaceable. I genuinely viewed her as a representation of my courage, my power, my commitment to survival. Even my love, in a strange way. Bel truly mattered to me, more than any other physical object I could think of.

Once I'd finished recasting the new shell over the dome tent (using anonymous dust), I spent a good half-hour cleaning up the bulk of the trash we'd accumulated in the clearing over the past year. Foil wrappers, white plastic grocery sacks, empty cans, pill bottles, wadded-up paper towels, plastic cutlery—as much waste as possible went into a fifty-gallon Hefty bag I'd managed to disentangle from a clump of brambles near the creek. The goal wasn't perfect cleanliness: the goal was to clean up enough garbage so that we'd be living a little less like pigs, and we'd be attracting a little less attention to the spot where our "magic fucking teepee of invisibility" (as Harmony had called it) had been pitched.

Once the area looked reasonable, I went to work on my own appearance: sponging myself off with a wad of paper towels and leftover water from an Aquafina bottle; using Harmony's hand mirror and makeup kit to fix my face (not up to her level, but close enough); and finally, spending some long-overdue time getting my hair right— unraveling the Havanas, combing everything through with my fingers, and doing my best DIY take on the classic big-box braid, finishing it off with a coiled-up red bandanna for some added flair. Feeling better than I had in a while, I took one last look toward the tent (still invisible), skipped across the creek using the stepping stones, and vaulted the boundary fence, landing in a thatch of long yellow weeds growing at the periphery of the Walmart parking lot.

• • •

Five damn minutes.

That was how long it took for the stupid-ass attendant to start knocking on the fitting room door in the middle of my experimentation, talking about "Excuse me, miss? Is everything fitting how you expected? Or can I help you find another size?" as if I needed special assistance, when all she was actually doing was pulling an Anne the Librarian and checking up on somebody, making sure I wasn't trying to steal the $11.99 summer swing dress I'd brought into the room with me (purely for show—I wasn't going to buy it or steal it or anything).

"No," I said through the door.

"No?" the attendant replied. "Like, no it doesn't fit? Or no, you don't need any help?" Her voice came out slow and thick—she sounded dopey as hell (or doped-up out of her mind).

"I mean no," I snapped. "As in, get away from me, I don't want to talk to you."

There was a brief pause before the dumb cow worked up the nerve to knock again.

"Miss?"

"Oh, my Lord. Are you serious?"

"If you're finished with the room, we have customers out here waiting."

"Does it look like I'm finished with the room?"

Another pause.

"Well. I don't know," she said. "But we do have a policy on time spent in the dressing room."

"Oh, really? And what is it?"

"Uh. What is what?"

"The policy, dummy. What is Walmart's official rule on how long I get this fitting room for?"

Silence.

"Well," the attendant droned. "All I know is that we have customers waiting."

"Noted. You have customers waiting. Got it. So if there's nothing else, I'll let you know when I'm damn well finished. You'll know as soon as I walk out the door."

That seemed to do the trick.

Now that I had some privacy, I got back on task.

Where was I?

Oh, yeah—carefully fashioning Bel into a flexible, form-fitting, head-to-toe, badass body sheath. Something I could easily step into and out of, something I could wear like a uniform as I moved through the world. A bodystocking made purely out of layers of blackened dust.

That was the easy part.

Within a matter of minutes, I was done: I had transformed myself into a living, breathing, walking shadow. When I caught a glimpse of myself in the mirror, I looked almost like a fissure in the world itself, an empty space where a girl used to stand. No facial features, no defining characteristics. I was the physical manifestation of shade, of dusk, of nightfall. I could have easily passed as a real-life apparition, a revenant—someone's soul gone rogue—and I realized immediately that, at some point, I would probably give that a try.

As for now, it was time for the next step—the truly difficult part.

Just as I'd done with the tent, I needed to adjust each individual grain of dust—its angle and spacing—in order to change the direction of incoming light waves. One grain would direct the light to the next grain, which in turn would direct the light to the next one, and so on, multiplied by thousands, until the light's path had been dramatically and intentionally altered. Instead of ricocheting off of (or being absorbed by) my body and being registered by somebody's eye, the light would travel *around* it, as though I weren't even in the room.

I got down to business. And let me tell you something: business was booming.

Maybe it was because of my prior experience with masking the tent, or maybe I was just *feeling myself* at the moment, but the process went much quicker than it had before, with much better results. My reflection in the mirror dissolved within minutes, fading away parcel by parcel—my limbs, my pelvis, my torso, my face—until the mirror showed nothing more than the closed door leading outside into the hallway.

I had disappeared. The effect was stunning.

Until I moved.

As soon as I began to walk around the fitting room, the illusion broke—I could see glimpses of my shadowy form as it blinked in and out of view. I quickly realized what the problem was: I had configured Bel to bend light coming from one specific location only. As I moved from one part of the room to the next, the lighting was constantly changing, which meant that the configuration of dust particles—the angles, the spacing between them—would need to change along with it. The arrangement would need to be dynamic, ever-evolving. This led me to yet another problem that I hadn't considered: multiple viewers with multiple perspectives. What the hell would I do, for example, if I was in the middle of a crowd, with potential eyewitnesses on every side of me—front, back, and both flanks? How would I be able to bend light around my body from every angle, all at once?

I heard a knock at the door.

"Miss?"

It was the attendant again.

"I need you to come out now," she said. Her voice sounded sterner, more focused, than it had before. "Security is here with me. So, yeah. It's time."

I checked my reflection again. In spite of all my efforts, I could still see swaths of dark dust, like patches of soot, whenever I moved—I had *almost* vanished, but not completely. The whole exercise suddenly seemed hopeless. Now that I'd added motion to the mix (not to mention the goal of being invisible from multiple angles simultaneously), the task had become too complex—I couldn't wrap my mind around how to accomplish it.

There was another knock at the door.

"Miss?"

"Hold up one second," I said distractedly. "I'm almost finished. Just wait."

"We can't wait any more, miss," the attendant said. "You need to come out now."

I heard the sound of a key in the lock.

Before I could react, the handle turned and the door swung wide open.

Panicked, I froze in place like prey, standing stiffly in the middle of the cramped fitting room, too afraid to take another breath.

There were two people in the entryway: a squat white woman with long brown hair and glasses, and a drowsy-looking man in a security guard uniform—he looked Ethiopian, Somali, or something else East African, I wasn't sure.

"What in the name of all things?" The woman gasped.

She looked around the room with her mouth wide open like she'd just returned to her parking space and found it empty. She got down on her hands and knees, lowered her face to the tile, and peered into the adjoining stalls through gaps underneath the dividing walls, then climbed to her feet, brushed off her pant legs, and turned to the guard.

"Good Lord," she said, shaking her head. "You heard her voice, didn't you? I swear she was in here only a half-second ago."

The security guard shrugged, his eyes half-lidded.

"You wanted her out," he said. "She's out. Everything is good, then. Why complain?"

The woman turned and scanned the fitting room again, seemingly looking right through me. "Well. That's right, I guess," she said. "But, still. How bizarre is that?"

The guard shrugged again.

"What does a child caught stealing do?" he said. "They run away. So she crawled underneath." He pointed toward the floor. "Not that bizarre, really."

The woman frowned, continuing to look around the fitting room, hands planted on her hips. She clucked her tongue a few times. "Well, at least she didn't have time to make off with anything."

Without warning, the woman marched headlong into the room, beelining toward the blue vinyl bench where I'd set the dress—I had to practically leap out of her path and press my body flat against the nearest wall to avoid being bowled over.

The woman picked up the dress, shook it out, and draped it carefully over a meaty forearm. She looked around one more time and shook her head in seeming bewilderment before walking out, leaving the door open behind her.

I waited until I was sure they were gone, then quietly exhaled and stepped away from the wall, my heart still hammering. I had no idea how in God's name I'd made it through the previous five minutes without being spotted—the illusion I'd put together had been respectable, yes, but it hadn't been ready for primetime.

Had it?

I checked my reflection in the mirror.

There was nothing to see.

I was gone—as gone as I could get. The illusion had somehow turned flawless, perfecting itself, at the very moment that the fitting room door had opened, and I had no idea how I'd managed to pull it off.

Staring in disbelief, I paced back and forth across the stall, wildly waved my arms over my head, and leapt into the air again and again as though the floor underneath my feet had suddenly turned to fire. No matter what I did, no matter how I moved, nothing about my appearance changed—the illusion held fast. All I could see in the mirror was the half-open door behind me: the blue-painted plywood with its brass hinges, the stainless-steel clothes hook, the disability placard mounted underneath. I had disappeared entirely.

Still invisible, I exited the stall and slowly walked out of the fitting area, left the Young Miss clothing section, and cautiously stepped out onto the main retail floor, scanning the face of every man, woman, and child that I passed, searching for any sign of recognition, any acknowledgement of my existence, any evidence whatsoever that I had been detected—but there was none. I was the very definition of *alone in the middle of a crowd.* Playing like a poltergeist, I knocked a plastic jar full of bath salts from a display shelf onto the floor and watched for some sort of reaction: a judgmental stare, a smile, a frown, a raised eyebrow. Anything. A few passersby looked down at the jar when it struck the tile, but not a single person even glanced in my direction. Based on their (non-)reactions, you'd think that the jar had fallen over purely by chance. Feeling emboldened, I walked up to a random clerk standing nearby and whispered *hello* into his ear, causing him to flinch wildly and wave his hands around his head like he was batting away a swarm of angry bees. (I was sorry for it later, but it was kind of funny at the time.) After that, I searched for the busiest aisle I could find, stopped at an intersection between the Pharmacy Center, Home & Office, Sporting Goods, and Cosmetics, and planted myself in the middle of a crowded thoroughfare. Shoppers approached me from every side—pushing carts, corralling their children, carrying armfuls of products, sipping from coffee cups or soda cans—and every single one of them was seemingly oblivious to my presence. Matter of fact, I had to sidestep and weave almost constantly just to keep from being trampled.

Before long, I declared the experiment a categorical success— nobody, not a single soul, could lay an eye on me—and without giving it a second thought, I lifted my body into the air, my arms spread wide and head thrown back, and spun myself around and around in slow, balletic circles only inches above the heads of shoppers walking by. I let myself laugh out loud for the first time in a long time, watching as the masses underneath me stared up at the ceiling and searched in vain for the source of the phantom sound.

I was free.

And there was more than that—something that made it even better: holding onto my freedom would no longer require a show of force. I could simply vanish, taking my freedom right along with me wherever I went.

For the first time, I had the ability to move through the world unnoticed, without scrutiny, and without fear—of accidentally stepping over a line and entering the wrong state, the wrong county, the wrong city, the wrong district, the wrong side of town, the wrong street, the wrong building, the wrong level, the wrong room, the wrong *space*, and inadvertently speaking the wrong words, at the wrong time, to the wrong person or set of people, and winding up shot with automatic weapons or beaten into a vegetative state or sexually assaulted and then disbelieved or subjected to racially-charged insults, thinly disguised or overt. All of those fears—fears that I had lived with for as long as I could remember, even at the age of twelve—would eventually peel away like a snakeskin and be forgotten in my wake. Not because the threats themselves had disappeared, but because I had.

• • •

I left the store, still shocked by what I'd accomplished.

The dust that covered my body had responded on the fly to changes in my environment, adapting dynamically, and it continued to do the same as I walked toward the rear of the parking lot. The evolution was happening so naturally that I couldn't even be sure I controlled it anymore. The configuration of particles was shifting constantly all around me, adjusting to light, positions, and angles: every time I moved, it felt like my skin was crawling across my muscle and bones to compensate.

As I approached the boundary fence, I noticed something else had changed—the sunlight. Even though it was close to noon (without a cloud in the sky), I could feel only a fraction of the sun's normal warmth. It made sense. I was literally wearing darkness like a shroud; the light simply couldn't reach me the way it used to.

I climbed the rickety chain-link fence.

When I landed on the other side, I heard the sound of Harmony's voice coming from the direction of the tent. It came as a surprise—I hadn't expected her back at camp before the evening.

And there was something else, too: although I couldn't understand a word she'd just said, the tone of her voice was all wrong. She'd sounded upset.

"Harm?" I called out.

I took a few steps forward and stood on the edge of the riverbank, listening, but all I could hear was the burble of the creek in front of my feet, the rollercoaster car laboring up the first lift hill, its tow chain clacking rhythmically, and the sound of the nearby freeway, a deep rumble—the city's resonant breathing.

"Harmony," I shouted.

A few seconds later I heard her scream.

• • •

I burst through the dust barrier surrounding the tent and tore open the front flap, popping the zipper teeth apart and leaving the surrounding nylon in tattered shreds.

I saw two white boys—maybe sixteen or seventeen years old—both of them tall and lean, both of them down on their knees. One was straddling Harmony's stomach with his back facing me, looking over his shoulder, while the other one knelt alongside, a cell phone in his hand—recording video, probably. Everybody was clothed, but that didn't make a damn bit of difference to me; I knew that what I was witnessing was wrong.

Both boys looked terrified.

Neither one was focused on me at all. They seemed to be eyeing the opening I'd just created in the tent—and that was when I remembered:

I was invisible.

"What the fuck," said the blonde one with the phone. At almost the exact same moment, the other boy—pale and dark-haired—

70

said pretty much the same thing.

Ignoring them both, I moved further into the tent and saw that the boy on top of Harmony was pressing his hand firmly against her mouth, leaning into her face with his weight—the back of her skull had created a depression in the earth beneath the fabric of the tent floor. Nostrils flaring, she clutched the boy's wrist with both hands, trying to pry it loose. Her eyes were darting wildly in pools of dark mascara.

I didn't have a plan.

I just acted.

Dropping the veneer of invisibility, I stripped the dust from my body in a flurry that swirled around me like a sandstorm as I lifted myself from the tent floor, my body coiled in a rigid crouch, my arms spread to either side, my mouth open grotesquely wide like the mouth of a stone gargoyle.

I was screaming at the top of my lungs.

• • •

The tent was silent.

"Are you okay?" I whispered.

I knew the answer already—she wasn't—but I didn't know where else to start.

Harmony and I were sitting side by side with our legs touching, my arm draped over her shoulder, while the two boys—unconscious, battered and bloodied—lay face down on the blankets in front of us like corpses ready for the river. In my anger, I had hurt them. I had injured them in ways that would require hospitalization. Like a young child playing a game of war with two plastic action figures, one gripped in each hand, I had taken the bodies of these two boys under my control and clapped them together—again, and again, and again— simulating the essence of combat, until they'd both gone completely limp. But they were still breathing. And every once in a while, I heard one of them groaning as though caught in the grips of a terrible dream.

I pulled Harmony in closer.

"Hey. Real talk. Are you okay?" I asked.

"Yeah," she said. "I just got scared, I think. Nothing really happened."

I looked at her for a few beats. "You're serious? That was nothing to you?"

"You know what I mean."

"Actually, I don't," I said. "What I just saw? I mean, damn Harmony. That wasn't nothing."

She shook her head. The lower third of her face was still bright red from the force of the boy's hand.

"I just got scared for a sec," she said. "I'm not even sure why."

"You're not sure why?"

"Not really."

I almost pushed things further, but I decided to leave the situation alone; there was no point in arguing with her. She saw the incident—her life—in her own way, and nothing I could say was going to change it. I knew that, even back then.

"Who are they?" I asked, kicking one of the boys' arms with the toe of my shoe.

Harmony stared at me like I'd asked her for the name of the prime minster of Liberia.

"How would I know?" she asked.

"You don't know them?"

"I mean. Sort of. But not their names or anything."

"Okay. But what about where they came from. How they got here."

Harmony shrugged again, then started playing with her hair—head cocked, twirling a pigtail with an index finger, running her tongue across her front teeth. I knew that habit of hers, that affectation. The only reason she engaged in it was because she thought it looked cute—cute enough, she hoped, to distract from how obviously uncomfortable she was.

"Harm," I said, trying to be gentle. "If we knew something

about who they are, it might help us know what to do next."

She looked down at her lap. "I'm not sure."

I was losing my patience. "Come on, Harmony. Who are they?"

"Boys," she said, as though no further explanation was needed.

"Boys? That's it?"

"They're from State," she said. "I don't know. I met them the other night—it was a party somewhere. Some fraternity."

"They're college students? As in, they go to fucking college?"

Harmony shrugged by way of a response. I noticed that her hair-twirling had picked up speed.

"So, you met some frat boys at a random party—I got that. But then you decided to bring them back here. To our invisible tent." I shook my head. "That actually seemed like a good idea to you? Shit, Harmony."

She stopped twirling and glared.

"Don't try and put this on me," she said. "What happened wasn't my fault."

"I thought you said it was nothing."

"Fuck you, Tal."

"All right, look," I said. "I'm not blaming you for what these assholes did. That's on them. I'm talking about being careful. Careful with my secret, I mean. I'm not trying to advertise myself out here, Harmony."

"I can't believe you're thinking about yourself right now. That's some selfish bullshit, Tallah."

I thought about it.

She was right.

"I'm sorry," I said. "All right. Just tell me one thing and then I'll drop it."

"Fine. What."

"When the boys saw the tent and everything. What did they do? Did they say anything when they saw it?"

"Whatever. I don't remember. *Cool. Right on.* Something like that. They thought it was camouflage or a hologram or something. I don't know. They didn't really care that much about it—they just wanted, you know, to go inside."

"Shit, Harmony."

"Yeah. I know."

We sat together in the tent and debated our next move.

It didn't take us all that long—the options seemed limited.

In the end, we agreed. Right or wrong, we didn't feel as though we had any choice but to leave the Jungle—to leave the city, maybe even the state—and never come back. The way we saw it, the only real alternative would have been to call the police and offer our version of that afternoon's events (including a plausible explanation for the injuries the boys had suffered). And who the hell would have believed a couple of dirty street kids—nothing but whorish jailbait, in the eyes of the law—over a pair of college fraternity brothers?

Harmony was already halfway out of the tent when I paused, staring down at the two boys, still unconscious.

"Hold up," I said.

Harmony froze in the entryway. "We need to go, Tal."

"I know that. Just hold up."

I hesitated. I knew what I wanted (needed?) to do, but I couldn't decide whether or not I should.

"What, Tallah? What's wrong?"

"I don't know," I said. "I think I might need to do something else."

Harmony waved her hands, urging me forward. "Like?"

"I'm not sure. Something more."

"More? The fuck you mean, more? More what?"

I gestured toward the boys. "More to them."

"As in, hurt them some more?"

"Yes," I replied. "I mean, not exactly."

"Then what do you mean? We need to go, Tallah. We don't

have time for this."

"I know that. I know." I paused, rubbing my face with both hands. "Listen. These two assholes right here? All right, yes, they're beat up a little bit right now. But they'll recover from it. Good as new. But what about us?"

Harmony stared at me. "Us?" she said. "Shit didn't even happen to you, Tallah. It was me."

"Whatever. I'm a part of this too, Harmony."

"So what then? You want to kill them? Cut off their cocks—what, exactly?"

I thought about it for a little while before an idea came to me. I'm not sure why I thought of it, even to this day.

"Their thumbs," I said.

"Their thumbs?"

I nodded. It felt like the right decision.

"Here's what I think," I said. "These motherfuckers need a reminder of what they did. A permanent reminder. And you know what? When they look down at their hands and see two empty spaces where their thumbs used to be—that shit doesn't fade. I think they'll remember us."

Harmony was staring at me as though I'd come unhinged.

"So you want to leave them with eight fingers each. That's your idea?"

"Yeah. It is."

"What the hell will that do, Tallah? It's not going to make them better at being boys, if that's what you're hoping for. So get that shit out of your head. If anything, it'll make them worse."

"Maybe. Maybe not. But either way, they won't forget."

"Forget?" Harmony's eyes were wide. "Think about it, Tallah. You appeared out of thin air like a ghost and started *floating*, right before you picked them up off the ground and gave them both a beat-down of a lifetime—two grown-ass boys on the fucking swim team. I think they're going to remember today just fine."

"They're swimmers?"

"I guess so. Yeah. I mean, that's what they said they were, at least. What does it matter?"

That settled it.

I knelt down next to the dark-haired one and took hold of his wrist.

"Tallah. Listen to me," Harmony said. "Don't."

I ignored her.

Staring at the boy's hand, I imagined the way he must have used it to slice through the water's surface, making a clean entry, before pulling through the rest of the stroke—optimizing propulsion and minimizing drag. I wondered how often his hand had made that motion—thousands of times? Hundreds of thousands of times? And how many times had he used that same hand to stifle a young girl's scream?

Harmony snapped her fingers a few times.

"Tallah—hello? Do not do this. I'm serious. I told you—nothing even really happened. I just freaked out a little bit, okay? It's not that big of a deal."

I heard Harmony's words, and I even thought about them for a moment—was this a big deal or not?—but it didn't take me long to decide. It was. To me, it was.

Still holding the boy's wrist, I closed my eyes and pictured the structures underneath his pale skin. The thumb is the first digit of the hand—the outermost digit—and in Latin, it is called the *pollex*. The thumb is composed of bones called phalanges, two of them, joined together by hinge-like joints that enable it to flex inward toward the palm. Of the five digits, it is the only one that is opposable to the other four.

"Tallah. Please don't. It won't help us. Nothing will be different."

I think I knew she was right, even then. But I didn't listen to her.

tallahassee

Harmony and I left the state of California and moved to Florida.

We started off living in a pay-by-the-hour motel called The Alhambra, located on the south side of Tallahassee, which—as we saw it—was about as far from the Bay Area as you could get without leaving the continental United States. I couldn't say we had a good reason for choosing Tallahassee over the hundreds of other options, honestly. Believe it or not, Harmony chose it because of the name— more specifically, because it had my name at the beginning. Seriously. That was the reason. I think it might have been Harmony's quirky way of thanking me for agreeing to move across country with her, for sticking by her side when the going got rough. This is your city, she told me. It was named after you, so that's where we're going. Go on: take me down to Tallah Town.

The quality of the motel was about what you'd expect: a double-bed with no box-spring, a window with no air-conditioner, a TV with no cable or remote, a lamp with no shade, a bathroom with a shower but no actual bathtub, and a whole mess of cockroaches with absolutely no common courtesy. In many ways it was worse than living outside in the Jungle, but it did have one major advantage over our previous living situation: it had an actual front door that locked with a deadbolt and a thick privacy chain. The difference may have only been a psychological one, but it helped somehow.

Room 17 was our home sweet home. It was on the ground floor, right between the front office and the ice machine. You had to be an adult to rent a room, so Harmony told the night manager she was twenty-one years old, even providing a (fake) California driver's license to prove it, but he wasn't buying her bullshit—not for one second. Only when Harmony offered to lift up her shirt and let him take a few pictures did he have a change of heart.

With a rent bill due at the end of every week, we had to get serious about making money. For me, that meant cleaning rooms at the motel in the mornings and working a cash register at Wendy's during the night shift, but I'll be honest: my foray into the world of honest work lasted less than a month. After that, I turned to petty theft to help pay the bills, using my abilities to steal small amounts of cash from rich people's wallets and purses without anybody noticing.

As for Harmony, she made her money doing something else—I wasn't exactly sure what she did all day, to be honest. All I knew was that it was lucrative and that it was against the law. I didn't want to know any more detail than that.

• • •

During my time in Tallahassee, I wore Bel on my body any time I went out into the city alone, no matter where I was going, no matter the time of day. She was, in the most literal sense, my second skin. In the mornings, after a shower I would dry off, dress in something light and form-fitting, and then use my abilities to coat myself in a layer of fine dark powder, after which I would promptly vanish. I had gotten so skilled at working with Bel that the process took about as long as putting on a t-shirt and a pair of shorts. Unfurling the dust like a skein of cloth, wrapping my entire body in its ghostlike folds, and instantaneously adapting the surface to whatever light happened to surround me—all of these things had become automatic. Habitual. I quickly reached the point where invisibility felt far more natural to me than social interaction, where being inconspicuous felt more desirable than to be watched, and where the idea of leaving no trace as I moved through the world felt more admirable than making a noticeable difference.

I forgot how to make eye contact. How to exchange pleasantries. I followed people into places they'd always believed were safe and separate, listened to private conversations that I had no business hearing, stole things that I wanted while telling myself they were necessary, watched intimate moments—confessions, sexual encounters, an assisted suicide at a hospital bedside—that I had no right to witness, and through it all, learned more about the inner workings of the world in a matter of months than I had in my prior thirteen years of living.

I focused on two things only, both of them selfish: access and experience. Going places where I'd never been allowed to set foot, seeing and doing things I'd only read about in fiction, as long as nobody got too hurt in the process. If I managed to help a few strangers along the way—intervening when I saw something truly horrifying and preventable happening—so be it, but the needs of others were an afterthought, honestly. A side effect of the self-soothing drug I was taking.

The first bank branch I ever robbed was located at the front of a grocery store, opposite the checkout lines; it wasn't much more than a long wooden countertop, like what you might find in a classic diner, with five bank tellers sitting in a row behind it. No bulletproof glass pane in front of their faces, no dedicated security staff, no locked door to keep customers out. It looked more like a place you would go to rent a car than somewhere you would go to take out money. Which meant that they didn't keep much of it on hand: only what was contained in each teller's cash drawer, as well as a small matte-black safe tucked behind the manager's desk. But that was fine: a little bit of cash was all I was looking for. This wasn't one of those last-job-before-I-retire heists. There was no sense in being greedy.

I decided to do it on a Saturday morning. I knew from previous visits that the lines were shorter, but not so short that the cash drawers would have no reason to be open. That was the trick. I needed just the right number of customers—enough so that the tellers stayed busy processing transactions, but not so many that I ran the risk of bumping into someone and calling attention to my (invisible) self.

As I approached the counter, I saw only one teller working—a young light-skinned brother with long locs tied back in a swirling bun. His gold nameplate read Jabari. He was talking to an Indian woman with an infant strapped to her chest.

While they chatted about how the weekend was going so far, I ducked under the red guide ropes, approached the empty teller station to Jabari's left, and quietly climbed onto the counter, swung my legs over to the other side, and hopped down. The branch manager, a middle-aged white woman in a pink pantsuit, looked up from her computer screen and glanced in my direction for a moment before returning to whatever she'd been doing.

I crept over to Jabari's side and stood a few feet away, waiting as the customer struggled to fill out a yellow deposit slip. Her baby was kicking and grabbing at everything in reach, including the long chain attached to the pen she was holding.

"Can I help?" Jabari asked.

The woman smiled. "Please. Thanks."

As Jabari filled out the form, I studied the cash drawer mounted underneath the counter: its grey metal face had a single lock, a small silver dome with a vertical keyway. There wouldn't be much time to act once the drawer was opened. Within seconds, I would need to reach out, place a hand on one of the stacks of bills (the Benjamin Franklins if possible), and soak up some of that sweet, sweet paper, absorbing it through the dust shell around my hand (and thereby rendering it invisible). All of this, without accidentally bumping into Jabari or getting my fingers slammed in the drawer. No problem.

I didn't have to wait long—Jabari was efficient.

He stamped the back of a paper check and dropped it into a slotted wooden box.

"And then seventy-five back," Jabari said, pulling out a set of keys attached to a retractable cable on his belt.

He leaned forward in his chair and unlocked the drawer, opened it, and began flipping through the twenties section of the tray with an index finger while I slid up next to him and made a beeline toward the hundreds, moving quickly but cautiously, as though preparing to grab a snake behind its head. I placed a hand down on top of the stack, peeled off five or six crisp notes without moving a single muscle, and drew them up through the dust barrier into my palm. Jabari finished plucking a ten-dollar bill and a five-dollar bill from their respective slots in the tray as I slipped my hand safely out of the drawer.

I'd done it.

I took a cautious step backward.

That was when Jabari reacted.

As if driven by reflex, his hand shot out and took hold of my arm, clamping down like a dog's jaws around my wrist. He didn't even glance in my direction; he continued to stare impassively at the cash in his other hand, sorting through it with his thumb.

I almost screamed.

Before I could make a sound, he relaxed his grip, released my wrist, and it was over. Almost instantly. In fact, the encounter had happened so quickly that for a moment I thought I'd imagined it, that my mind had somehow made manifest my fear of being caught. Covering my mouth to keep from shrieking, I slowly backed away as Jabari locked the drawer, retracted the keys to the spool on his belt, and counted out seventy-five dollars onto the countertop.

• • •

That boy became my new pet project.

Over the next few days, I followed Jabari everywhere he went: to his dorm room at Florida State University, to an off-campus convenience store for a case of energy drinks, to a class on cognitive psychology, to a study group at a student lounge, to his fraternity's house, to a listening party for a band's new record (I didn't like it at all). Whenever I was around him, I kept my distance, staying on the opposite side of a room, keeping one or two bodies between us at all times. Remaining on my feet when he sat on a couch or in a chair, sitting only when he was lying down on his back, hovering near the exit, poised to run away at a moment's notice when he stood up again.

I don't know why I was so afraid. I could have ended Jabari's life with nothing more than a well-placed thought, and I won't lie—I was strongly considering doing exactly that. I thought long and hard about ending that young brother's existence, for the simple reason that he'd taken something profound away from me—my ability to pass unnoticed through the world, and by extension, my fledgling freedom—and because I had no idea why or how, I believed that he might need to be erased from the earth in order for me to get it back. I wasn't seeking revenge; I wasn't even angry. I was seeking reclamation. If possible, I would reclaim my former life by acquiring information, by learning what power Jabari evidently had over me, but I would reclaim it through violence if left no other choice.

On the fourth morning, I followed Jabari to the gym.

I stood in the entranceway leading to the weight room while he pedaled a recumbent bike on the main floor, his body swaying side to side. This whole song and dance with Jabari had gotten old—trailing after him, standing unacknowledged in his presence, watching, waiting, receiving nothing in return—and I was losing my damn patience with it. Like these poor clowns all around me trudging along on treadmills to nowhere, or endlessly picking up and putting down pieces of iron, or stepping up onto a plastic box just so they could immediately step off again, I was spinning my wheels. I needed to see some results.

Without thinking it through, I stormed over to Jabari and stood behind him, a couple feet back, and stared daggers as he continued to pedal at a steady pace, looking up at one of the TVs mounted overhead—ESPN was showing the worst highlights from yesterday's sports action.

I waited. For what, I wasn't sure.

The heart rate monitor on the bike's display read 117, then 115, then 113, then 114. The values fluctuated over time, but never rose above the 120 mark, and never dropped below 105. I watched for a while, mesmerized. There was something oddly intimate about seeing the current status of someone's heart stripped down and translated into numbers. Seeing a person's internal rhythm—something only they could feel—laid bare. It served as a direct window into the things he found effortless, as well as the things that taxed him.

Keeping watch on the monitor, I approached Jabari from behind and stood at his back, looming. Hanging over his shoulder like a scavenger. I was close enough to hear his patterned breathing; to see the sheen on his shoulders; to smell the scent of mint and lemongrass on his scalp.

I don't know why, but I decided to bring my hands forward and place them directly in front of his eyes, holding them there as if I were blindfolding him. For a moment it felt as though I was forcing him to use my flesh as a lens, but that wasn't accurate; he wasn't seeing through me. The reality was that I was forcing him to see *around* me.

I kept my hands in place for an uncomfortable length of time.

The numbers on the monitor began to change.

118. 122.

137. 153.

164. 170.

176. 181.

• • •

That night, I watched Jabari pace the floor of his dorm room, shirtless, drinking a brownish liquid straight from a plastic bottle and murmuring what sounded like religious passages to himself, his long locs bouncing off his shoulders as he shook his head in an agitated rhythm. From time to time, he poured a slug of liquid onto his hands and randomly flicked his dripping fingers as though issuing blessings to a congregation, before gliding his wet palm across his forehead, his cheeks, his lips, his throat. It was as if he was consecrating himself.

I stood in the corner nearest the front door, my muscles tensed, primed for flight. The dorm room's main living area was decently sized—two other roommates shared the space—so I had a reasonable area in which to maneuver, but I preferred to stay as close to the exit as possible in case I needed to get away from whatever this was, this bizarre ritual. This homespun exorcism in progress.

I wasn't sure why I had come here in the first place. Or what I was waiting for. Hoping for, maybe. After what felt like almost an hour, Jabari dropped the bottle onto the carpet and stood, swaying next to a half-open window. He put both hands over his face. I could see his shoulders shaking, and before long, he let out a hoarse sob.

A better person than me would have felt sorry for him. But I was pragmatic. I needed to understand him, not pity him—I needed data, not mindless sentiment.

"I'm sorry," Jabari said through his cupped hands. He let them fall and looked around the room almost accusingly. "Okay? I'm sorry. You hear?"

I stayed silent.

Soon he began pacing again, more fiercely this time, and before long, he'd picked up the bottle and resumed his bizarre, alcohol-drenched sacrament.

"I'm sorry for reaching," he said, raking his fingernails down his chest. "I dared too much. I did things." His voice trailed off. "I know that I've been wrong to question you like I did. The presence."

I wasn't sure what to do or what to think.

Was I supposed to be responding to all this? Or letting it run?

"I know it," he continued, still talking to the air, still anointing himself, still stalking the room. "I should have known my place, though. My earth. I should have let you be. Please, talk to me. No no no no no. No, that's wrong—don't talk to me. No. Don't. It needs to be what you make it, not what I pray it. To be whatever it may be."

I was at a loss.

"Are you even there still?" he asked.

Was I supposed to answer that?

"Yes," I said softly.

Oh, shit.

What the hell did I just do?

Jabari's eyes widencd.

He cast the bottle aside and rushed in my general direction with his arms spread wide open, scanning the room wildly, as though trying to corral a small animal that had managed to wander indoors.

On instinct, I stopped that drunk-ass lunatic dead in his tracks. I took hold of him, seized his body, and lifted it clear off the floor, pinning his arms down to his sides and locking his ankles together at the bone.

Inexplicably, with tears in his eyes, he smiled broadly. Beaming. He looked like a lost child who'd just seen his mother come running from the middle of a crowd.

"Are you taking me?" he asked.

"No," I replied, but it sounded too severe, too booming. "No, I'm not," I said softly.

Jabari's face fell.

"But it's you, right?" he asked desperately. "You're the Being One. Aren't you?"

Am I the Being One?

I thought about it.

I don't see why not.

"Yes," I answered. "I am the Being One."

"And are you mine?"

That one was easy. No pondering required.

"No," I replied. "I'm not anyone's. But maybe I can help you."

• • •

I stayed with Jabari into the morning hours.

As far as he was concerned, I was the Being One.

Being One, he would say, can you answer a question?
Being One, I don't understand.
Being One, why does this have to be true?
Being One, I have been hurt so many times.
Being One, where is the place that I came from?
Being One, is there something for me to finish?
Being One, I am so glad you found me.
Being One, you are the flesh and the blood and the life.

It was overwhelming.

I found myself simultaneously reassuring him, correcting him, advising him, and lying to him, boldface. I had no idea what I was doing (or what I might have been doing *to* him in the process), but I didn't stop. I couldn't, both because he seemed to need me to continue, and because from my point of view, our entire dynamic—his raw, naked vulnerability, my clear superiority, his thirst for an authoritative voice, my desire to be heard, to let my thoughts pour out—was too novel and too intoxicating to give up.

"Being One?" Jabari said.

He was laid out on the sofa, which meant that I felt safe enough to be seated. I'd chosen a spot on the carpet near the door.

"Yes?" I answered.

"Are you real?" he asked.

"I am. Very."

"Are you sure about that, though? Because this doesn't feel real to me," he said. "I think I might be dreaming it all. You know? Lucidly. But still stargazing. Checking my eyelids for holes, as my dad used to say."

"Maybe."

"But then again, I mean. Damn. This sure does feel like I'm here—right here. In the world, I mean. Not up in my synapses. But down here in the thick of it."

"I think you are."

"All right, then," he said, adjusting his position. He looked like he'd just had an epiphany. "So if that's all true—if you're real, and if I'm real, and if nobody on the outside is dreaming all this—then where have you been, Being One?"

I hesitated.

"Where have I been?"

"I mean no disrespect by that, you know? I'm just asking. I've needed you around sometimes. Earlier in my life, mainly."

"I'm sorry," I said.

"No no no. It's all right. Just, if you can—please stay close to me. I don't always need to hear you, but I need to know you're there."

I saw an opening.

"How do you know I am?" I asked.

Jabari paused. "What do you mean?"

"How do you know that I'm around? If I'm not speaking, I mean."

He let out a sigh, turning his focus back to the ceiling.

"I'm not sure," he said. "The room breathes different, I guess—or maybe it holds its breath. I don't know. But the light doesn't fall the same way. You make waves in the ozone that I can feel. You're atmospheric." He made imaginary rainfall in the air with his fingertips.

"Um. Okay. But you don't see me, right?"

"What do you mean?"

"I mean with your eyes. You can't see me."

"Not with my eyes. No. I can't see you."

• • •

"Being One?"

"Yes, Jabari."

It was early afternoon, and we'd barely changed positions over the past few hours. Jabari's roommates would be returning soon from a vacation trip (jet-skiing or something), and so we didn't have much time before his real life would resume. Which I was glad for; I needed a break from this.

"I have a question," Jabari said.

"All right. Go ahead."

"Can I request things from you?" he asked. Judging by his sheepish tone, he expected a negative response.

"Request things?"

"Yeah."

"Maybe," I answered. "It depends. What do you want?"

Jabari paused. He seemed to be thinking long and hard about his answer.

"I just want things to be better," he said.

I waited.

"Um," I said. "That's good. But can you be more specific?"

He seemed hesitant.

"Can you protect me?" he finally asked.

Even though his focus was on the ceiling, I could see the tears in his eyes.

"Protect you from what?"

"I don't know—everything," he said. "Look. I'm hated, Being One. You know? I'm the hated one out there."

"I understand. And I'm sorry. But I can't help you with that."

The truth was that I could have—I could have protected him from almost anything. But only if I stayed around, which I wasn't planning on doing.

Jabari turned to look in my direction. "You can't?"

"No. I can't. But if you think of me during those moments when you're unsafe, you'll be stronger. And then you can protect yourself."

Jabari didn't respond. I could tell that I'd disappointed him.

"What else?" I asked.

"What do you mean?"

"What else would you ask for, if you could?"

He shrugged. "Just help, I guess. With everything. With making it. Getting by."

I wasn't sure what he meant by that.

"How about small things?" I asked. "Could I help you with those?"

He nodded. "Yeah. Okay. Definitely."

• • •

In the beginning, it was like being a genie let loose from a lamp.

Jabari would ask for ordinary things—for a little bit of extra cash, for his roommate to be pranked (I made his bedsheet fly around the room like a ghost while Jabari took video with his phone), for an unpopular professor's car doors to be jammed closed on a permanent basis, or for a bottle of vintage bourbon to make its way out of the downstairs neighbors' window, fly up the side of the building, and come to rest in his waiting hand. Those kinds of things. At first, Jabari was clearly uncomfortable asking me for what he needed (wanted?), and I was equally reluctant to fulfill his every asinine wish, but it didn't take long for us each to see the light. His appetite was whetted when he witnessed the extent of my capabilities, and as for me, I quickly grew to relish granting or denying his requests at my own discretion, with no explanation required.

But it didn't last.

Soon Jabari's requests became less concrete, less material. Less here-and-now. More long-term, more long-shot. He wanted to have his spirit renewed, to have his wrongs pardoned, to be cleansed. To have his future told, to have his successes preordained, mapped out for him. To have his family cared for after he passed on. He wanted knowledge—a reason to keep going. A reasonable explanation for the tragedies of his life, and my assurances that they wouldn't happen again.

• • •

"I need to go now," I said quietly.

Jabari and I were on opposite sides of one of the bedrooms adjoining the main living space, with the door closed and music playing. His roommates had been back for a few hours—they were busy eating takeout noodles on the couch.

"What do you mean?" Jabari asked.

"I can't stay here," I said. "I need to go someplace else."

"Really?" He looked absolutely crushed.

"But I want you to remember that I'm still with you—I see you, Jabari. We're connected. Even if you can't feel me, it doesn't mean I'm not nearby."

I sounded ridiculous. But I was doing my best to part amicably; for some reason, that was important to me.

"I don't understand, Being One. Did I do something wrong?"

"No. Of course not."

"Then why?"

I didn't have an answer ready.

The truth was that I'd gotten the information I came for: namely, that Jabari was able to sense my presence because, although he seemed nice and well-adjusted in most ways, he was fundamentally weird as shit, which hopefully meant that he was an anomaly. The exception to the rule. In any case, he wasn't a threat, which had been my main concern, so I felt that my work here was finished. It was time. I was exhausted and starving and had to pee, and there was no way in hell I could help Jabari in the way he needed me to—he was clearly not a weekend project—so what was the point in staying?

"I came to teach you something," I said. "And you've learned it."

"Learned what?" He sounded desperate. "You taught me so much, Being One. What was the most important lesson to remember?"

• • •

When I finally made it back to the motel room, Harmony was not happy.

"Bitch, you cannot— cannot—just disappear and not tell me where you went," she said. "Not overnight."

She had one white towel wrapped around her head, and another one wrapped around her waist. Even after all this time together, I still hadn't gotten used to her insistence on casual nudity.

"I'm sorry," I said. "Shit was crazy. I'm sorry."

"I mean. You don't even bother to turn on the phone and call me?"

Harmony was right. I kept a pre-pay phone in my pocket, but it was always off—I couldn't be getting texts and shit while invisible—so I usually forgot I even had it on me.

"I'm sorry. Okay?"

"You should be fucking sorry."

"I am."

"Good," Harmony said.

There was an awkward silence in the room.

I gestured toward the bathroom. "So are you done in there? I need to shower."

"Yeah," Harmony said, shedding both towels onto the floor. "I need clothes. Can I borrow something?"

"Whatever you can find."

I gathered up the two towels while Harmony started digging through the cardboard box where I kept all my shit. Clothes, bags, sodas, keepsakes, feminine hygiene items, gum, extra deodorant sticks—everything. Well, everything except for my money.

Just as I entered the bathroom, I heard Harmony gasp—loud enough that I jumped a little. It sounded like she'd been electrocuted.

"Oh my God, Tallah," she cried out. "Are you fucking serious?"

"What?"

"These," she said. "These, Tallah. I can't believe you and your sick ass. What the hell is wrong with you?"

I rushed out of the bathroom to see what she was going on about.

That was when I saw them on the floor:

Four severed thumbs, little more than thin white bones stitched together by shreds of desiccated skin.

"Seriously, Tallah," Harmony said. "You have some kind of mental problem."

I didn't say anything. I couldn't remember making the decision to save them.

• • •

A few days later, I fell ill.

I didn't have the energy to do anything other than lie on the bed, drink lemon-lime Gatorade, stumble to and from the toilet, and watch one of the three shitty channels available on the nineteen-inch TV.

The symptoms felt almost flu-like: nausea, fatigue, fever, body aches, and shortness of breath.

But I was worried that my problems were caused by something else, something non-viral: the use of my abilities.

For over a year, I'd been acting a fool, plain and simple, using my abilities indiscriminately, on an almost daily basis—and on many of those days, nearly constantly—without restraint, without considering the consequences to my body, without remembering the lessons of my father. I couldn't help but wonder if my recklessness was finally catching up with me. And if it was, would that stop me from continuing?

• • •

On my third day spent in bed, Harmony came home at lunchtime carrying a styrofoam carton of *rojo posole* stew and a white plastic spoon.

"How's my sick little bitchy bitch?" she asked, setting everything down on the nightstand. She was dressed simply—ripped jeans and a green t-shirt with a tree icon on the pocket. Same old pigtails, but the purple had faded out.

I rubbed my eyes. "Hey."

"It's all for you. Enjoy that heat, girl."

"Thanks, Harm."

"You're welcome," she said.

I sat up in bed and stuffed a pillow behind me, punching it into shape. I picked up the soup and the spoon, sat back, cracked open the lid, and peeled it back, letting the steam escape. Drops of condensation slid down the clear plastic.

I paused, spoon in hand.

Harmony hadn't moved from the bedside. She was twirling her hair so ferociously that I could see a collection of loose strands wrapped around her finger like silken threads.

Shit.

"What's wrong," I demanded. "Don't try and be cute. Just tell me, Harmony."

"What?"

"I said no bullshit. What's wrong with you?"

"Nothing," she said, wide-eyed. "Geez. Everything is fine. Brilliant, actually."

I stared at her. "For real?"

"Of course! I was about to tell you that I have some people I want you to meet. That's all."

Shit.

"What kind of people?" I asked.

She shrugged.

"What kind, Harmony?"

"My kind, I guess," she said, winking. She seemed to be enjoying my annoyance, which only increased it. "They have an idea to tell you about—my idea. And I want you to promise me that you'll actually listen for once. Okay?"

"When."

"When what?"

"When do we meet?" I asked.

"Now."

"Now?" I set the soup carton back on the nightstand, slopping a bit of red liquid over the edge. "Harmony, don't be stupid for once. Look at me—I'm sick. I don't want to talk to anybody right now, not even you."

She flipped her hands dismissively. "Stop. You look great. And I can tell you're feeling better because you've got that mean gleam back in your eye. It's back, which means that you're back, love. I can tell. Don't try and lie."

Harmony was right—I was feeling much better. But that didn't mean that I was excited about meeting a bunch of "her kind" just twenty-four hours after I'd been down on my knees in front of the toilet, puking my guts out.

"Whatever. Fine." I whipped the blankets off of my feet and started climbing out of bed. "Where's this thing happening?"

"Here," Harmony said.

I paused, one leg hanging off the mattress.

"Don't tell me," I said. "They're waiting outside right now, aren't they."

Harmony smiled.

She left the room and came back a few minutes later with a tall white man by her side. He was in his twenties, wearing a black t-shirt that said The EAST across the front (it looked like the name of an edgy rock band). Brown curly hair down to his shoulders, skin that looked like it had seen weather—from work outdoors, not from play. I wasn't sure how I knew, but this man wasn't a beach bum or even a hiker: he was somebody who built things, or took them down, out in the elements.

"This is Elijah," Harmony said, curtsying for some bizarre reason. "Decorah is also here, but she wanted to stay outside."

"Hey," I said, nodding to Elijah. I was leaning against the wall near the TV, my arms crossed.

"Hi, Tallah," said Elijah.

He smiled, closed the door, slotted the privacy chain, and locked the deadbolt.

I had to endure their irritating small talk for a while.

Obviously, Harmony was trying to break the ice between us before getting to the damn point of the exercise, but I wasn't having it. You could let that shit stay frozen, as far as I was concerned. Sometimes ice is the only thing keeping you from falling through the surface and going under, from being pulled down into the cold and murky depths of something worse.

I kept a stern expression, responded to every question with as few words as possible, offered nothing personal about myself, and ignored all of Harmony's feeble jokes and (supposedly) amusing anecdotes, until Elijah finally got serious.

"I don't know what Mony told you, Tallah. But we could use your help moving our inputs and outputs. Literally and figuratively."

"Mony?" I said.

Harmony raised her hand like a schoolgirl. "That's me."

"Ah," I said. "Well, Elijah. Our friend Mony hasn't told me shit. So you're gonna need to start from the beginning."

"There's a lot to explain," he said. "More than I want to say at the moment. But in the end, I'm talking about a whole lot of Amp we need to sell."

I waited.

"Amp?" I said. "Sorry. I don't know what that is."

"Amp is weed, but with something extra—it's dipped in formaldehyde. Then pre-rolled before sale."

I wasn't sure I'd heard that correctly.

"Formaldehyde?"

"Or any kind of embalming fluid," Elijah said. "Yeah, I know, right? But people seem to really go for it."

"So why do you need my help?"

Elijah stared at Harmony for a few seconds. "You really didn't tell her anything, did you."

Harmony shrugged and started tugging on a pigtail.

"Okay," Elijah said, returning his attention to me. "Mony let me know some things about you—good things. She said that you carried yourself well and that you could handle certain special tasks, handle them better than anyone she's ever seen, in fact. And I've chosen to believe her. So I want you to come work with me—notice that I said 'with' not 'for.' Nine days out of ten, you won't be asked to do a thing. The risk is low and the money is right."

That last bit piqued my interest, but that didn't mean that I was sold on the proposition.

"Sounds like you're doing pretty good without me."

Elijah shrugged. "You're right. We are doing well. But that doesn't mean we couldn't be doing better."

"I'm thirteen."

"So what?"

"So what do you need me for—to be your runner?" I shook my head. "You want me to stand out on the corner and raise up when the cops roll on you?"

"We don't distribute like that."

"What, then?"

"First of all—your age? It's a good thing in my book," Elijah said. "Your gender, too. Both are advantages in this game, as I see it, because they make you unusual, and therefore unexpected. But those things are nothing without the mind to back them up. And I'm told that you have a mind for this. That's why I'm here."

I glared at Harmony, but she was too chicken-shit to make eye contact.

"Mony told you a whole lot of things, sounds like," I said.

Elijah grinned. "She did. And a whole lot of what she told me sounded far-fetched, to be honest. But a few things turned me into a believer. Four things, actually."

"Four things?"

"Four of these," he said, making a fist with each hand and extending his two thumbs.

• • •

One thing about Elijah that I learned right away: he was long on sweet talk, short on facts. Everything concrete that I learned during an hour's worth of chitchat with that man could have been summarized in a couple of breaths.

Basically, Elijah wanted me to serve as a combination between a logistics manager and brute enforcer—not the only one on his team, but one of several. In his mind, a thirteen-year-old whom he'd known for less than a day was an ideal candidate to help him deliver life-sentence-sized shipments of Amp from a major deepwater seaport in Jacksonville all the way to Tallahassee along Route 10 without attracting attention, to deliver the product to individual dealers in the city, and—in the spirit of one-stop, full-service treatment—to rough up anybody who didn't pay the new higher prices he was demanding.

Granted, I wasn't your everyday teenager, but still.

Harmony walked Elijah outside while I waited at the door, ready to confront her the moment she returned.

When she walked in, I didn't hesitate.

"You have got to be the dumbest," I said. "I swear to God, Harmony. Or is it Mony? You are so beyond stupid, I can't even believe it."

Harmony raised up her hands in mock surrender. "Calm down. They call it *relaxing*. It's fun. You should really try it sometime."

"I'm serious. What did you tell him about me?"

"A lot."

"A lot? Oh, my Lord, Harmony. What the hell for?"

"Look. I'm sorry, okay? He was cute and I was a little bit drunk at the time, and I started saying things. I'm sorry."

"You are such a stupid-ass, I swear."

"I know. I'm sorry."

"Fuck your sorries," I said. "What exactly did you tell him?"

Harmony shrugged. "Just things. I don't know. Elijah, he's way into all this *oneness* and metaphysical shit and *the connection* and everything. The natural world is powerful, and we are a part of the natural world—he likes to say that. He believes in some pretty out-there stuff, like mind reading and out-of-body experiences and moving shit just by thinking about it. So I told him about you. I couldn't help it, Tal. It was just so applicable."

I rubbed my temples—there was no getting through to this ignorant fool.

Whenever I had a problem with Harmony, regardless of its severity, it could never be resolved because she couldn't handle my righteous anger, my justifiable rage—at least not in its truest, purest form—and I knew it. Which meant that any time I tried to settle a legitimate issue between us, the process instantly degenerated into a pointless song and dance in which I offered the most watered-down, listener-friendly version of my grievance while she proceeded to deflect every word I said with her trademarked charm, a tactic I had somehow conditioned myself to tolerate, and maybe even to seek out.

"And the thumbs?" I asked.

Harmony picked something off of her lip, looked at it, and wiped it on her pants.

"Harmony."

"Right. Sorry. Yeah, I told him the thumb story. I had to, Tallah—it's an amazing story, and it gave you a crazy amount of street credibility, which matters a lot in this industry. Okay? I'm sorry."

"I swear. I know you're smart, Harmony. I know you are. But

you are so fucking stupid sometimes."

"Unfortunately, that's true," she said. "But I love you so much, Tally-girl. You know that, right?"

• • •

Since meeting Harmony, I had thought several times about leaving her behind and setting off on my own. But in the end, I'd always decided to stay.

The reasons were complicated, but they never involved issues of basic survival—I'd always known that I could take care of the hard-edged needs, the non-negotiables of my existence, without anybody's help. My reasons were softer than that. They involved fear—not a fear of starvation or exposure or assault, but of loneliness. Without Harmony, I had absolutely no one, and every time I'd ever considered starting over alone, I imagined spending my days and nights in solitude and silence, with my name and my face and my whereabouts and my story utterly forgotten, and I couldn't endure the thought of it. As much as I'd wished to be invisible to the outside world, that was only because the kind of visibility it offered—the mercilessly negative kind—was almost unbearable. The truth was that I wanted visibility, but on my own terms, in my own way. And although Harmony's personality was difficult beyond imagination, and although she brought with her an awkward assortment of baggage (more than half of which I was expected to help carry), she represented my only opportunity to be seen as anything other than a shadow.

But I was feeling different lately. The meeting with Elijah had changed things.

Up to that point, as far as I knew, Harmony had only been involved in petty criminal shit, same as I was, which meant that we'd only had the potential to ruin each other's lives in predictably petty ways. But now? Harmony was involved in something massively illegal, something that only career lawbreakers—professionals—would ever attempt, something from which ordinary lives like mine could never recover. And whether I agreed to help Harmony or not, I would be affected by the outcome of her actions if I chose to stick around.

• • •

Staying cooped up in the motel room was making me crazy, so I left the next morning and got out into the world—and did so, for the first time in ages, as a visible person. No Bel shell for me. Not today. It wasn't because I was desperate for human interaction or *to be seen* by somebody; the reason was purely practical. I needed to get a couple of errands done—errands that would require me to be more than just a ghost.

First, I paid a visit to the free clinic over at Coventry for a proper checkup, the last thing in the world I wanted to do. I felt just fine—better than fine, actually. But if I was planning to continue using my abilities at will (which I was—no question), then I needed to be sure that I wasn't killing myself slowly along the way. This meant going to the damn doctor and submitting myself wholesale to the healthcare process: the appraising eyes on me, the body measurements, the pages of intake questionnaires, the discussion of my history, my choices. The advice. The needle. My blood collected in two clear vials. The cold instruments manipulated by latex-gloved hands. The open-backed gown over my shoulders, and the sound of tissue paper crackling underneath me as I lay down on the exam table. I hated every second of every moment of the experience, but I felt the exam was important, so I pushed through with it.

The final verdict?

I was healthy.

Mostly.

The nurse practitioner did think that I might be suffering from mild depression, PTSD, and a generalized anxiety disorder, but I didn't give a shit about any of that—I was concerned about my body, not my mind. Body-wise? I was all right. Better than all right. Matter of fact, when my blood work came back from the lab down the hall, the physician assistant said that my results were *enviable*—as in, worthy of jealousy, very desirable—even for someone young. The numbers were *optimal*, she added.

I felt so relieved.

But at the same time, I couldn't understand: Why was I doing so well? What had I done differently than my father had?

After leaving the clinic I grabbed some pulled-pork nachos for lunch at Taco Libre to celebrate, then headed to the Leroy Collins Public Library (the coolest-named library in the world) over on West Park Avenue, where I checked out a few books in hardback—memoirs and autobiographies. This was for business, not pleasure; I was doing research. Reading about the lives of others helped me to think more clearly about my own, and since I was trying to make a major decision about my next step (whether to focus on maintaining what I'd already built, or to blow up everything and start fresh), I needed all the help I could get.

The last item on my list that day was to check on Jabari.

He'd been in the back of my mind ever since I'd left him (forsaken him?) the other night. I was worried: Had I caused some kind of lasting damage? Was Jabari still able to function, having discovered the Being One—something so obviously meaningful to him—and then having lost it, in such a short time? Was he worse off now than he had been before I came around?

Unsure of what I would find, I went out looking for him.

First I tried the bank branch in the grocery store. Jabari wasn't standing behind the counter, and when I asked the manager about him, she told me that he wasn't working that day.

After leaving the store, I tried the other places Jabari and I had gone together (unbeknownst to him, of course). Wearing Bel to make sure no one saw me coming or going, I searched for Jabari everywhere.

The auditoriums where his classes were held. The library. His dorm room. The fraternity house. One of his friends' apartments. The gym.

I tried. But I wasn't able to find him.

• • •

That night, the door to the motel room opened while I was dozing in bed.

I reached blindly for Harmony in the dark.

My hand fell on a cold patch of mattress where her body should have been. I felt around for her, but she wasn't there.

I turned over to face the door.

"Harm?" I whispered.

A yellow neon glow from the outside spilled through the open door into the entryway.

I squinted, blinking.

"Harm?"

The light slowly faded as the door closed. I heard the sound of the deadbolt engaging, then the privacy chain sliding into place. With the heavy blackout drape over the window, I couldn't see a thing other than a thin line of light from underneath the door.

I sat upright, my heart pounding.

"Harmony?"

"It's not Harmony," said a man's voice. "It's me."

The voice sounded familiar.

"Elijah?"

"Yes," he said.

I flashed a quick glance toward the bathroom—the light was off and the door was wide open.

"She's not here, Elijah."

"I know that," he said. "She was with me. Just now, I mean."

Oh, shit.

Elijah had known I would be here, alone, and yet he'd come anyway.

"I need you to go," I said. "You can't be here."

My eyes were beginning to adjust. I could see the outline of his body against the wall.

"I'm not playing," I said. "I'm telling you to leave, Elijah."

"I understand that. I do."

"Then go."

I waited. But that motherfucker didn't move an inch.

I needed to be clearer, apparently.

"Look," I said, straightening. "I don't like hearing myself talk how I'm about to talk, because it's not my nature—not usually. But listen, Elijah. I will fuck you up—if I have to do that, I will. And I mean it. Like, permanently fuck you up. Scars and rehabilitation and traction and surgery and shit. On that level."

"I understand."

"Well if you do, then you need to be up out of this room. Now."

"Make me go, Tallah."

I couldn't believe what I was hearing.

"I'm supposed to make you go?"

"If you can. Yes."

"Oh, I can."

"Then do it," he said.

"What for? You need some kind of proof that I can handle myself or something?"

"Yes."

Unbelievable. This asshole.

"Well you can forget that," I said. "I'm not anybody's dog. I don't work for you."

"Not yet, maybe."

"Not ever."

I was able to see him now—his silhouette had gradually taken on detail. I could see his eyes, his mouth. His teeth.

"I'm going to try and hurt you now, Tallah," he said.

"You're what?"

I saw him reach into a pocket and take something out. A hunting knife.

He unsnapped the catch and pulled the blade from its sheath.

"Disarm me," he said, stepping forward. "Take the knife, Tallah."

That was enough.

Without even blinking, I stopped that devil cold in his tracks, staring him down as he stood like a store mannequin at the foot of the bed. I didn't take the knife away—that would have been what he wanted me to do. Instead, I took control of his entire arm from shoulder to fingertips and forced him to tighten his grip on the handle. To squeeze it. Wide-eyed and paralyzed, Elijah watched helplessly as I twisted his wrist to change the blade angle and began to drive his hand slowly in a downward direction—straight toward his waiting thigh.

Now I had that asshole's attention.

"All right, that's enough, Tallah," he barked. "That's enough."

Unfortunately, it wasn't enough, not for me.

"Stop. Okay?" he said. His tone had softened. "I believe you, Tallah. That's enough. Please, stop."

"I thought you wanted proof, Elijah."

"No. No. I believe you. I fucking believe you, all right?"

The tip of the steel was around an inch away from making contact with his thigh, in a spot halfway between his knee and hip.

"I don't think you're convinced," I said. "I want to really convince you."

"You have, all right? You have. I'm convinced. Jesus, I'm so convinced. I'm convinced, okay?"

I'd heard all I needed to hear.

I locked his jaws closed, straightened and stiffened his tongue, and tightened his vocal cords, until the only sound Elijah was able to produce was a series of desperate whimpers.

"I tried to tell you," I said quietly. "I tried. Remember that."

Proceeding slowly, by a few millimeters every second, I lowered the blade until the tip pressed into the denim fabric of his pant leg and broke through, pushed into the surface layers of his flesh, and sank three or four inches deep into the muscle of his leg, eventually embedding itself into the underlying bone. Unable to speak a word, Elijah groaned and wailed through gritted teeth, thrashing his head wildly through it all.

• • •

I tossed Elijah a hand towel for the bleeding and sent him, limping and still mute, out the door into the night.

Hands trembling, I turned on my phone and called Harmony.

There was no answer; her mailbox was full.

I fired off a few text messages.

Where are u stupid?

Call me.

Come home when u get this pls.

I need u.

No response.

While I waited for Harmony, I worked on cleaning Elijah's blood from the carpeting to pass the time. Pouring cup after cup of water onto the stains and scrubbing furiously with a bath towel, down on my knees, tears streaming down my face. Hard as I tried, nothing seemed to change. The carpet was dark brown and wildly patterned, which helped, but the discoloration was obvious—all I could do was hope that it would look better once it had time to dry.

Just after midnight, the door opened.

It was her.

"What the hell, Harmony," I snapped.

"What?" She dropped her shoulder bag on the floor, closed the door, and locked the deadbolt.

"Where were you?"

Harmony smiled. Suddenly she looked absolutely ecstatic.

"You did it," she said.

"Did what?"

She walked over to where I was kneeling on the floor, held my face in her hands, leaned over, and kissed my forehead.

"You passed, you crazy bitch," she said. "You fucking did it."

That was when I understood: Harmony already knew what Elijah had done.

The only question was whether she'd known in advance, or whether she'd found out afterward. But it didn't matter. Either way, I felt betrayed.

I pushed her hands away.

"What the hell?" she said.

"You knew that asshole was coming here, and you didn't tell me?"

Harmony hesitated.

"I mean, I guess so," she said. "Look. Elijah just needed to know this was for real. I told him. I tried to. And part of him believed me, but part of him needed to see for himself. You know how people are."

"He had a knife, Harmony."

She shrugged. "It's not like he was really gonna do anything with it. The knife was for show. To motivate you. I knew you could handle it."

I couldn't imagine how this idiot could be so casual about this.

"Good to know you have so much faith in me," I quipped.

"Of course I do."

Harmony went to the nightstand, pulled out a half-eaten snack-sized bag of Fritos from the top drawer, shaped the bag into a funnel, and emptied it into her mouth.

"But damn, Tal," she said, chewing. "Did you really need to take it so far with him?"

I stared at her.

"Seriously?"

"Yeah, seriously," she said.

"So I wasn't gentle enough?" I asked. "When I stopped that asshole from attacking me, I should have, what—toned it down?"

"With the whole leg thing? I mean, yeah," she said. "You have to admit—it was a little intense, right?"

"You've got to be kidding."

"Well, he was pretty pissed, Tallah," she said. "He couldn't exactly talk at first. But he seemed pissed."

"So, let me make sure I understand. Somebody breaks in our place—your fucking boyfriend—and pulls a knife on me. You knew about it and didn't tell me. But you think I'm being intense."

"He didn't break in—he had a key. And he's not my boyfriend, Tallah. He's just a guy."

"That's your answer?"

Harmony shrugged. "What do you want from me? I mean, damn, Tallah. All I'm trying to say is that you don't have to be such a psycho Black bitch all the time. Is that so fucking hard for you?"

That was it.

I couldn't do this anymore.

Without another word, I threw the blood-soaked towel onto the carpet and got on my feet. I stormed over to the cardboard box in the corner, fished through my belongings, and shoved whatever necessities I could find into a backpack: protein bars, a few bottles of water, a windbreaker.

"What the fuck are you doing?" Harmony asked.

I didn't answer.

"You need to relax, Tallah," she said. "You did it. Be happy for once in your shitty little life. I swear to God."

I threw on some clothes, zipped up the backpack, and shouldered it. I ripped a blanket from the bed and shoved it underneath my arm, slapped my card key and cell phone down on the nightstand, and stormed out the door.

the foundation

I used to dream of Tallahassee after I left the city.

I dreamt of the heat. The way it would rise up from the blacktop in a rippling, vaporous haze, as though everything in front of me was being consumed by an ethereal flame.

Sometimes I thought it might be true—that the flames were real, not a dream, and that the world around me was actually burning itself to the ground without my knowing. Could there be an invisible blaze burning everything, all around us, constantly, but we just aren't able to see it clearly unless the conditions are just right? Unless someone who has already seen it, decides to show us?

I decided that the answer was yes. The fire was real and it was with us, always, but because we couldn't see it every day, most of the time we could ignore the fire completely and live our lives as best we could in blissful ignorance. But the fire was growing—that was the problem. It was growing. And one day the fire would grow so large and hot that it wouldn't matter any longer whether we were able to see the flames or not, because we would be able to feel them. All of us would feel them equally, because by that point, the flames would be burning us alive, and everyone we had ever cared about would be disappearing before our eyes. But by then, it would be too late to do anything to save ourselves—too late to fight the fire, to try and cut off its fuel supply, to extinguish our own bodies. Too late for anything, because the fire would have already taken on a life of its own, and it wouldn't need you, or me, or anyone else as a witness—it wouldn't need to be seen in order to be felt—not anymore.

• • •

I had no destination in mind when I fled the city.

Fueled by loss and anger, I wrapped myself in Bel and took to the skies. Screaming through the night air. Higher than the cloud cover, far past the pollution of light, to the point of sheer blackness. Distant starshine and the scythe-like moon. It was so hard to breathe at those heights. Almost impossible. And it was so cold—colder than I'd ever been in my life. I didn't care where I was at the moment, where I had been in the past, or where I was going next.

• • •

At first light I touched down somewhere in the wild, surrounded by dense thickets of evergreen and hardwood cypress. A blackwater river was cutting sluggish channels through the floodplain. Leaves and light were falling. I heard the steady thrumming of cicadas somewhere deep in the forest.

I knelt down. I plowed my hands into the soft earth, gathered two fistfuls of soil—no different from the soil my people once worked with their hands—and cast it into the air over my head. Infusing dust into the atmosphere. *There should be no choice but to breathe the ground that my people bled for. It ought to reside deep within your lungs. Make you retch.* I reached out with my mind, whipped the dust into a frenzied devil, and brought it together into a single mass, then added to it, augmented it, drawing soil from the ground on every side of me, building the mass into a cloud, a thunderhead, a stormfront. A tempest of earth. I lifted the whirling mass higher, raising it above the tree canopy, continuing to feed it from below, to expand it, to turn it monstrous. Soon the mass grew large enough to cast a looming shadow, to blot out my view of the sun, to generate its own sound—a low-pitched droning—that reverberated through the clearing. I took this dark nebula, my galaxy of debris, and spread it like a stain across heaven, extending the darkness as far as I could make it reach—north, south, east, and west—continuing to feed the mass from the ground below, from the atmosphere on all sides. Before long, the veil of dust extended for what looked like tens of miles in every direction, all the way to the horizon. I brought the outermost boundaries of the dust veil down to the ground, securing them there, creating a nebulous dome that covered as much of the forest as I could encompass. Shutting myself inside, shutting the rest of the world out.

I tore into the trees.

Without lifting a finger, I destroyed entire swaths of forestland, clearing everything in front of me from the understory all the way to the canopy, ripping out any sign of life—old-growth hardwood, grasses, ferns, saplings, groundcover, shrubs, wildflowers—uprooting it all, violently sweeping it aside and out of the dome, forming a massive heap of intertwined timber and assorted foliage reduced to an almost unrecognizable pulp. In seconds, I laid waste to solemn glens and overturned vast, lofty groves that had stood for generations; stripped valleys and hills all the way down to the bedrock; turned green fields into vacant lots, whipping up a monsoon of debris—wood splinters, shards of rock, clay deposits—and unearthed a writhing mass of sightless organisms, pale and soft-bodied, from the darkest subsoil. Sending swarms of wildlife—flurries of panicked birds, wild-eyed game animals, hordes of insects—scattering to the four winds. As easily as a child might blow seed florets from a dandelion, I swept through thousands of acres of raw woodland and left nothing but devastation and scorched earth in my wake. Diverting rivers, draining wetlands, emptying lakes. Altering ancient topographies and gutting whole geological strata, blending the constituent layers into one. It was wanton. Ruin for the sake of ruin. The air was a permanent haze of dust. Leaves fell in a deluge all around me like paper fliers during wartime.

• • •

I awoke on open ground, in a bed of pine needles and damp earth. Something was drifting lazily through the air above my face— grains of pollen or dust. Seeds with thin stalks and tufted crowns like

parasols. It was midday—I could tell by the sun's position overhead.
But the shadowy dome that stretched across the open sky had the same
effect as a solar eclipse, giving everything a dull, burnt-orange hue,
making the world seem slightly darker than it actually was.

I sat up slowly.

My backpack was lying in the dirt next to me. I pulled it into
my lap, unzipped the main compartment, dug out a water bottle with a
missing label, and forced myself to drink slowly, to take only a few
small sips. I unwrapped a peanut butter protein bar, tore off half, and
shoved the entire piece into my mouth, folding the rest inside the
wrapper and stashing it in a side pocket with a drawstring closure.

Still chewing, I took another sip of water then put the bottle
away. I got on my feet, dusted myself off, and shouldered the
backpack, adjusting the straps.

I was standing in the middle of what looked like an empty
field—a vast stretch of farmland, recently turned over. Seemingly
limitless. It extended all the way to the horizon on every side. No
trees, no plant life, no animals. Only rich black soil mixed with
remnants of the forest that used to grow there, the forest that I had
unthinkingly gutted and wiped clean from the earth.

I started walking.

I didn't have a destination in mind, or a plan—at least none
that I could have articulated. I wasn't sure what I was hoping for. Like
a shell-shocked survivor in an apocalyptic wasteland, I arbitrarily chose
a direction to call "forward" and pushed ahead.

I heard a helicopter: the churning engine and the blades. I
scanned the sky, squinting, but I couldn't find the source—the veil of
dust arching overhead was transparent, but it definitely affected
visibility.

I kept walking, pausing periodically to listen, to stare skyward,
and eventually I spotted them—not one, but three helicopters. Two

from the forestry service, and one emblazoned with the logo of a local news station: WTXL News.

I was still wrapped in Bel, so I wasn't worried about being seen (invisibility is the greatest source of bravery). Shielding my eyes with a forearm, I stood directly underneath the choppers and watched them circling slowly above the surface of the dome, all of them seemingly unwilling to descend any further and risk crossing the dark barrier below.

Watching them made me realize something. At the moment, the dome was nothing more than a layer of loosely held-together dust, as easy to pass through as a beaded curtain in a doorway. When I'd created it, I hadn't envisioned the dome as a way to keep people out (or as anything at all, really)—it was a product of rage more than a product of conscious strategy—but now I could see that the dome could act as a layer of defense. I just needed to solidify it, to tighten the connections between the particles by increasing their attraction to one another until I'd forged a stout shield. A kind of border wall around my new territory.

It was simple.

I thinned out the surface of the dome by removing some material (to maintain overall transparency) and ramped up the forces that held the remaining particles together, transforming the dome from a gauzy veil into a hard tempered shell. It wasn't indestructible; I didn't think anything was. But it was secure. I didn't have to test it with my hand to know—I could feel it with my mind somehow.

• • •

I spent the rest of the day exploring.

Instead of traveling by foot, I took flight. One part research, one part release. I barnstormed over the ruined land below, surveying the extent of the damage while trying (unsuccessfully) to come to terms with the fact that I was the cause, that I had singlehandedly destroyed an entire ecosystem. I couldn't wrap my mind around what I'd done.

Once I found the outer edge of the dome, I traveled the circumference until I'd gone full circle, giving me an overall sense of the area's footprint (shockingly big). After that, I started exploring the interior. I wasn't systematic about it; I used whatever strategy came to mind: following the path of the sun on its arc, moving perpendicularly to the path instead, flying in straight lines or zigzagging at random intervals. I wasn't sure how many miles I covered in total, but one thing was certain: I never saw a single living plant or animal inside the dome—even the insects I'd unearthed seemed to have wormed their way back into the darkness. Only fragments of former lives were visible. Fallen leaves. Half of a bird's nest. Bark chips. Broken shoots of juniper. The cloven hoof of an animal, a deer maybe.

Eventually I spotted a tangle of splintered brush half-buried in the dirt and decided to stop there—to make camp, I hoped, using the broken branches as a shelter. It was a psychological need, not a physical one. The atmosphere inside the dome was peaceful and still (and seemingly temperature-controlled?) like the inside of a terrarium, so I didn't need any protection from the elements, but I wanted something around me, something home-like. A basic lean-to made of sticks would do fine. I just needed something to serve as a barrier between me and the outside world, something other than the dark surface of a dome thousands of feet in the sky.

As I pulled the branches from the ground and shook them off one by one, I heard something—engines churring, blades whipping the air. The sound of helicopters on approach. Dozens of them, judging by the volume. Soon I saw a dizzying array of searchlights sweeping across the dome's surface, their beams breaking apart and turning diffuse as they filtered through the lens of dust and entered the interior.

I dropped the branch I was holding and stared skyward. As far as I could tell, most of the choppers in the convoy belonged to the media, and a few others were clearly law enforcement. But it was the last two that were the most unnerving: a pair of military gunships with long turrets mounted on either flank, hovering menacingly like twin dragons.

do you want to be famous?

Over the next two days, the scene at the dome became a media-driven shitstorm.

At any given moment, dozens of choppers could be seen canvassing the area from above, while every square inch of space on the ground along the circumference was occupied by some combination of a camera crew, a newscaster, a special science correspondent, a blogger, an online video personality, a website curator, or a thought-leader/tastemaker out on assignment. News vans with satellite antennas on their roofs. A huddle of protestors holding signs with slogans about deforestation. Blue-green portable chemical toilets in a long row, set back from the crowds. A food truck selling *nikuman* pork dumplings (a few of which I managed to snatch from the pickup window after sneaking out of the dome with Bel). Everything was lit up by massive light towers with banks of flood lamps in three rows of six, like what you would see at a baseball game at night. I quietly stood by and listened to random people—everyone from off-the-grid hippie types to buttoned-down businesspeople—offering their unique theories about the phenomenon unfolding before them (atmospheric disturbance? geographic formation? government technology? alien weapon?), but it didn't take long for me to decide that I'd had enough of the circus for one day. It was time to find a quiet place to sort things out.

This had clearly gotten way out of hand.

Creating a spectacle hadn't been my original point. Nothing had been. Neither the destination I chose (a forest in the middle of nowhere) nor my actions upon arrival (destroying said forest and creating a giant dust bubble——?) had been part of a larger, mad design on my part. It was the exact opposite. Everything I had done since I'd left Tallahassee had been a result of impulse, not calculation. I had acted on instinct, on pure emotion, and right now I was seeing the consequences—all of them obvious, in retrospect, but unexpected in the heat of the moment.

And there was something else happening that I hadn't expected.

I liked the way it all felt.

Not the public attention—I didn't need or want that for myself as an individual. But the power? Yes. The power to mobilize an entire population, to cause the deployment of critical resources, to dominate the news cycle. I enjoyed these things far more than I would have imagined.

I'd caused a scene. And for whatever reason, I felt good doing it.

I was about to reenter the dome and return to camp when someone standing in the crowd caught my eye—a young Black man shifting anxiously from one foot to the other, wringing his hands, and peering over the heads of the masses in front of him as though late for an appointment and waiting on a train. He wore what looked like camping clothes—army-green cargo pants, a light-blue denim shirt, and brown hiking boots—and on the ground beside him was a frame backpack with a sleeping bag and a foam bedroll strapped to the metal scaffolding with crisscrossed bungee cords.

I recognized him right away. His long locs were bundled under a black knit cap, but I knew him. It was Jabari.

I approached and stood silently behind him, a few feet back.

I waited, wondering.

Would he feel something?

Would he notice that I was here? Even as he stood among all these people with distractions on every side of him, would he be able to sense me? To pick me out of a crowd using nothing but vibrations? Did I matter to him that much?

After a few seconds, Jabari turned his head slightly to one side.

"Being One?" he said softly.

I felt my eyes well up.

I couldn't have explained the reason why, exactly.

"Yes. I'm here," I managed.

I stood shoulder to shoulder with him.

He continued to stare straight ahead as if he were alone.

"I knew I'd find you here," he whispered. "I knew the second I saw all this online. I just knew."

"You were right."

He wiped both eyes with the back of a hand. "Thank you. Thank you for being here."

"Why did you come?" I asked.

"Why?" He almost laughed. "For you, Being One."

I wasn't sure what that meant.

"For me?"

"To be a part of it," he said, looking around. "To join this—whatever it is you're doing out here. To join you."

"But I don't know what I'm doing," I said.

Still staring straight ahead, Jabari smiled. To a person passing by, it might have looked like he was remembering something—a funny story—or maybe thinking of a specific person, someone he was looking forward to seeing. "It's all right," he said. "I want to be here when you find out."

"I can't let you, Jabari."

His face fell. "What do you mean? Why not?"

"I don't want this for you," I said. "This isn't life. Not your life, at least. This is something else."

"Are you testing me?"

"No. This isn't a test," I said. "I'm being honest. Look around you—do you really want to be a part of this?"

"You're here," he said. "That's all I need to know, Being One. This is what I want."

"You don't. Trust me."

"I do," Jabari said.

Shit.
I was at a loss.

Living on a dirt lot with no address, no modern conveniences, no family, no friends, no means for survival, and no future—in short, my existence—was the last thing Jabari should have wanted for himself. And I knew that if he'd known the truth about me, that I was a charlatan, a thirteen-year-old playing God, he would have never offered himself up to it. But there he was, and the thought of having someone staying with me underneath the darkened dome, sharing days of perpetual dusk, was too tantalizing to ignore.

"I need to ask you something," I said.

"Of course."

"Do you want to be famous?"

His brow furrowed. "Do I want to be famous?"

"Yes. And be honest," I said. "It's all right either way."

He seemed to give the question some thought.

"Are we talking about the kind of famous that gets somebody rich?"

"No," I said. "I mean, not at first anyway. Look. Just answer the question. Do you want to be famous or not?"

Jabari shrugged. "Not really. I mean—if it happened? All right, fine. But it isn't a life goal or anything. I was a psychology major, so, yeah."

I noticed that he said "was."

"But you're not against it," I said. "Being famous."

"No. I'm just good either way."

"Then come with me."

He looked confused. "How?"

I started walking toward the dome. "Follow the sound."

Using my abilities, I carefully carved out a path through the crowd ahead, moving individual people and pieces of equipment to either side with as little force as possible, trying to make it seem believable that a normal human being could have been responsible. Staying a few steps ahead of him, I created just enough space for Jabari to pass through unhindered.

"Walk," I said.

Jabari did.

Wearing the oversized frame backpack, Jabari made his way through the channel (the gauntlet?) that I had built for him. I heard scattered murmurs and a few expletives from the surrounding crowd: What the hell, asshole? Who the fuck are you supposed to be? But most of the onlookers stayed silent and watched him pass, wide-eyed, mouths closed.

"It's okay," I said. "Keep going."

Jabari slowly approached the surface of the dome and stopped short. Staring up at the barrier like a child bellying up to a skyscraper, he waited.

"What do I do?" he asked under his breath.

"I told you. Keep going."

Jabari hesitated.

"Go on. It's all right," I said.

"Okay, Being One."

Jabari paused, closed his eyes, took a deep breath and stepped forward.

• • •

I led Jabari to the campsite.

For some reason I didn't fly him in. I made him walk.

It seemed appropriate somehow—the requirement of struggle. His boots sinking into the soft earth with each step. The burden he carried on his back.

Was the labor worth it to him?

How much would he be willing to suffer for what I was offering—without even knowing what it was?

A battery of helicopters circled overhead while Jabari set up the tent. I watched as he linked the fiberglass poles and threaded them through canvas loops in the outer shell; as he bent the poles into position, giving shape to the overall structure, and secured them; as he pushed stakes deep into the ground at each corner with his heel.

When he was finished, he spread out the foam bedroll and sleeping bag on the nylon floor and sat down just inside the tent opening, much like I used to do back in the Jungle. He pulled off the knit cap and shook out his hair. Before long, he was checking his cell phone and sipping from a metal canteen.

I wasn't sure what I should do.

I had just invited a strange boy to come and live with me—an invisible entity whom he idolized—in a field of dirt under a homemade dome. Yes, Jabari seemed kind, smart, and he was definitely attractive in the tortured-artist-damaged-wanderer category, and I suppose that I low-key liked him in a way, but was I really planning on playing house with him for any length of time?

What was my next move supposed to be?

"Being One?"

Jabari's eyes were wide. He was staring down at the phone display. "I'm all over the news feed," he said. "Correct that. I am the feed. The whole damn thing is me."

"Are you surprised?"

"No—not that it happened. That part doesn't surprise me, I guess. But seeing it live is a whole different story. And the quickness?" He shook his head. "Yeah, I guess the speed did surprise me, to be honest."

He went back to the screen, thumbing through pages and pages of stories, by the looks of it.

"Oh, damn," he said.

"What?"

"My mom," he said. "Shit. They talked to my mom—already. She's got a quote and everything on here."

"What did she say?"

"For one thing, that I've never gotten into any trouble before. Which is bullshit."

He paused for a few seconds.

"Anything else?" I asked.

"Yeah." His voice quieted. "That I should come home, and that she hopes I do. And that I'd be welcome."

"Maybe you should do that."

Jabari lowered the phone. "I can't." His voice hardened. "I'm staying here with you, Being One."

"But are you all right with that?"

"It doesn't matter what I am. This is what I signed up for."

• • •

A few hours later, we received a message from on high.

Not from God or anything, unfortunately.

From one of the police helicopters.

"Mr. Warner," said an amplified voice—a woman's voice. "By order of Title 36: Resource Protection, Public Use, and Recreation, you are to leave this area immediately. Your actions are considered trespassing under federal law."

The message was repeated three times.

Once the speaker clicked off, I looked at Jabari. He was lying on the sleeping bag with his bare feet crossed at the ankles. His boots were just outside the tent opening.

"What do you think?" I asked.

"About what?"

"Leaving."

"I've been telling you already," Jabari said. "I'm staying here with you."

"She sounded serious."

"I'm serious."

"Okay, Jabari."

"Okay, Being One."

• • •

That night, I scattered the helicopters above us like moths.

Nobody got hurt. I just waved them away as if I were the wind. My goal was to create a no-fly zone around our camp—a five-mile-wide buffer in every direction—so that Jabari could get some sleep.

While he was busy dreaming, I did some thinking.

If I really planned on staying here for any significant length of time, I needed to build something, especially if Jabari was going to be living here with me. Nothing elaborate. It didn't even need to be permanent. But if we were going to call this place our home, then I—we—needed something more than just a nylon tent and a hole in the ground with a few sticks for a roof.

I made a decision.

I was going to build.

Eager to begin right away, I left the dome, rocketing into the black sky, wheeling off in the direction of the crowds I'd seen earlier. The first task on my list was the most important one, I thought. To get us a bathroom. Or, rather, to get *him* one. (I realized that it needed to be "his," at least in name, because the Being One—whatever it was—probably didn't need to use the bathroom.) And since I couldn't singlehandedly build an onsite plumbing system plus an underground sewer network, I was going to do the next best thing—steal myself a port-a-potty from The Man.

When I reached the boundary zone (my name for the most popular area along the circle where the dome met the earth), I saw plenty of activity—journalists and cops, mostly—but the crowds were much sparser than before, I assumed, because of the late hour. I didn't waste any time. Reaching out with my mind, I targeted the last portable toilet in a row of about fifteen and coated it with dust that I siphoned off from the atmosphere, peppering the structure from all sides until it looked like it had weathered a sandstorm. After that, I began adjusting the positions of the particles dynamically, causing them to shift in response to ambient light, until the entire structure melted out of view. Without hesitation, I lifted my new (and newly invisible) toilet into the air, pivoted toward camp, and headed off. No witnesses, at least none that I'd noticed. As far as I could tell, I had just pulled off the perfect Hygiene Heist.

It wasn't until I set the port-a-potty down at the campsite that I heard the banging.

And the yelling.

Somebody was inside.

"Oh, shit," I said.

I let the coat of dust slip off and fall to the ground.

"It's all right," I said through the door. "You're safe now—everything is okay."

Slowly, the door opened, and a woman peered out. I wasn't sure, but she looked like she might be Black like me—her rich brown skin, tight corkscrew curls, and full lips gave off the right kind of vibe—but it was hard to tell. She wore a blue silk button-down and brown slacks with a gold-link belt. It was a nice look. Classy. Sharp. (The pants were down around her calves, but still.) She looked about the same age as my dad was when he was shot.

"Hi," I said. "Are you all right?"

The woman didn't answer. Seemingly dazed, she pulled up her pants and fastened them slowly, staring at the campsite like someone who'd just awoken from a coma and was trying to piece together where she was, how she'd gotten there, and how much time had gone by since her last true memory.

"It's okay," I said. "You're safe now."

The woman started swaying side to side; she looked like she was about to pass out on her feet.

I rushed over and took her arm by the elbow to steady her, but she immediately cried out, pushing my hands away.

"It's all right," I said, louder than I'd planned.

The woman recoiled even further, retreating through the doorway and shifting into what looked like a street-fighting stance.

That was when it dawned on me.

I'd completely forgotten that I was invisible.

Shit.

"I'm sorry," I said. "Look. Look." I quickly sloughed off Bel and funneled her into my palm before slipping her into my back pocket. "See? I'm the same as you. Everything is okay."

The woman stared at me, open-mouthed.

Oh, damn.

What the hell did I just do?

"You hit your head on something," I lied. "I think you might be confused still. Just relax. Okay?"

There was no response.

I didn't push the issue. After everything this poor woman had just been through, I decided to give her some time to acclimate. It only seemed fair.

Gradually, she uncoiled.

Her body returned to a non-combat posture, but she kept her distance from me, staying just inside the doorway. Staring out, evaluating her environment—or her options, maybe. Over time, her breathing slowed and her shoulders seemed to relax. She pulled her phone from her back pocket and started tapping on the screen, glancing up at me warily from time to time.

I decided that I'd waited long enough.

"I'm sorry, okay? It was an accident," I said. "I can help you get back to wherever you need to go."

The woman continued to tap and swipe the display as if I wasn't there.

"Just please don't tell anyone about me," I said. "That you saw me out here. It's important. Okay?"

Nothing. No response.

I decided to try a different approach, one that had never come naturally to me—making friends.

"My name's Gabriela," I said, choosing a name randomly out of nowhere. My voice sounded sing-songy, which I hated. "What's yours?"

The woman finally looked up.

She said something in a language I didn't understand. Spanish, I was pretty sure.

"Huh?"

"Guadalupe. Gwah-dah-loo-pay. That's my name," she said. "It's from a famous Spanish soap opera." She shook her head. "Sorry—I don't know why I told you that."

Still holding her phone out in front of her, Guadalupe stepped out of the port-a-potty and onto the dirt. She spent a few seconds staring at the crude lean-to shelter, the tent, and the dome overhead. Finally, she put her phone away and focused on me.

She smiled.

It looked like the real thing, too; she wasn't faking it, as far as I could tell.

"Nice to meet you, Gabriela," she said, extending her hand.

I took hold of it—her skin was warm. "You too."

"Sorry about how I'm acting," she said. "This is just very strange to me. All of this."

"It is pretty strange. I agree."

"So, then. Help me to understand. How did you get inside of this place?" she asked.

Uh oh.

This was not a conversation that I wanted to have.

"I don't know—I just did. Why?"

"Well, I have a daughter around your age," Guadalupe said. "Fourteen, fifteen?"

"So?"

"So I would worry for her if she was out here alone. That makes me worry for you."

"I'm not alone."

Guadalupe glanced toward the tent.

"I see that," she said. "Is Jabari Warner your friend, Gabriela?"

"You ask a lot of questions."

She smiled again. "That's true. I do ask a lot of questions," she said. "This is my job—I work for a magazine. If you want, I could tell your story there."

"I don't."

That was mostly true. A part of me did want my story to be told, but not by somebody else—I either wanted to tell it myself or keep it to myself. Those were the only two options.

"Did you do all of this, Gabriela?" Guadalupe gestured to the ground all around us, to the dome overhead. "Are you the one who took away the forest and built this shield against the world?"

"I told you. I don't want to talk to you."

"That's fine," Guadalupe said. "I understand."

"No—that's not good enough. I want you to swear," I said. "Swear that when you leave here, you won't talk about me. You can tell everybody that you found a way in here but you don't know how." My words were coming out like a threat; I needed to be softer. "Please. I'm serious. I don't want to be part of your story."

Guadalupe held up her hand, palm out—a promise salute. "I swear," she said.

"All right."

"But I need a favor from you, too," she said, nodding toward the tent. "Let me take some photographs of Jabari Warner. And let me speak to him, just for a little while."

"Why?"

"For proof that I was here, where no one else can be. Look, to be honest, I already took photographs of everything here—including your face. I won't use it unless you say it is okay; don't worry. But you have to give me something, Gabriela. Let me at least see Mr. Warner."

"Bitch, I will rip that phone out of your pocket."

"Calm down," she said. "I sent the photos to my email already. Just work with me, Gabriela—I don't want this to be ugly."

I thought for a while about what that little blackmailing witch was telling me.

"So if I let you take a picture of Jabari, you'll leave me alone?" I asked.

"And speak to him. Take photos and speak to him. Both. Then, yes."

"He's asleep," I said. "I don't want you bothering him."

Guadalupe paused. She seemed to be thinking.

"All right," she said. "Then just a couple of photographs. One. Two. Boom. Then I go. Okay?"

I didn't feel like I had much of a choice. Unless I was willing to hurt Guadalupe or take her prisoner, which I wasn't. Letting her snap some pictures of Jabari seemed like the best way to keep my face out of the public eye.

In any case, Jabari was already all over the news—how would one more article make a difference?

"Okay," I said. "A few pictures. But that's it."

"Fine. Pictures it is."

"Fine."

I quietly unzipped the tent opening and held one flap to the side while Guadalupe got the shots she wanted. It felt wrong—like a violation—allowing Jabari to be photographed while he was asleep, without his consent, but I let it happen anyway. I was more concerned about my anonymity than my morality at the time.

When she was finished, I sent her on her way. On foot.

But before she left, she handed me a glossy-black business card. Guadalupe Calderón, Editor-at-Large, it read.

• • •

"I have a question, Being One."

It was morning.

Sunlight streaming in through the layer of haze overhead gave the landscape an otherworldly feel, as though we'd been stranded on the dust plains of a remote planet. Jabari was lying on his back in the tent, hands behind his head, while I sat cross-legged just outside the opening.

"Okay," I said. "Go ahead."

"Why me, Being One?"

Oh, shit.

Here we go.

"You mean, why are you here?" I asked.

"Sort of. What I mean is—of all the people struggling out here on the third rock, you know? Why did you reach out to me?"

I thought about it for a while.

"You sensed me," I said. "And nobody else has been able to do that. So that's how we met. I didn't reach out—I didn't even want to be found."

"But what are you?" he asked. "I mean, no offense—sorry. I

thought you were like my brio guide or something, but now I'm wondering. Are you some kind of angel?"

"No."

"A ghost?" He shook his head. "Honest to God, sometimes I think I may have already died and moved on. Like maybe this is the Elsewhere Between, and you're trying to decide if you're going to build it into heaven or hell for me."

"So why did you come?"

"Because I believe that you're good. That you're doing good work out here," he said. "Is that true, though? Are you good, Being One?"

I wasn't sure how to answer that.

So I didn't.

"Listen, Jabari," I said. "This is important, so listen. You are not dead, okay? I told you—this is real life. All of this. So don't worry."

He looked deeply relieved. "It's real?"

"Yes," I said. "I'm not magical. Just think of me as your friend."

"Okay. I can try that."

"Good. Now, can I ask you a question?"

Jabari's eyes widened. "Of course, Being One."

"Where are we?" I asked.

The question was genuine. I really didn't know how far I'd traveled since leaving Tallahassee.

Jabari didn't respond right away. It seemed as though he knew the answer but didn't want to tell me for some reason, like a child who was afraid of getting into trouble.

"I'm not sure how I'm supposed to answer," he said. "Is this another test?"

"No, Jabari. I wasn't even testing you the last time you asked me that. I really want to know the answer. For real. What is this place?"

"All right. Well, this used to be a national park," Jabari said.

"Is that what you mean?"

"Used to be?"

"Yeah. Apalachicola National Forest—something like five miles out of Tallahassee. The news said that around seventy percent of it is gone now. Four hundred thousand acres."

"Oh, shit."

Jabari's brow furrowed. "It seems like you're surprised."

"I am."

"You're surprised by that?" he asked pointing outside. "You were the one who cleared everything out. Right?"

I didn't want to own up to it, but there was no use in trying to lie.

"I was," I said. "I just didn't know how much I'd done."

"I'm not questioning you, Being One," Jabari quickly added. "I'm sure you had a good reason for doing what you did."

That was true—I did.

Rage was my reason.

After everything I'd experienced in my life, I felt that I had a right to be angry—I would have never apologized to anyone for that— but my actions? Wiping a forest from the face of the planet? I was absolutely sorry for that. There wasn't anything I could do to walk it back at this point, but I hoped that I could find some measure of redemption by what I chose to do with the land. By turning it into something that mattered.

"I need to go get some things done, Jabari," I said.

He nodded. "Okay."

"But I have to tell you something first." I took a deep breath. "I accidentally let someone else into camp last night. A reporter. And she took a few pictures before she left. Some were of you."

"Last night?"

"Uh huh."

"So I was asleep," he said. "She caught me sleeping? Really?"

"I'm sorry. Have you checked the news today?"

Jabari turned over and fished around in his backpack. "My

phone's almost dead. I brought a few spare batteries with me, but I'm trying to save them, so I've been staying off."

"Okay. If you decide to check your feed, don't be surprised at what's there. The pictures are probably all over."

"Mom will love it," he said. "Her boy, out here making a name for himself by sleeping in a tent."

• • •

The next step in my plan was to find a better dwelling. Something with permanence. Something that the wolf couldn't blow down with a single breath.

I knew I couldn't build a structure on my own, so I needed to find something pre-fabbed. Luckily, my conversation with Jabari had given me an idea of where to look—out in the woods. I was going to scour what remained of the forest in search of something called an emergency cabin.

Maybe even two of them.

I wasn't sure whether these cabins even existed, much less whether I could find any, because the only place I'd ever seen one was on TV. A couple of years earlier, I'd watched a movie where a bunch of white folks decided to climb a steep mountain in a national park in Alaska (because simply being themselves was apparently so safe and comfortable that they needed to introduce some risk) and they found themselves trapped in a blizzard with no food, water, or shelter. The two people in the group who didn't die of exposure managed to find a small building where they waited out the storm in relative comfort: an emergency cabin. The cabin was bare-bones—a couple of cots, a few blankets, a camp stove, and a plastic bucket for a bathroom—but it was a solid roof over their heads. It did the job. A real-life Florida version of the cabin (if there was such a thing) might not be equipped with blankets, but it would definitely include the main structure, which was all I really needed.

I flew out of the dome and started my search.

It wasn't until I'd passed far beyond the boundary zone that I began to see trees again. Scattered individually at first. Then small isolated groves, pushing from the soil at awkward angles like strange oases in a desert. Before long I came upon mountainous drifts of castoff vegetation, the centuries' worth of growth that I'd managed to eradicate in only a moment's time. Vast mounds of dying foliage the size of small municipalities sprawled across ravaged fields as though uprooted by a tsunami and left to rot, steaming and putrefying in the sun. Only after I'd borne witness to all of these terrible things did I finally discover the untouched areas of the forest—acre upon acre of continuous woodland that had somehow escaped my reach. The contrast between these lush areas—whole and unblemished—and the devastation I'd seen only moments earlier made my actions seem all the more appalling, all the more despotic. Practically indefensible. I suddenly understood the true depth of what I'd done, and I burst into tears.

After what felt like nearly an hour of wasted effort, I caught sight of something—a sliver of chrome glinting through the tree canopy ahead. Sheet metal, maybe, or possibly a length of corrugated drainage pipe. I descended past the canopy into the understory, pushed through a screen of needled limbs, and quietly touched down on a low ridge along the edge of a clearing.

At its center was a small mobile home.

The building immediately reminded me of the beige-and-white portable classrooms at my old elementary school, the ones we were forced to use after a fire broke out in the primary wing. It had a simple shape—almost like a basic cargo shipping container—and was mounted on a travel-trailer frame with axles, wheels, and a tow hitch. Black solar panels lined the metal roof; an oversized plastic water tank stretched from the foundation all the way to the eaves; and some sort of grey electrical box with the word Yamaha on the face—it looked like there was a car engine inside—had been bolted to the trailer frame on one end. Wires ran from the electrical box directly into the side of the house.

A green woodcut sign affixed above the front door read Ranger Outpost Area A-12.

I'd found a ranger's station.

I studied the structure from the clearing's edge, scanning the barred windows for hints of movement, listening intently. In spite of the fact that I was literally invisible to the naked eye, I still felt the need to be overly cautious, to be almost obsessively aware of my surroundings at every moment. The thought of approaching the building and discovering something unexpected left me terrified, even with the seemingly limitless power I could use to protect myself.

I waited and watched.

There were no obvious signs of movement. All I could hear was the chirr of insects boring into the bark of the surrounding trees. A random whippoorwill's calling.

As far as I could tell, I was alone.

I stepped into the clearing and made my way to the front of the building, got up on my toes, and peered through a window at the interior.

Oh, my sweet Jesus.

It had everything.

Eight metal cots arranged in two rows. A kitchenette with a two-burner cooktop, a microwave oven, and a full-sized refrigerator. A round wooden table with six chairs pushed in tight. A desk with a computer. Even a pretty nice-looking TV set.

The place was so incredible that I almost gift-wrapped the entire thing in dust and snatched it from the earth on the spot, but I stopped myself. I couldn't be reckless. Not after what had happened the previous night with Guadalupe. The outpost seemed to be empty, but I couldn't ignore the possibility that somebody was inside. I needed to be certain.

I went around to the front door, climbed a set of fold-out stairs, and quietly tested the knob; it turned freely, but a combination padlock had been threaded through a metal hasp toward the top of the jamb. That was a good sign. Somebody had secured the building from the outside and walked away; it was impossible to imagine a reason why anyone would still be inside, effectively imprisoned in the outpost. Feeling more confident, I popped the U-shackle loose, letting the lock body fall to the dirt, and opened the door.

The interior consisted of one continuous living space with two side doors at the far end, opposite the kitchen. Both were closed. With the exception of whatever was behind those two doors, I could see almost everything in the outpost from where I was standing in the entryway. The place looked deserted.

I stepped inside, letting the door swing shut behind me.

The air was sweltering. It was difficult to breathe—I felt like I was inhaling cotton with every breath.

I made a quick pass through the main living area, double-checking the desk, the rows of cots, and the kitchenette before heading to the far end and standing in front of the two closed doors.

I pressed my ear against each panel and held it there for a few seconds, then knelt down and checked for light coming from underneath. There was no obvious sign that someone was waiting on the other side.

I tried each knob. The one on the left was locked, so I decided to start with the one on the right.

I slowly opened the door.

It was a bathroom—for the love of God, this place even had its own bathroom. A sink, a composting toilet, and a walk-in shower unit. Unbelievable, the amenities in this place.

I moved on to the other door, stripped the tumbler mechanism on the lock, and opened it.

The room was around the size of a closet.

It was empty except for a wall-mounted rack full of black hunting rifles with long, cylindrical scopes. Twelve, maybe fifteen guns in total. Dozens of boxes of bullets were stacked on a shelf underneath.

• • •

I took the entire structure back to camp.

"Daaaamn," Jabari murmured as I unveiled my find.

The mobile home looked a little bit lonely sitting by itself in the middle of a vast dirt field, but I had to admit—it did look good.

"It's all yours," I said. "For as long as you want it to be. Welcome home."

"Thank you, Being One."

"Any time."

Jabari spent a few minutes circling the structure, pausing periodically to inspect a specific feature or, perhaps, a flaw. At one point, he knelt down to check the hitch assembly, reaching into the mechanism and adjusting something with his fingers, and then he climbed up onto the trailer frame to take a closer look at the grey Yamaha electrical box with the engine inside. He circled the box until he found a label and, after a few seconds of reading, hopped back down onto the dirt, backed up a few paces, and stared in the direction of the building's roof.

"Is everything okay?" I asked.

Jabari smiled. "Better than that. This place has got power, you know? I'm talking about real power, too—enough to run real shit for a real long time, actually."

"You mean the panels?"

"Those are part of it, yeah. But that box over there? That's an electrical generator—a good one, too. It runs on regular gas, the kind that you can buy at any pump station. That generator is the real source—"

He abruptly cut himself off, as if he'd gone on for too long and wanted to give me an opportunity to speak.

"Sorry, Being One," he said, shaking his head.

"Why?"

"You know all this. Everything I'm telling you—you know already."

"No, Jabari. Really, it's fine. Go on."

"Are you sure?"

"Of course," I said. "Please, tell me everything."

We spent a long time touring our new place.

As it turned out, Jabari's dad used to have a job as a general contractor, so he'd learned a lot about how things worked over the years.

According to Jabari, the generator could produce enough electricity to power everything inside the mobile home—overhead lights, water heater, A/C unit, computer, TV, microwave, refrigerator, cooktop—all at once, for as much time as we needed, as long as we kept feeding gasoline to the generator's engine block. And that wasn't the only piece of good news. The plastic tank affixed to the side of the house turned out to be a ten-thousand-gallon storage unit, capable of piping water on-demand to the faucets and shower head inside the home—and the tank was almost completely full.

The fridge, on the other hand, was not.

It had eight bottles of water (two already opened), a few raspberry yogurt containers, a half-eaten block of orange cheese with mold growing on one edge, and six green apples—those were the only consumables.

But there was something else sitting on one of the shelves inside the door. It wasn't edible, but it was definitely notable.

Six vials of a clear liquid labeled *fentanyl citrate*.

Jabari looked it up on his phone— fentanyl citrate was the name of a large-animal tranquilizer, four orders of magnitude more powerful than morphine. The ranger outpost must have kept the drug on hand in case of random run-ins with black bears or Florida panthers—anything large and potentially dangerous living in the forest.

Jabari and I agreed to leave the vials where they were. The last thing I was worried about was a wild animal invasion in a place with no trees, but I thought the drug could be useful as a medicine if we ever needed it. I was far more concerned about food. There was only enough to sustain us (correction: him—the Being One probably didn't need to eat anything) for a few more days at most.

I decided it was time to do a little shopping.

• • •

I spent the next few days stockpiling supplies, which is another way of saying that I stole with complete and utter abandon.

I hit Morales' Grocery in Tallahassee and walked out with two cases of Top Ramen packets (chicken flavored); a wooden pallet stacked with bottled water; every bag of Doritos stocked on the shelf, regardless of flavor; and every sixteen-count box of protein bars in the Health & Nutrition section—around thirty of them in all. Dozens of boxes of cereal, cartons of milk, bags of fruit, jars of peanut butter. A bulk bin full of trail mix. Entire display racks full of chocolate and gum.

I stormed the Target on Apalachee Parkway and came away with six red shopping carts full of clothing for both Jabari and me (mostly Jabari), a toolbox with a complete set of hand tools, toilet paper rolls, cleaning supplies, personal hygiene items, a DVD player along with a library's worth of DVDs, and a PlayStation video game console.

I crashed the Ace Hardware over in Hanley and helped myself to anything useful I could think of: light bulbs, power strips, a flatbed full of hardwood lumber and fasteners, rolls of duct tape, eighty-pound bags of Portland cement mix, packets of gardening seeds, water hoses, extension cords, folding chairs, one of every power tool stocked in the tool cage, and half of the potted plants on display in the Outdoor

Garden Center.

I snatched vehicles clean off the road—a pickup with a confederate flag decal, a construction backhoe, a Chevron fuel tanker truck, various contraptions I didn't even know how to operate—leaving their occupants standing on the side of the roadway, trying to sort out what had just happened to them.

The more I stole from the world, the more invigorated I felt, which pushed me to take more and more and more, but it wasn't the act of stealing itself that gave me such a rush—I didn't enjoy being a thief. It was creation that fueled me. Building something new from the things I took. Something that could last into the long-term. This was what left me breathless as I rampaged through the aisles of store after store, through street after street, wrapping up whatever my heart desired into a package of dust and whisking it back home.

• • •

Jabari moved into the outpost and made it his own.

He not only slept there; the outpost was where he spent most of his waking hours. In the morning he would exercise (yoga, handstand pushups), eat breakfast, shower, then lie down on one of the cots to check the latest news, respond to messages from both friends and foes (he'd become quite the overnight celebrity), and scribble on a dog-eared notepad—his journal, by the look of it. Periodically, he would talk on the phone with a police negotiator named Ellen (the cops had gotten hold of his cell number early on), who would find a hundred different ways to ask him what he wanted—his list of demands—as though he were a hostage-taker on a plane. "I don't want anything," Jabari would answer. Or "I just need some time," he would say.

Jabari's afternoons were laid back; he spent his time watching DVDs, playing video games, napping, paging through speculative science-fiction novels, or studying textbooks with names like *Discovering Behavioral Neuroscience* and *Theories of Developmental Psychology*. When evening fell, we usually ate dinner together (which meant that I watched while he ate) and talked about the future of the camp—what we hoped our community of two could become. It was during these long discussions that I learned what Jabari truly wanted for us: expansion. He wanted more. More members, more infrastructure, more independence from the rest of the world, more change. More difference.

As for me, I continued to make my home outside, underneath the lean-to, with my blanket folded into a bedroll on the soft earth. During the day (when I wasn't spying on Jabari), I would go out on supply runs, walk around downtown Tallahassee thinking about plans for the future, steal from whatever restaurant happened to catch my eye, or go to the library and read what the media was saying about our situation (which was nothing good).

As far as I could tell, the entire world was watching us. Because of the no-fly zone I'd established, the only pictures of our camp (other than the ones Guadalupe had taken) consisted of grainy satellite images with little to no detail, which meant that most of what was being said was nothing but wild guesswork and theorizing. News articles speculated wildly on the nature of the dome itself (extraterrestrial?), the identity of Jabari Warner (Black extraterrestrial?), and the rash of mysterious thefts that were taking place all over the greater Tallahassee area (super-aggressive Black extraterrestrials?). The only thing that seemed clear from the articles I read was the fact that somebody, somewhere, was making a whole lot of money from the unfortunate tragedy at Apalachicola National Forest. News outlets making cash off clicks, advertisers pulling in revenue from the products they pitched during commercial breaks, environmental non-profits raking in donations to restore the devastated ecosystem, the tourism industry cashing in on a record number of visitors to the area, companies selling t-shirts and other memorabilia with slogans about the dome ("I got dome at the dome" had my vote for the worst of the bunch). Maybe all that money changing hands was the real reason why no one had made a concerted effort to try and evict us yet. Maybe the spectacle we were creating was just too good for business.

● ● ●

We started to build fires at night, bonfires that raged high enough to send light dancing on the concavity of the dome overhead.

I would haul in heaps of downed trees from the outskirts of the forest, and Jabari and I would sit together and watch them burn to white ash as night fell around us. The fires served a functional purpose—we would use them to incinerate trash—but the true purpose always felt more ritualistic than practical, more tribal than logistical. Staring off into the blaze, Jabari would tell quiet stories about his life—about his parents' divorce, his mom putting him out on the street when she found him with another boy (Jabari was into boys, it turned out), his struggles in college, his dreams for tomorrow—and I would quietly listen, offering my opinion or advice when asked, but never speaking otherwise. It wasn't because he was too self-centered or too fragile to allow it. Jabari would have made room for me to speak whenever I pleased; in fact, he would have clung to every word I had to say. I chose silence. I didn't care to make a single sound unless I had to. I was content to sit quietly in the glow of the blaze and watch the flames as they returned the remains of the woods—and in some small way, my most recent mistakes—to the marrow of the earth.

● ● ●

"I need to talk to you, Being One," Jabari said.

It was late morning. Jabari was sitting across from me at the table in the outpost, spooning yogurt from a plastic container.

"Okay," I said.
"Hear me out, though. All right? Promise me."

"Just say it, Jabari." I was losing my patience fast lately—even the littlest things were getting on my last damn nerve for some reason.

"Growing the rolls," Jabari said, putting his hands together to make the shape of a picture frame. He looked excited, as though he'd just offered a grand revelation. "That's what I want to talk about. Germination, maturation—the next level. You know?"

"No, Jabari. I don't know. Use plain English, please."

"All right—so there's these five brothers I know from school, and they're ready to join us out here. To be part of the movement. The march onward. I've been knowing them a long time—they're good folks."

"Brothers?"

"Fraternity brothers." He smiled. "I mean, it's a Black fraternity, so these brothers are *brothers* and all, but yeah. Just five of my boys signing up for the campaign, you know? What do you think?"

I wasn't sure what I thought.

Five more people in camp? More than tripling our numbers? Fraternity brothers?

"Being One? You still with me?"

"Sorry. I'm just thinking," I said.

Jabari put another spoonful of yogurt in his mouth.

"All right if I talk while you think?" he asked.

"I guess."

"Okay. So, here's my elevator pitch. First of all, these aren't random acquaintances I'm talking about—this here is family. I'm not trying to invite some strangers in off the street to come stay with us, not while we're just getting started. And unless I'm mistaken, we do need bodies, right? If we ever want to build this place into something real, it's going to require hands. Hands we know. Hands like ours."

"This place is already real."

"I know that," he said. "I know that. Look, I'm not trying to disrespect what we've got going here. I'm just acknowledging the fact that we want more."

"You want more."

"We both do. Come on. We talked about this, Being One. We both want the same thing here—to prosper. To go beyond."

Jabari was right—we had talked about it. And the truth was that I did want our camp to turn into more; I just wasn't sure *what*, exactly. And how could we ask anyone else to join us unless we knew what we wanted our community to become, so we could teach them what we stood for? But then again, maybe the only way to figure out our identity was to let more people in and decide together along the way. I just wasn't sure.

"Do they know about me already?" I asked.

Jabari didn't respond. He stared down at his hands.

"Jabari. Did you tell them about me or not?"

"No, Being One."

"Were you planning on it?"

"I don't know," he said. "I guess not, Being One."

"So what then?" I said. "I'm just supposed to act like I don't exist?"

"In the beginning, maybe."

I couldn't believe what I was hearing.

"You want people to think that you created all this," I said.

"Not necessarily, no. But I think it might be better for the movement if we put a face on it. That's all."

"What movement, Jabari? You keep saying the word movement like we've got something big happening in this dirt field."

"We do, Being One," he said. "We've got something no one ever gets, at least not on a large scale—we've got a chance to wipe the slate. To start over and do better the second time."

"You sound so stupid right now."

Jabari smiled. "I do—I know. That's because I am stupid when it comes to this project. And I know you agree with what I'm saying. Which is why I think that we should keep things how they are, for now—let folks on the outside dream up all their conjecture about me and what I've done here. I won't confirm or deny any of it. Just keep that mystery alive. I'm telling you—leaving them guessing and grasping at straws will make this story everlasting. It won't ever quit."

I stared at him.

"So you want me to do all the work," I said. "Keep my mouth closed. Let you stand up front with your head held high. For the sake of the movement."

"Damn, when you put it that way," he said, shaking his head. "Look. Most folks on the outside? They already think I'm the one who perpetrated all this madness. That I'm the guilty party. So I get both the glory and the blame for it. The love and the hate, the backers and the death threats. So all I'm saying is maybe that's okay, for now. Maybe we just keep things rolling the way they've been rolling. I mean, you were the one who said I'd be famous—so you must have known this would happen, right?"

I had to admit: it was a fair argument.

When I stopped and thought about it, this scenario—as truly bizarre as it was—had unfolded pretty predictably once it had gotten started. Of course Jabari was front and center; I had helped place him there.

"You already lied to them, didn't you," I said. "Your little frat-boy friends. You told them that you were the one who did all this—the forest, the dome, the camp. Everything. Right?"

Jabari shrugged. "They assumed whatever they assumed. That's what people do."

"But you didn't tell them any different."

"Like I told you—we need to put a face on the movement right now," he said. "Nobody's trying to take anything away from you by letting a bunch of strangers believe that I made these miracles happen. And it doesn't have to be forever, either. We just need to serve the higher purpose first."

"And to serve the higher purpose, I need to not exist."

"That's not what I'm saying," he said. "Nobody's trying to tell you not to exist."

"What, then?"

"Just do what you've been doing. But let's keep everything

between you and me until we get this thing off the ground. You know? Do what we each do best."

"So I'm supposed to do all the work, but stay in the background."

"No. We'll work together, like we have been," Jabari said. "We'll each sacrifice what we can—I give up my safety and my privacy by putting myself in the crosshairs; you give up your chance at recognition by staying safely in the shadows. That's what I'm saying."

I thought about it.

I didn't know what the right decision was, but I was tired of arguing.

"Okay," I said.

"Okay what?"

"We can try them out—on probation, though. If I don't like somebody, they get bounced."

● ● ●

Jabari scheduled a phone conference with the five brothers— the Fab Five. He called it "the last sit-down of the Alphas before the dawn."

Part of the reason for the call was to finalize the details of the brothers' transition to dome life—where and how they would pass through the barrier, what they would bring with them, when they would speak to the media, and what the messaging would be—but another reason for the call was to give me a chance to listen in on the discussion through the speakerphone. To give me a first impression of who I was dealing with.

Darius, Franklin, Malik, Allen, and William—those were the brothers' names. The loudest and funniest one was Dare (Darius). Both Franklin and Malik were quiet and serious. Allen was the most outwardly political of the group ("we've got truth and crew on our side, so these cowards need to fall back"). And William seemed anxious about the entire plan in general—appropriately so, in my opinion. The whole idea of a group of college students abandoning their friends, their families, their studies, their jobs—their entire lives—in order to create a new, more just society beneath a mysterious dome sounded completely insane on its face, even to me, and I was the one who'd started it all. But each and every brother, even William, seemed willing and able. Over the course of the conversation, the Fab Five came across as honest, sincere, and ready to put in work, which was a good place to start as far as I was concerned.

Did they also come across as a bunch of sexist fools? Of course they did—they were boys. An hour-long call provided more than enough time for boys to be boys, as they say. Thankfully, there was nothing deeply anti-female; the piggishness on display was pretty tame by most standards (a few bad jokes mixed with a general ignorance of male privilege). But it was still the same old mud-bathing at its core. It bothered me a little bit, I must admit, although I didn't say anything to Jabari about it. I didn't want to sound weak, or even worse than that: divisive to the movement. Not "down for the cause" enough. So I kept my mouth shut. I was pretty sure Jabari wouldn't be friends with any true girl-haters, though, so I wasn't too worried.

All in all, I felt comfortable with the Fab Five coming onboard. There was an obvious love among the group, nobody seemed to have any obvious ulterior motives, everybody was given an opportunity to speak his mind, and the overall vibe was one of openness, trust, and a genuine uncertainty about what was going to happen once they reached their new home, which I appreciated. Uncertainty was a plus in my book. The last thing I wanted was to build a community with folks who thought they had all the right answers before we even got started.

• • •

Jabari and I spent the day getting ready for the arrival of the brothers. Putting fresh sheets on the cots, cleaning the kitchen and bathroom, stocking up on everybody's favorite foods and drinks (alcoholic, mostly), and the biggest task on the agenda—laying hands on three new portable buildings. Adding real estate had been Jabari's idea. One new building to serve as a sisters' cabin (in anticipation of the glorious day when sisters actually joined us), another new building to serve as a recreation room with arcade games and a pool table, and the last new building to serve as a meeting space—basically a room full of office chairs, a large table, a white board, and a coffee-maker.

Instead of scouring the forest for another outpost, I decided to be more direct this time. I headed over to *The Mobile Home Source for the Sunshine State*: Clayton Homes of Tallahassee, Florida. The MHI Home Center of the Year. (I'd seen their commercials on Animal Planet.) Clayton Homes had a thirty-acre lot packed with ten different models of mobile homes, all of which were labeled with fancy slave-owner names like The Madison and The Lafayette. I dropped down onto the lot in broad daylight (wearing Bel, as always), checked out a few different floor plans when no one was around, and eventually settled on one VonGadsden and two Calhouns, wrapping all three structures in coats of dust for the trip home.

On my way back to camp, I stopped at Target, Home Depot, Mike's Billiard Supplies, and The Furniture Warehouse (leaving the three mobile homes hovering around thirty feet above the ground outside each store) to pick up what we needed to make our new living spaces both comfortable and functional: generators, electrical wiring, plumbing materials, lamps, chairs, office supplies, fold-out cots, bedding, TVs, a few PlayStations, a pool table—anything I could think of. I brought the entire haul back to camp, set up the buildings in the configuration I thought would work best (a loose rectangle with the bonfire pit at the center, leaving our collection of vehicles off to one side), and left Jabari to sort out the rest of the details: getting the generators up and running, arranging the furniture to his liking, collecting the leftover trash and piling it high inside the fire ring.

We were as ready as we were going to be.

By this time tomorrow, the Fab Five would be official members of our camp.

That night I sat on the ground next to the bonfire, exhausted, watching as sparks climbed into the air and wheeled around in mad circles like smoldering moths before dissipating into the black. Small flares flickering out like lost signals. As I listened to the steady churn of the flames, the cracking of wood, I could feel myself starting to doze off, my chin drifting toward my chest.

"Police," someone said. It was a man's voice. He was somewhere behind me. "Stay right there."

I whipped around and saw a six-member SWAT team spread out into a single straight line, positioned at the edge of the firelight's reach. Every rifle was raised to shoulder level, and every barrel was aimed squarely at Jabari, who was seated in a folding chair on the opposite side of the fire.

"Keep your hands open and visible," one of the officers said. He spoke quietly, as though trying not to startle anyone. "Stay calm. Do not move."

Jabari didn't move. Staring directly into the flames with his hair shaken loose and his expression stoic, his brown skin ablaze with light, he looked every bit the vision of a revolutionary: powerful, free, and implacable. Lion-like. Staunchly defiant even in his compliance. The ordinary chair beneath him had turned into a throne.

Before I had a chance to think, one of the officers—a tall white man wearing a black helmet and tactical goggles—slung his rifle over his shoulder and pulled a stun-gun from his belt, took two steps forward, aimed it at Jabari and pulled the trigger, ejecting two dart-like prongs attached to long trailing wires that looped behind. The prongs struck Jabari directly in the chest above his heart and stuck there, embedded in his skin, immediately sending him into frenzied convulsions as the electric current surged into his body. His eyes squeezed closed. His jaw locked open and his fingers curled. Spasming wildly as though the chair itself had become electrified, his body careened and heaved back and forth, rocking with greater and greater violence until the chair tipped to one side, spilling him headfirst into the heart of the fire.

In seconds it engulfed him. Tissue, hair, clothing. Flames poured down his throat like an incandescent liquid as he tried to scream, to catch his breath. He had fallen into something viscous, some kind of bubbling, sap-like gel—the remains of a large sheet of thick plastic packaging—that clung to his body like a coating of napalm, giving fuel to the fire and accelerating its spread.

Terrified, I whipped up a torrent of soil from the ground below, crested the cloud into a wave, and crashed it down onto the blaze in a deluge, smothering the flames and sending plumes of smoke and dust skyward. I quickly stripped Bel from my skin and siphoned her off into my palm, spread her over Jabari's trembling body like a crude salve, and lifted him gently into the air, leaving him suspended a few feet above ground to relieve any pressure on his blistered flesh. I kept him visible; I needed to be able to see his tangible form, as ravaged as it was. Invisibility would have felt too real, too final, as though he had actually disappeared and left me behind permanently.

I turned to face the team of officers.

They seemed just as frightened as I was.

Before they could make things even worse, I went on the attack, starting by ramping up the weight of the officers' weapons until they dropped like cast-iron dumbbells from their hands, striking the earth with enough force to bury them from view.

• • •

I was in a wild panic.

Holding Jabari's dust-covered body like a delicate artifact, I took to the air and flew toward the boundary zone, dragging the officers in a writhing mass of flailing limbs behind me. As I passed through the dome's outer barrier, I flung the officers to the ground in a tangled heap like playthings—eliciting gasps and astonished stares from the crowd below—and sped off toward the city lights in the distance.

Jabari didn't make a single sound during the trip into Tallahassee.

Silent and motionless, he lay in front of me like an ancient sculpture, a badly eroded relic extracted from the earth.

• • •

I ran, screaming at the top of my lungs, into the fluorescent-lit lobby of Tallahassee Memorial's Trauma Center, the first hospital I'd managed to spot on my way in. I found an open gurney in a hallway near the entrance, placed Jabari's body on the white vinyl padding, and released the sheet of dust that covered him, drawing it into my hand like an unveiling on a stage. The charred, red-cracked crust of his skin. His raw and featureless face, his empty eye sockets, little more than dark craters. Cradling Jabari's head in my hands, screaming for a doctor, I looked around the room at the startled expressions on the faces of onlookers—both patients and employees—as they tried to make sense of what they were witnessing: a young man burned beyond belief, appearing from a dust cloud as if by magic. No one came to us. No one even made a move in our direction, as far as I could tell. Help him, I screamed. Someone please fucking help him.

• • •

I'd barely slept.

Lying on Jabari's cot inside the outpost, I held his damaged cell phone in my hand, running my fingers along the sharp ridges of its blackened case, scratching the corner of the bubbled glass display with my thumbnail. The phone still worked somehow. And it was unlocked—no passcode required. I opened the email program and scrolled through the messages in his inbox but didn't read any of them. I closed the program and thumbed through his list of text messages, but my mind didn't register any of the words I'd seen.

Jabari was gone.

Since I wasn't a relative, the hospital had refused to release his body to me. But I had insisted—incapacitating two orderlies, one security guard, two doctors, and a nurse before wrapping Jabari carefully in a white sheet and leaving Tallahassee Memorial through a broken window. If his mom wanted to come and claim him, fine. She could come claim him from me; it wouldn't be from them. I felt a sense of ownership, even though I knew I didn't have the right to.

After leaving the hospital, I had brought Jabari back to camp and laid him to rest in the soil underneath the lean-to, in the place where I'd slept. This would be his place now. I'd spent most of the night sitting cross-legged beside him, thinking about the mistakes I'd made—the lies I'd told him about my identity, and how those lies had led him to this place in the wilderness, putting him in harm's way. I was responsible. I knew that. But I couldn't accept the truth of it, not in any significant way. Instead, I had already pushed Jabari's death deep into the folds of my brain and started the long and arduous process of shielding myself from the reality of what I'd done, the part I had played. Burying his memory wouldn't be quick; it would take time. But I had already proven myself capable of living with horrors, even those of my own making. I would eventually find a way to protect myself from the past, as I always had.

By the time dawn arrived, I had left Jabari's gravesite and started searching the dome's perimeter for the location where the officers had entered. It hadn't taken me long to find. The officers had breached the barrier in the most straightforward way possible: by tunneling underneath using excavating equipment. Burrowing in like rats. I was disgusted with myself for having allowed it to happen.

I collapsed the tunnel. And to discourage anyone else from trying to dig their way inside, I created a hard-packed layer of clay substrate just underneath the soil around the boundary zone; anyone who wanted to cut into the ground by more than a few inches would probably need an explosive device to make a dent. It felt like the best I could do. Unless I decided to ship every single cop, soldier, journalist, and random rubbernecker all the way back to Tallahassee (which I would have done if I didn't want the media attention), I was going to have to live with a degree of risk.

I yawned, stretched my arms, and sat upright on the cot.

It was time to do the task I had been dreading all night. I opened a browser on Jabari's phone, called up a news site, and started paging through the stories published over the last few hours.

I saw exactly what I'd expected.

I saw myself.

Absolutely everywhere.

Images and videos of last night's events—body-cam footage of my encounter with the police; security feeds from the hospital hallways; cell phone clips uploaded by random strangers in the waiting room or outside the dome in the boundary zone—all of which showed me casually performing a wide variety of godlike feats, such as appearing out of thin air, creating raging dust storms, tossing grown men around like household knickknacks, and perhaps the best of them all: flying clear across the night sky like an aircraft. Not levitating, not floating. Straight-up, Superman-level flight.

I was all over the world.

And to make matters worse, the media had quite naturally made the connection between me and my father, so these stories weren't just about some nameless, faceless negress out on a rampage. They had my identity, my history, associated with them. All of it was public information now.

In fact, there was only one thing that hadn't gone viral overnight: Jabari's murder. The single act that had precipitated all the events that had come after; the police had obviously kept the video of that part under wraps. The only footage I could find of Jabari showed him after he'd already been burned alive, as though the reasons behind his murder—the questions of who, when, where, why, and how—were incidental, without any real consequence.

I read and I read until I fell asleep on the cot, and when I woke up a few hours later, I started reading again.

At one point, I noticed the date written in the byline of one of the articles.

My birthday had passed only a few days before.

I had turned fourteen without realizing it.

• • •

That evening, I approached the boundary zone on foot. Visible to the world. Whether I liked it or not, it was time for me to be seen. I was dressed simply—jeans, a plain black sweatshirt (hood up), and red Converse trainers. A small graphite sphere—my Bel—was hovering above my right shoulder, bobbing lightly. Knowing that she was nearby and at-the-ready made me feel safer somehow, more prepared.

It was dark inside the heart of the dome, but closer to the outer barrier, the landscape was bathed in the glow of multiple light towers with rows of bluish flood lamps focused toward the interior, bright enough to cast shadows across the barren ground. As I came closer, I heard the steady hum of generators, the voices of the gathering crowds, the churring of a helicopter blade. I saw police officers squinting through the scopes of sniper rifles; countless video cameras with black lenses lined up in tiers like the glossy eyes of spiders; hordes of demonstrators hoisting signs with my name scrawled across them; and what looked like a full regiment of National Guard troopers wearing green fatigues and holding automatic weapons tight against their shoulders.

As I approached the edge of the dome, the sounds of the crowd increased, swelling into a crescendo, before trailing off to an eerie silence. Shielding my eyes from the glare, I looked around at the guns, the cameras, the faces of soldiers, journalists, demonstrators, police officers, concerned citizens, and vendors. Expressions of terror, confusion, curiosity, or hate. Whatever these people may have thought of me, their silence felt almost like a unanimous show of respect; it was as if I was being offered a chance to speak my mind at the outset.

But there was a problem with that idea—the idea of giving me time and space to deliver a message. The problem was that I didn't need to be listened to, not anymore.

It was too late for that now.

At this point, all I needed was for them to move aside.

I raised one hand in the air and proceeded to part the crowd. Slicing the throng down the middle to create a corridor, a way through. Bulldozing people and equipment with significantly more force than I had when I'd done the same thing previously, with Jabari. I wasn't out to injure anyone, but it was a subtle show of strength. I wanted to give these fools an in-person demonstration that they could actually feel, and would continue to feel in the days that followed, in case they had any lingering doubts about who they were dealing with.

I continued to push and shove the crowd—eliciting a chorus of shouting and screams—until I'd formed a ten-foot-wide passage leading up to the dome's outer surface.

I waited, holding the corridor open, keeping everyone at bay.

Soon there were five young brothers wearing frame backpacks making their way along the path toward me.

I started my fifteenth year off right.

By letting my light shine.

From the moment that the Fab Five joined the community, I established myself as the de facto leader. Age be damned. I may have been the youngest (and the only female), but I was also the most powerful by a mile—by several hundred-thousand miles—so I wasn't about to take a backseat to anybody, especially not somebody new.

One of my first tasks as leader was to explain to Darius, Franklin, Malik, Allen, and William exactly what had happened to their brother Jabari. Even though I was afraid of what their reactions might be, I led them to his gravesite, told them the story as quickly as I could get it out, and left them alone to grieve in their own way, watching and listening from the front stoop of the ranger outpost. There was silence among them for a long time. But then, huddled reverently around the lean-to as if it were holy ground, the five brothers spontaneously locked arms at the elbows and softly hummed a song that I'd never heard before, swaying gently side to side, until Allen (the political one) spoke some words that I couldn't make out, words that left the other four nodding their heads in agreement.

Later on, I helped them settle into camp.

I showed them around the community: the ranger's outpost (my home), the recreation room, the sisters' dorm, the meeting space. I repeated what I remembered Jabari telling me about the electrical generators, the solar panels, the water storage reservoir, the fuel tanker truck. I pointed out some of the more unusual amenities of their new home: the fire pit, the chemical toilet, the redneck pickup, the construction backhoe. I helped them move their things into the recreation room, which would serve as the brothers' dorm until I had a chance to go back to Clayton Homes and pick up something new.

"Why can't we just take that?" asked Dare, nodding toward the sisters' dorm as he hauled one of the cots out of the outpost. Dare (the funny one) was a dark-skinned brother with a six-inch afro shaped into a perfect curve and a full beard to match. He wore thick, black-framed glasses, slightly tinted. I was pretty sure they were purely for fashion, not vision.

"Because it's the sisters' dorm," I replied. "That's why."

"Yeah, but come on." Dare stopped and looked at each of the other four brothers in turn. "You see any sisters here?"

"I don't," I said. "And that's a problem we're about to fix."

The community grew quickly after that. More quickly than I would have thought possible.

It all started with active, selective recruitment. Dare reached out and chose people—Black folks—whom he'd known since childhood, whom he'd met at college, or who had made a name for themselves in the Tallahassee area (for doing something positive) and he courted them, gauging their interest in joining the still-young movement. The movement toward *what*, we still weren't sure, but toward something new and different and good. Something radically good. Dare applied a degree of pressure to convince them, using Jabari's death to point out the obvious need for large-scale changes in the way we lived, but he only pushed so hard—anyone who joined us needed to be freely committed—and plenty of people immediately declined the offer. Most did, in fact. Often emphatically. The fact that my presence put our camp under constant scrutiny by the government tended to work against us when it came to attracting members. But those who did say yes tended to jump in with both feet, often bringing others along with them, who in turn, often suggested the names of other folks who might be open to joining the cause. Before long, the recruitment process had taken on a life of its own, with new brothers and sisters petitioning to enlist in the movement with each passing day.

In the beginning, I had insisted on interviewing every single potential newcomer, vetting them against my own internal set of community standards, and making the final call on their eligibility for membership, but that approach had proven impractical almost right away. The volume of petitioners was just too high.

I put together a leadership council to make decisions for the camp community—ten sisters, five brothers, the Fab Five, and me.

The *Baraza*, we called ourselves. The Swahili word for council.

We tried our best to serve the people's interests—I genuinely believe that. But the process wasn't pretty. Members of the Baraza gathered daily around the conference table in the meeting space (which we named the Baraza House) and discussed the state of the community with an unmistakable sense of self-importance and a fair amount of disdain, as though we'd each created at least a dozen brand-new, all-Black, dome-covered, progressive societies exactly like this one within the last few months and couldn't understand how the other council members could be so fucking obtuse about how to get it done right.

One thing I learned really early as a member of the Baraza was that when you put a whole bunch of supposedly enlightened folks in one place to make decisions together, what you get is a whole lot of arguing, posturing, jockeying for position, and complaints—a whole lot of competition to see who can sound the most enlightened. What you don't get is a whole lot of progress. At least not right away.

And another thing I learned—if you want to be a leader, it doesn't always pay to be the youngest one in the room. Especially as a female. When it came down to my powers, yes, I got my due respect from the rest of the council, but when it came down to my ideas—my thoughts on how my powers should be applied—the Baraza tended to treat me like a third-class citizen. Like a blunt instrument. A means to an end. Lift this, move that. Fetch this, build that. It wasn't as if they didn't allow me to speak—I had my chances, and when they weren't offered, I took them anyway. The problem was that I was always drowned out by louder voices, bigger-sounding ideas, and more sophisticated delivery.

I could have refused to go along with the Baraza at any time, of course. They couldn't have forced me to do a damn thing even if they'd had the entire population on their side, but I went along with their plans willingly nine times out of ten. The reason for that was the camp itself: I believed in it. Building a new community had become a dream of mine, and I felt like the Baraza offered the surest opportunity to fulfill it. I trusted them, bottom line. These twenty individuals, with their sword-sharp minds and their statesman-like facility with language. Their strength, like the strength of lions. I believed in these sisters and brothers with all my heart and soul.

Having said that, the attitudes on display around the conference table were pretty damned egotistical at times. It wasn't as if we'd been formally elected or anything; I had selected myself and then handpicked the folks I'd thought would best represent the larger group. Period, end of story. So it wasn't like we had a Mandate From The People to act like a bunch of pompous tyrants. There was no such mandate. Yes, decisions were being made and implemented successfully in spite of all the bickering, but I knew that it wouldn't work that way forever. Folks outside the leadership team were already fussing and grumbling about all things Baraza-related. In spite of the fact that the community had grown (and even begun to thrive) under our watch, it was still small enough that gossip—especially the negative kind—spread quickly from mouth to ear.

Before long I developed a daily routine.

1.) Managing logistics—food, water, housing, utilities—which often meant going out into the city on elaborate supply runs.

2.) Working with the Baraza to plan for the present and future. To develop an official charter. A one-, five-, and ten-year plan. A set of laws and the means to enforce them, as well as a set of consequences if the laws were broken. A way to protect ourselves from the outside world—a way that didn't involve relying solely on my abilities.

3.) Meeting with new recruits, which usually involved (a.) asking why they'd chosen to join us, (b.) showing them to their living quarters, and (c.) performing a few tricks with Bel to prove that I truly was the badass dragonslayer they'd seen on their video screens back home.

4.) Conducting security sweeps of the dome interior. Predictably, as our population increased, so did the presence (and aggression) of the authorities, both police and military. It seemed as if we were constantly under some form of attack. Tactical units with heavy weaponry, body armor, and assault vehicles. C4-explosive charges. Plasma cutters. Attempts at breaching the dome became an almost daily occurrence. I was forced to interrupt my schedule at least once every couple of hours to reinforce the dome's surface, to corral a group of interlopers and cast them out on their asses, or simply to patrol the landscape from above, to make sure we weren't about to be ambushed by a random group of men with automatic rifles.

• • •

"Power grows from the gun," Allen said. He was tall, built like a sprinter, and had a clean-shaven head that developed a sheen when he got animated, which was often. "It's the only thing that can free anybody—Panthers said so, Malcolm said so. Even King had a fucking arsenal in his living room. So who the hell are you to say it ain't so?"

"All of them died by that same gun," a sister said—her name was April. "Remember that. Don't try and downplay it. I'm just saying."

We were in the middle of our morning session, and the leadership council was sitting around the conference table in the Baraza House. Security was the topic, as it often was. Guns, specifically. We had already taken the step to gather all the known firearms in the community (including those I'd sunk into the earth during my confrontation with Jabari's murderers) and locked them in the outpost closet—those guns weren't the point of today's discussion.

The issue on the table was whether we should lay our hands on more. Whether or not we should arm every human being in the community, in fact. Whether we should turn the idea of universal gun ownership into official policy.

The arguments went back and forth for hours: one side talking about self-defense and the other side talking about self-destruction, with neither side giving up an inch of ground.

As for me, I wasn't sure what to think.

On one hand, I desperately wanted to offload the responsibility for keeping the community safe. The pressure of serving as the dam that held back the floodwaters of the outside world was proving too much for me to handle alone.

But were guns the solution?

Did I really want to live in a place where everyone was carrying?

It took several meetings and hours of debate. But the decision was eventually made to arm the populace. To place a rifle—not a pistol or anything else concealable—into the hands of every sister and brother living under the dome. Remington 700s, AR-15s, M4 carbines, automatic shotguns, Ruger deer rifles. I went out into the city and collected everything I could find, including crates full of ammunition. We took this collection of weapons, added the rifles from the cache in the ranger's outpost, and distributed a single firearm and a box of ammunition to every member of the community.

When folks finally got hold of their new rifles, they generally fell into one of three camps.

There were the militant, raised-fist types who treated gun ownership as a radical act of self-preservation, believing that the weapon was a necessary tool to save their lives in the absence of government protection (or, the presence of government hostility). They saw the rifle as a key to the great and heavy lock around their necks. As such, they treated it with a certain kind of reverence and awe. Around half of the folks in our community fell into this group.

But there was another group, which I'll call the stupid-ass gun-headed fools. These were folks who, within seconds of having the rifle in their hands, started taking pictures of themselves in various wannabe thug-life poses and posting them on their social media accounts. Thankfully, this group was in the vast minority.

The final group consisted of those who were terrified by the entire proposal; these people grimaced and held their rifles at arm's length as though they were venomous asps, only agreeing to accept them into their homes out of a sense of duty (or, perhaps, simple peer pressure). If these folks had felt they had a choice, they would have locked the gun in box somewhere and never touched it again. Unfortunately, I counted myself as a member of this group.

• • •

"Lil Sis. You seen this?" Dare asked, sliding his phone across the conference table in the Baraza House. He called me Lil Sis. Everybody did, actually—at least, everybody who knew me as anything other than the bad boss bitch in charge.

I picked up the phone and looked at it.

I saw a news story with a headline that read, "Welcome to the Terror Dome: The Occupation is Now Armed." A grainy image captured by either a satellite or a high-altitude drone showed a group of our residents—maybe a hundred or so—brandishing rifles like members of a citizen brigade.

"Shit," I said.

"Exactly. Shit."

A beautiful sister sitting next to me—her name was Tressie—leaned over and checked the display. "So what?" she said.

"So, I've never been a big believer in the idea that all press is good press," Dare said.

Tressie shrugged. "Good, bad—whichever. It makes no difference. Out here, we are what we are, and we do what we do. They say what they say. It makes no difference."

"You think we're untouchable," Dare said. "I hear that. But we're not."

"She makes us untouchable." Tressie nodded toward me.

"Maybe. But what if we didn't have her?"

"We do."

"For now," Dare said. "Either way, scaring the white off of everybody on the outside? I don't see how that can be a good thing for us."

"I didn't say it was good. I said it doesn't matter. Not as long as we got Lil Sis with us, it doesn't."

"You think so, huh?"

"I do. Think about it for a second, Dare—what's really changed by the existence of this story? So they know we've got guns now. I thought that was the point. To put everybody on notice."

"The point was to put the feds on notice. The feds—not everybody. We don't need the entire world aligned against us."

"Because it's not already?"

"I'm just saying. We don't need any more help being feared, do we?"

"Honestly, Dare. We should be past all that by now," Tressie said. "We've already jumped off the ship and started swimming in open water, looking for land that none of us can see yet, and you're sitting here talking about *what they think of us*. What they think? Brother, what you need to be doing is concentrating on your stroke."

Tressie had a point.

We had already taken over hundreds of thousands of acres of government land, stolen hundreds of thousands of dollars' worth of private property, and we were on pace to attract more than a hundred thousand new residents—Black residents—over the course of the coming year. Would a picture of our people holding a bunch of rifles really make a difference?

"That's some smooth rhetoric, Tress," Dare said. "Really. But I'm talking about concrete direction. The direction of us. We've all agreed—if we're going to build this place into something that lasts, we can't depend on Lil Sis to protect us forever. We've got to go straight at some point—get out from under this dome and plant a flag in the sunshine. Stand up instead of hiding."

"Who's hiding? You? 'Cause I know I'm not."

Dare snorted. "You're living under this little girl's protection like the rest of us, aren't you? Shit." He shook his head. "Everybody's a revolutionary when they've got somebody else's shield up in front of them. But we need to get ready to face the world when nobody's around to guard us, Tress. And I don't think that a bunch of pictures of us carrying weapons is going to help."

"Is that what your problem is? A girl protecting you?"

"What?"

"You heard me," Tressie said. "Maybe your ego can't handle accepting protection from a female."

"Um. I'm sitting right here," I said, waving my hand.

"You're reaching now," Dare said to Tressie. "You really think I've got a problem living under this girl's roof? I'm here, ain't I?"

Tressie shrugged. "Check in with yourself. That's all I'm saying," she said. "You're sounding pretty dismissive talking about getting coverage from 'that little girl' like you couldn't imagine anything worse."

"You got me wrong, Tress."

"Sorry. But either way, my point stands," she said. "The pictures make no difference. If people on the outside want to be scared, let them be. Eyes forward, Dare. Keep aiming forward, always."

That wasn't the end of the discussion. They kept on going back and forth for a while, but I'd stopped listening. I was irritated by the fact that they hadn't seemed to care what I thought about the subject (and hadn't even acknowledged my existence, for that matter), but something else was bothering me more than that. As much as I didn't want the community to rely on me for its survival (too much pressure), it made me sad to hear them planning for my obsolescence—hoping for it, in fact. Working actively toward ending their dependence on my abilities. After hearing them talk about the future of the community, I was left feeling like they were suggesting that I wouldn't even be part of it—not like I would step aside, but like I would be gone.

• • •

It wasn't long before the camp could no longer be called a camp. It was a town. A proper town made up of shared dwellings, structures with dedicated purposes (medical, trading, education, religion), and reliable public utilities. Over the course of a few weeks, a group of sixty engineers had managed to drill three freshwater wells, establish a trash collection and disposal schedule, install a solar panel array on the roof of every building that didn't already have one, and set up a system of above-ground septic tanks to handle waste.

The organization of the town itself also took shape. Homes and other structures were laid out in a grid-like pattern with rough-cut dirt roadways running in between. A broad town square was established with the fire pit at its center and Jabari's gravesite at one end, marked with a proper headstone. Previously unused land on the outskirts was divided into forty-acre parcels, each of which was assigned to a different group of residents to tend communally. Militias were formed—multiple teams of women and men who'd agreed to take up arms and patrol the dome in jeeps and pickup trucks that I'd commandeered from the outside.

Even with all that, the town still wasn't much to look at. But it was light years ahead of where it had been when we'd started out with a lean-to made of sticks and Jabari's ragged tent. And regardless of what it looked like—plain, handmade, and held together with little more than ingenuity and sheer will—it was working, and it belonged solely to us.

The Baraza thought it was time to give our home a name. Eventually we settled on Fort Mose.

• • •

Nighttime was community time in Mose.

Just after dusk, almost every living soul in town—thousands and thousands of heartbreakingly beautiful souls—would show up and show out around the bonfire in the town square. Just being there. Being together, being magical. Being each other's business. Making music, making friends out of acquaintances, making time. And laughing. Lord, the laughter coming from the square was so resounding at times that I swore I could hear it echoing off the ceiling of the dome, hundreds of feet above our heads.

I never joined in, though.

Sitting alone on the roof of the ranger's outpost, my knees held tightly to my chest, I closed my eyes and listened to the chorus of voices rising up from the courtyard below me, listening in the same way that someone might listen to a song. These are my people. I hear them, the sound of their lifeblood. Implacable. Even with my eyes closed, I see my people's brilliance, sheer and sinuous as a bolt of silk.

• • •

Folks used to watch me sometimes, especially in the beginning; I could feel their stares as I moved heavy equipment from place to place, delivered a load of fresh supplies to one of the metal quonset huts, or arranged a line of mobile homes into a perfect cul-de-sac shape. I used to wonder what they saw when they looked at me, how they interpreted my actions, and what sorts of judgments and assumptions they were making about me, their adolescent leader, at any given moment. I wondered what their thoughts would taste like if I could drink them unfiltered, like groundwater drawn from the cistern of a deep well.

Soon their opinions became perfectly clear.

According to the gossip mill, a good number of folks in Mose saw me as an over-exposed, ego-tripping, unstable, bossy-ass, immature, high-yellow house negro with too much power—a power that most likely sprang from an unholy arrangement with the devil himself.

Overall, it was a valid critique.

These people (my toughest critics) either feared me for what they perceived me to be, or hated me for the same. And I knew that I could never change their minds about who and what I was—these were not the types of folks you could win over—so I didn't try. I just stayed away from them as best I could.

The next group (my second-toughest critics) saw me as an oddity. More bizarre than dangerous. They interpreted my power as a mutation that, while beneficial in many obvious ways, marked me as separate and distinct, alien and out of place. Utterly foreign to everything they stood for. The fact that I kept a ball of dust hovering in the air above my right shoulder as I went about my daily business probably didn't help to normalize my image, but the truth was that these folks were going to view me as an anomaly either way. For weeks, they had watched me perform strange and often unsettling feats of magic on a routine basis—after everything they'd witnessed, I would never be normal in their eyes. No amount of soft-shoeing or kowtowing during the off-hours could have possibly undone the psychological effects of having seen countless displays of uncanny, voodoo-like trickery. I was branded. Forever exotic and outlandish. Unusual and unwanted.

But, thankfully, there was one more group: the awestruck.

These were the folks who immediately stopped what they were doing and stared with obvious admiration whenever I walked by, who asked me to sign pieces of memorabilia with a permanent marker, who posed with me for selfie after selfie and posted them to social media, who occasionally reached out and touched my hand or my arm with the kind of solemn reverence typically afforded a prophet or a saint. They invited me to sit and eat with them, asked how I was feeling if I seemed down, thanked me regularly for what I was doing for Mose, and sometimes even referred to me as their friend, as their saving grace, as their way forward, or as their one way out. These were the people who kept me from giving up. Without them, and without the memories of my mother and father, I wouldn't have been able to carry on.

• • •

One evening, I was running a solo patrol along the dome's outer rim, taking a quick pass around the circumference to get a sense of the crowd's behavior, size, and composition—the ratio of law enforcement to military to media personality to private citizen—when I noticed that the number of protestors had noticeably grown. There were hundreds of them now, maybe thousands, and they had divided themselves into two distinct groups. Both loud, both seemingly angry, and—as far as I could tell—both exclusively Caucasian.

One group was familiar to me: the environmental protestors. They'd been camped outside the dome from the very beginning, chanting and waving picket signs with statements about deforestation, reclaiming the planet, Mother Earth, and becoming a force for Nature. Statements like Waste is a Terrible Thing to Mind. Green is the New Black. Will Work For Trees. Will Your Children Be Able to Breathe When Tomorrow Comes? None of those things were new; I'd seen it all before, countless times. But there was one change in the group that was impossible to overlook—their clothing. Almost every single protestor was wearing a black t-shirt with *The EAST* printed across the front and *The Environmental Action Sovereignty Trust* printed across the back. If they hadn't been holding picket signs, they would have looked almost exactly like the audience at your average indie rock concert.

The other group, however, was a whole different animal.

These were the white supremacists. They came to the dome to protest what they clearly viewed as a Black uprising. A takeover. This group of demonstrators was diverse (in every way other than race, though weirdly, there were a few brown faces), consisting of young and old, rich and poor, women and men, formally and casually dressed, radical and conservative in their rhetoric. Some were heavily tattooed, leather-clad, and armed with aluminum baseball bats, ball-peen hammers, long hunting knives, and deer rifles, while others were clothed in dress shirts and khakis, armed only with mobile phones and coffee cups. There was everybody in between, also—white folks who reminded me of teachers I'd had, store owners I'd been in confrontations with, social workers I'd been assigned, parents of friends I used to have during my former life, a life that felt as distant to me now as the moon. Some protestors were hoisting up signs printed with familiar imagery like swastikas, iron crosses, the snarling faces of Vikings with horned helmets, and eagles clutching bolts of lightning in their hooked talons, but there were also signs printed with slogans that I hadn't seen before, seemingly benign slogans like Free America Rally, Love your Race, Blut Und Ehre, 14 Words, AKIA, and One-Hundred Percent Nation. America First. A boy who couldn't have been more than half my age was gripping a rifle in one hand and a sign in the other that read, "Florida is an Open-Carry State…As Long As You're Going Hunting."

I watched the chaos for as long as I could stand it.

As I started to leave, I noticed someone familiar in the crowd of protestors—he was standing on the environmental side, which was preferable to the alternative, but it didn't make me feel all that much better, honestly. Like the others standing next to him, he wore a black shirt with The EAST written across the front. It was Elijah, Harmony's friend from the motel.

When I got back to town, I walked slowly along a quiet and nameless dirt road that someone had carved into the earth only weeks earlier. A line of young cypress grew along the shoulder; they'd been planted just a few days ago. In their own stark way, the saplings were beautiful. They could never undo the immeasurable damage I'd done to this place, but hearing the sound of their leaves in the wind felt like another small measure of redemption. One more incremental step in the agonizingly slow process of renewal.

I was headed roughly in the direction of home, but was in no particular hurry to get there. Just putting one foot down in front of the other, trying to clear my mind of everything I'd seen in the boundary zone and replace it with something good. A reminder of why I was here, maybe. A convincing reason to expect anything in the future other than the eventual fall of Fort Mose, the loss of our freedom, the taking of our lives. The punishment of an entire people. Given the magnitude of the forces amassing against us outside the dome, I wasn't left with much reason to hope for anything other than a quick ending. But I wouldn't allow myself to quit, not now. I didn't know what else to do other than carry on.

I had almost reached the ranger outpost when I noticed movement in the distance, off to my right. Someone in the shadows across the town square who I didn't recognize—a thin, light-skinned brother wearing a black sweatshirt with the hood pulled up. He was alone, in a mad rush, and clutching something bulky in his arms, holding it tightly to his chest. It could have been anything: a package of food, a bundle of clothing, extra parts for a broken machine, a package containing medicine, a bag with a laptop inside. Anything. But it didn't matter; the sight of an unfamiliar man racing through the darkness was unsettling somehow—an all-too tangible reminder that Fort Mose no longer belonged to me, in spite of how much I liked to imagine it did.

The town had grown. It had grown well past the point where I could walk into a room or through the center courtyard or down any random dirt road and recognize every face I saw. Those times were far behind us; I'd already known that was true, but obviously hadn't accepted it, which was something I needed to change. Clearly I was going to have to get comfortable with the idea of living shoulder to shoulder with strangers again—people whose faces I wouldn't be able to place and whose origins, beliefs, and motivations I would never fully understand. I would need to learn to live with uncertainty again—either that, or I was going to have to start keeping a close eye on some brothers and sisters whom I didn't fully trust. One or the other, or maybe both. I wasn't sure.

• • •

It didn't take long before I'd decided.

Fuck uncertainty.

I didn't want to live with it.

So instead of accepting the fact that Mose was changing into something I couldn't control, I did the unthinkable—I launched a calculated campaign to run surveillance on my own people. Keeping tabs on folks. Watching them in their homes, in the town square, in the streets, as they worked, as they tried to unwind, and as they slept at night. Not all the time, of course, and not everybody. Just those sisters and brothers whose shady behavior gave me cause for concern: grown men who leered at my body for too long, women who stole from Mose's trade store, the soapbox pundits who criticized the leadership too loudly without adding anything productive to the conversation, or folks who simply weren't pulling their own weight around town. Wrapped up in Bel's shadowy folds, I followed these people when they thought they were alone, watched how their behavior changed when they were in the public eye, and listened to their supposedly private conversations about every topic under the sun: their family, their lovers, their so-called dearest friends, the jobs they used to have before coming to Mose, the lives they hoped to build once Mose had finally come of age, assuming that it ever would.

It was addictive. Even better than the surveillance I'd done in the past. Back then, spying had felt more like anthropology—studying a foreign culture up close as a purely academic pursuit—but spying in Mose felt much more visceral. More personal. I kept telling myself that I was doing it for the right reasons—to learn more about my neighbors so I could become a better one myself, to increase the security of the community as a whole, to help me make more informed decisions on behalf of the larger group—but the truth was that I enjoyed the shit out of every moment. Otherwise, why would I have continued? My efforts never yielded a single piece of actionable intelligence concerning the safety of Mose, never provided any inside tips that could have helped the Baraza council with more effective decision-making, and never made me a better person by even the slightest margin. It was criminal voyeurism perpetrated against my own people, plain and simple. And by indulging in it, I had given away another scrap of my soul for perhaps the thousandth time. On top of all that, I hadn't even accomplished the one thing that had set me on this twisted path to begin with: I was never able to find the light-skinned brother I'd seen that night in the town square. It was as if he'd never existed at all.

• • •

One of the forty-acre plots of land was mine to care for, all on my own. I took responsibility for tilling and preparing the soil, for planting the seeds, for irrigation, for the harvest. I didn't sow the entire farmstead—it would have taken too much effort, even with my abilities. Instead, I carved out a five-acre tract that I was able to maintain alone, growing potatoes, snap beans, squash, pintos, and sweet corn. The yield wasn't high, but for me, the yield wasn't the point. The process of working the land was what mattered—it was meditative. Gratifying, because my hand wasn't being forced. Liberating, because the land belonged to us.

One morning I stood alone at the edge of the field. My field. Hazy sunlight fell on crisp rows of seedlings, barely more than sprigs in the dark soil. I was working. Working on drawing a swarm of insects away from the leaves of the plants, all at once, without damaging them. Trying to separate pest from plant using only my mind. It was harder than I'd thought it would be, preserving the resource while eliminating the parasite feeding on it. I concentrated. My eyes were closed tightly. Over time, I began to feel thousands upon thousands of frenzied, writhing bodies deep in the meat of my mind, as though they'd somehow figured out a way to worm their way into my skull and burrow there.

I started to lift the mass of insects gently from the leaves, but then I heard a concussive blast in the distance and the spell was broken. It sounded like an explosion. Low and resonant, like an airplane colliding with a faraway building. Soon after, I felt the ground tremoring underneath my feet.

Suddenly it began to rain.

Nothing but a light mist at first. But seconds later, the heavens opened up and showered the earth in a torrential downpour.

Only it wasn't water falling from the sky.

It was dust.

The dome was collapsing on every side. Disintegrating. Pulverized into a fine, silken powder.

It was like a thick curtain falling over me—everything went dark.

I could barely breathe.

In a wild panic, I raced back to town.

Mose was in a state of chaos.

Brothers and sisters covered from head to toe in layers of soot-like sediment, running through the square as though fleeing the epicenter of a bomb blast. Screaming, calling out for each other. Some carried weapons in their hands at the ready, while others scrambled to take cover inside of mobile homes or portable buildings, slamming doors closed behind them. A terrifying number had collapsed onto the ground where they'd stood, either unconscious from a lack of breathable air or catatonic from clinical shock, while a handful of medical personnel attended to them as best they could.

Members of the Baraza were in the thick of it all. Calling out commands, trying to bring a measure of organization to the pandemonium. Allen, Dare, and a sister known only as Jones— wearing black bandannas tied around their mouths and carrying hunting rifles—had gathered together what looked like a crowd of hundreds around them, all armed. On the opposite side of the square, I saw April and Tressie trying to marshal folks indoors and out of harm's way, practically shoving them wholesale through open doors. As for me, I was paralyzed. Standing mutely next to the ranger's outpost, watching in disbelief as our fledgling society spiraled its way back down to earth. A nebulous haze of dust still hung in the atmosphere like smoke.

I looked up at the sky.

The dome was gone. Unfiltered sunlight shone down on Fort Mose for the first time in its existence, and—strangely—it didn't feel like a sign of renewal; it felt like the beginning of the end. Like exposure.

Suddenly, I heard the sound of engines.

Even over the crowd noise, I could hear the sound getting louder.

Someone from the outside was coming.

I lifted myself into the air until I had a clear view beyond the buildings' rooftops.

They arrived moments later, just as I'd feared they would.

Countless tactical police units. Officers riding four-wheeled ATVs in a cavalry formation, kicking up plumes of roiling dust in their wakes. Seven armored assault vehicles that looked like battle tanks mixed with prison transport units, with a row of gun emplacements installed along each side panel and a water-cannon turret mounted on every roof. Dozens of standard-issue police cruisers with lightbars flashing blue and red. Unmarked black SUVs. Within a matter of seconds, a low-flying attack helicopter knifed through the sky about fifteen feet above the ground, pulled up when it reached the town's border, and steadied itself, hovering menacingly, as at least twenty officers wearing brown fatigues leapt out of the open bay door and disappeared among the dust devils whipped up by the beating blades overhead.

Before I could process what was happening, there were boots on the ground all around us. Cops decked out in riot gear marching through the streets of Mose, shields raised and masks lowered, like an occupying army. Dogs that looked like wolves on long leashes. Canisters of tear gas skittering across the graveled walkways, pinging off of building facades, spewing out streams of white smoke that swirled across the town square like a rolling fog.

Gunfire rang out.

A series of heavy exchanges back and forth.

Bodies began to fall—Black bodies. The sound of our screams resounding through the streets was deafening.

I had learned about mythology once, during my old life. Back when I was still a student in elementary school—back when I was someone else.

For a class project, I'd chosen to research the mythology of the Scandinavian people, the Norse. Hammer-wielding, one-eyed, gold-toothed gods. Goddesses who donned feathered cowls, used the sorcery of the underworld, and rode into battle on monstrous timberwolves. Nine different worlds surrounding a central tree whose branches extended deep into heaven.

And valkyries.

Valkyries were the main reason I'd chosen the Norse: warrior women on winged horses, carrying spears tipped with lightning.

Choosers of the slain.

I rose up from the ground.

Eyes closed, I focused on drawing the swarm of police officers away from Mose. Separating them from us. Choosing. Every part of my consciousness converged on a singular task: to find and preserve my people while eliminating the forces that fed upon them.

It was much easier than I'd thought it would be.

• • •

"I see only one way," Allen said, leaning back in his chair, hands behind his head. "We pick six of those rollers outside, any random six, and shoot them square in their fucking backs. The end. Just bring everything into parity right quick, then send the rest of them on home. That's my humble suggestion."

The council was seated around the table in the Baraza House, arguing over the fate of the police officers currently imprisoned in the massive, twenty-foot-deep chasm I'd carved in the earth. Two hundred seventy-four cops in total. I had culled those men from our town, subdued them, stripped them of their weapons and clothing, and dropped them inside the pit like a group of zoo animals in an open-air exhibit. But now what? Tressie had already contacted the outside world and let them know that we'd taken hostages (and weren't afraid to hurt them), which seemed to be enough of a threat to keep the authorities from sending in more troops. As a matter of fact, our patrols were reporting that no one had dared to even set foot across the invisible line where the dome's outer boundary once stood. But how long could a stalemate like this last?

And what were we supposed to do with almost three hundred prisoners?

There was serious disagreement over that last question.

For some members of the Baraza, the idea of holding police officers as hostages was too much to process. These brothers and

sisters believed that we should take the moral high ground, turn the
other cheek, and return the officers unharmed, voluntarily, as a show
of good faith. As a dramatic demonstration of the fundamental
righteousness of our community. Imagine what the world would think
of us then, they argued. Imagine how the winds would shift in our
favor.

Other people on the council (the more militant folks) had a
different perspective.

For these sisters and brothers, the facts were as follows: The
cops had raided our town—our homes—and applied an unreasonable
level of force without warning or provocation. Six of our people, four
sisters and two brothers, had been gunned down as a result; a half-
dozen human beings erased from the earth for what amounted to
simple trespassing. To the most militant among us, there was only one
appropriate response to these events. Revenge. An eye for an eye.
According to their logic, the laws of vengeance were as self-evident as
the laws of physics. For any given force, there is a reaction force that is
equal in size, but opposite in direction. The only thing they disagreed
about was the number—how many of these motherfuckers should be
forced down onto their knees and shot in the head.

Some (like Allen) wanted to murder exactly six of theirs like
they had murdered six of ours, balancing out the death toll in the
current equation, while other members couldn't help but think
historically, remembering all of the blood that had ever poured from
Black souls at the hands of overseers across the centuries spent
surviving in the Americas. For these sisters and brothers, six dead
officers wouldn't come close to paying the debt we were owed as a
people. These folks were ready to kill every last cop we'd captured,
transforming the prison pit outside into a mass open grave.

Every Baraza member was either a dove or a hawk except for
one.

Yours truly.

I understood both sides, but I didn't believe that murdering our
prisoners or voluntarily setting them free would get Mose any closer to

what I saw as the ultimate goal: legitimacy. Official legal status as a recognized city-state. As a self-governing territory—shit, as an African-American reservation. As something, anything, as long as it was sanctioned.

To achieve this goal, I had my own strategy in mind: to return the hostages to the government, but not unconditionally. Not as a goodwill gesture, and not as proof of our moral superiority, but as a negotiating tool. I wanted to use the officers as leverage in a larger conversation, as a way to help secure the long-term future of Mose.

"We should send them back," I said. "Alive. But only after we get something first."

Everyone at the table looked at me. Their haggard faces, still dust-covered and bloodied, like the faces of prisoners in an internment camp.

"Like what, Sis?" Dare asked, shaking his head. "What would they possibly be willing to give us at this point?"

"Everything," I replied. "Borders. Recognition. Rights."

Allen snorted. "You think they're going to give us all that? For some pigs?"

I wasn't sure.

But one thing had become clear to me after today—Fort Mose wouldn't exist for much longer if we had to keep living our lives like this. Constantly under siege, constantly under threat of erasure. It wasn't sustainable.

"I can't defend us," I said.

"You can," Dare said. "You have."

I shook my head. The tears were starting to build; I wiped my eyes. "I thought I could hold them back long enough. Wait them out. You know? I thought all we needed was time and space to grow up. But they aren't going to leave us alone."

"Bitch lost her nerve," someone muttered—a sister, I wasn't sure which one.

I ignored her. "All I'm saying is that we need help getting Mose to the next stage. Help from the outside."

"Fuck the outside," Allen said. "The whole point of Mose is self-sufficiency. Not begging."

"I'm not talking about begging. I'm talking about living."

Allen snorted. "One thing I know? Living ain't always living, Lil Sis. Usually it's just dying slowly. And we've had more than enough of that already—that's why we came to Mose in the first place. For something different. That's the point."

"Whatever," I said. "We need help with this—believe me."

"Believe you?"

"What would you rather do, Allen? Go out and declare war on them? Use me as your weapon? Well, I'm telling you—I can't do it. We need to find a way to end this now."

• • •

I left Baraza House and went to the field. My own forty acres.

Night had fallen. With the dome gone, I was able to see stars again, more stars than I'd ever seen before in my life, in any place I'd ever lived before. The black sky and the sickle-shaped moon overhead. I walked slowly along a tilled row in the soil toward the center of the field, and soon I could hear voices—the voices of our prisoners. Moaning. Calling out for help. Cursing. Making threats that couldn't possibly be carried out. I heard my name mentioned more than a few times.

Flashlight in hand, I approached the edge of the pit—cavernous and steep-sided, almost canyon-like—and shone the light inside, sweeping the beam slowly across the prisoner's upturned faces. Their expressions of anger and resilience, resignation and terror. A few of the men were standing tall, but most had found a spot in the dirt to sit, leaning up against one of the walls or huddled with their knees pulled in toward their chests. Hollow-eyed, filthy, and clothed only in undergarments, the men looked nothing like officers of the law, nowhere near the ideal of Protect and Serve. Without weapons, without uniforms, they looked small and exposed, like dogs with their coats shorn off.

None of them said a word.

"You're all going home soon. Don't worry," I said. "I just have a question first. An easy one."

"Fuck you, bitch," a man shouted from somewhere in the dark. "You can't keep us down here."

"Who the fuck said that?" I demanded.

I shone the flashlight in the direction of the sound. Scanning the crowd.

"Right here," the voice said. "Here, bitch."

Eventually I picked out a tall, muscular white man wearing a tanktop and boxer shorts, squinting up at me. A heavily tattooed arm shielding his brow.

"You can't keep us down here," he said.

"Actually, I can. Motherfucker, I can cave in the walls of this hole and bury you as easy as shrugging my shoulders. So don't try and tell me what I can and can't do. I can do whatever the fuck I want to do. Right now, I'm trying to tell you what I'm *going* to do. So I suggest you shut your damn mouth and listen before I snatch that tongue out of your thick head."

I waited.

The man didn't respond.

"All right, then," I said. "Like I told you. I'm going to let you all go, but I have a question. You'll be free when I have the answer."

I paused, shining the light from face to face. A vast majority of the men down in the pit were white, but not all were; I saw brown and Black faces in the group as well. It didn't matter much to me, honestly. My question was the same either way.

"Six of our people were killed today," I said quietly. "Six human beings. So my question is simple. I need to know who's responsible for their deaths."

"They are," a voice called out.

It was the same overgrown, tattooed white man as before.

"They're responsible for their own deaths?" I asked.

"Nobody forced them to come here. Right? They chose to grab some fucking guns and put themselves in harm's way. And then along came harm. It's simple cause and effect."

"Then I'll ask my question a different way," I said. "Which one of you pulled the trigger on them? That's what I need to know."

"We all did," the man replied.

I stared at him; for a moment, I wasn't sure what to say. "Really? That's your answer?"

"All of us. We all pulled the trigger."

Almost immediately, I heard voices of dissent from the crowd. I didn't shoot nobody, a voice said. Speak for your damn self, motherfucker, said another voice.

"Shut the fuck up," the man barked. "You cowards need to learn to stand up. Either we all did it or none of us did it. Nothing else."

I paused for a moment, sweeping the light across the faces of the group.

"Is that the final answer?" I asked. "All or none?"

No one responded.

"Look," I said. "So you know, I'm not that chick who counts to three or any of that shit. Last chance is right now. Does anyone want to step forward and take responsibility for the deaths of my people?"

I gave them a few seconds to decide.

The inside of the pit was utterly silent.

Without another word, I took a step forward and plunged over the edge, descending upon the men as though I were riding a winged horse, screaming at the top of my lungs. Almost immediately, their screams melded into mine.

movin' on up, movin' on out

It was time to make my intentions known to the world.

I had thought I'd been clear. But evidently I hadn't been direct enough with my non-verbal cues. This time, things would be different; there would be no miscommunication. Shit was about to get laid out plain as day.

I knew that the only way to get my message across was through the media, so I arranged an in-person interview with Guadalupe Calderón, Editor-at-Large, for the following morning.

I had three goals in mind.

First, I was going to remind the world that we were holding hostages and, accordingly, were not to be fucked with.

Second, I planned to declare the independence of Fort Mose officially, and to make our desire for formal ties understood. I needed to change the perception of Fort Mose from a dangerous occupation movement made up of ragtag Black separatists, to a full-fledged sovereign state, similar to Vatican City in Italy. A walled-off fort within the heart of a host nation. Mose would still be viewed as dangerous, of course, but the hope was that a formal relationship with the government would make us seem like a controllable danger—one they could live with peacefully.

The third and final goal was mass recruitment. To take Mose to another level—the next plane of ascension, as Allen used to call it. Enough with the slow roll. It was time to grow the town for real.

Up to that point, we had tightly controlled the gates of Mose, only offering membership to those with direct ties to a current member. But that tactic needed to change if we were going to survive. We needed to open our doors to the broader community—the broader African-American community, to be crystal clear. There would still be a formal intake process, as there always had been, but the plan was to start encouraging any and all Black folks to apply from now on, not just friends or friends of friends.

It was a risky growth strategy (Manifest Destiny revisited), but it couldn't possibly be more American—steal a piece of land, clear out space, and increase the population at a breakneck pace until the rest of the world has no choice but to recognize your legitimacy.

By the way—all of these decisions? I made them on my own, without the Baraza's input. I'd come to a conclusion last night: if the people of Fort Mose were going to use me for my powers, then they were going to deal with my unilateral decision-making, at least some of the time.

I was ready to spread the word—Fort Mose was real, and it was open for business.

• • •

On the morning of my sit-down with Calderón, I traveled to the boundary zone in a red pickup truck, the one with the Confederate flag decal on the back window. She had chosen the meeting place— the borderlands. The place where our two separate worlds came together. For her, staging our interview in the most watched location on the planet was a way to gain maximum exposure for her personal brand, no doubt, which was fine by me. The venue met my personal goals for maximum exposure as well.

It would have been easier to fly myself in (and definitely would have added to my overall mystique), but I had a different set of goals in mind. The choice to drive the truck was about making an impression as a broader unit, a united front. Creating an indelible image of our community. When we rolled up to the boundary zone, the media was going to broadcast exactly what we wanted potential residents to see: something inspirational. One sister in the driver's seat, me sitting beside her, and four more sisters and three brothers kneeling in the truck bed, wearing dark dress clothes and holding rifles against their shoulders in broad daylight, underneath the sun. It was pure theater. Pure fiction. For starters, I didn't need any protection whatsoever, and in any case, my entourage consisted of a former pre-med student, an accountant, a grocery clerk, a mechanical engineer, three social workers, and a line cook at a diner. But none of that made a difference. When the picture of the nine of us was published in every single news outlet across the globe—which it undoubtedly would be—the message was going to be clear. We are together, we are independent, we are free, we are unafraid, and we are ready for you to join us in the wilderness.

As the truck approached the exclusion zone, I saw that the normal scrum of journalists had swelled into a seething, monstrous horde in anticipation of the interview. The fact that none of these hacks would get a chance to ask a single question didn't seem to bother them one bit (this was going to be a one-on-one conversation). As for Calderón, she was seated coolly in a folding chair under a white marquee tent with long metal poles stuck into the soil, a cluster of video cameras stationed on either side of her. She looked ready for anything.

I was too.

Because the nine of us were driving into an unprotected area swarming with police, National Guardsmen, and white supremacists (openly carrying), I had taken some extra precautions. Namely, I had siphoned dust from the atmosphere and fused it into a solid veneer, applying it to the entire length of the truck chassis, including the occupants in the rear. The barrier was sheer and translucent, allowing light to pass through with minimal distortion, but it was almost unimaginably strong—bullet-resistant, in fact, due to the surface angles (we'd tested it back in Mose with every caliber of firearm we owned). Of course, I would need to leave the protection of the truck when it was time for my conversation with Calderón, but I was ready for that as well. I would be relying on my Bel to shield me during the interview.

We were around twenty-five yards away.

"That's good enough," I said to the driver—I'd forgotten her name. Alicia? Aleeya?

She slowed down and stopped the truck. I summoned Bel, dispersed her over my body (keeping her surface transparent), and got out. I closed the door behind me and turned to the folks standing in the truck bed.

"Relax, everybody," I said. "Focus on looking good, like you do. This shouldn't take long." I glanced down at the fifty-gallon trash bag lying between their feet. They were standing as far away from it as they could without falling overboard. "Just make sure you're not blocking that when I call for it. I can't have you killing my vibe out here." I patted the truck's side panel. "Be right back."

Wearing a tailored black suit coat and slacks, my braids in an up-do, I lifted myself into the air (eliciting an audible response from the audience) and glided over to the canopy where Calderón was seated. A metal chair had been set up across from her. I sat down, crossed my legs, and folded my hands in my lap.

The humidity was stifling—it felt like I was breathing through a wet cloth—but I didn't let my discomfort show. Wearing a smooth and placid expression, I stared directly into Calderón's eyes.

"Good morning, Miss Williams," she said, smiling. "Thank you for agreeing to this."

"Good morning, Miss Calderón. Thank you for having me."

The two of us went back and forth for at least an hour while the world watched.

It felt like an endless tug-of-war. Calderón kept trying to pull me into discussing the status of the hostages, while I responded by dragging the conversation back to Fort Mose, to our goals and beliefs. In no uncertain terms, I let her and all her viewers know that Mose wasn't going anywhere, that we had our eyes set on growth, in fact, and that we were seeking formalized relations with the United States: a treaty agreement. She asked me whether last night's raid had changed anything about these plans. Yes, it had, I answered. It's made us stronger, even more determined than we were before.

"I have to bring us back around again," Calderón said at around the forty-five-minute mark. "The hostages. Where are they now? And what assurances can you give us that they're unharmed?"

"None," I replied flatly.

Calderón stared. For a moment, it looked like she'd forgotten the reason why we were sitting there.

"Can you clarify?" she asked.

"The hostages were harmed. So I can't give you any assurances that they weren't."

"They were harmed?"

"Yes. But I can tell you that they are alive, and that we plan to give them back. We just need the process started first."

"What process?"

I looked at her. *Seriously?*

"Everything I've been talking about for almost an hour," I said. "Making Fort Mose permanent. Legalized. Giving us our official seal."

"And if those things don't happen?" Calderón asked.

"They will. They're going to."

"I'm asking about opposition. What are your plans if your goals are opposed?"

I thought about it for a moment.

"Let me put it like this," I said. "We're here. We're not going anywhere. We would like to coexist with the rest of you peacefully, if you let us. But whether that's possible or not, Fort Mose is real and it's happening. Trust me—all of you will be far better off if the politicians accept this and sign off on a deal. Sincerely. I don't want to hurt anyone more than I already have."

"But you would."

I shrugged. "Not because I want to. But yeah, of course I would, if someone tried to hurt us first." I paused, staring directly into the lens of the camera over Calderón's left shoulder. "Look—please don't make me hurt anyone just to prove a point. All we want is independence for Fort Mose, and then you never have to hear from me—"

I stopped short. Someone standing in the crowd behind the camera had broken my concentration—a scrawny little punk-hippie chick with purple pigtails and a couple of nose rings. It was none other than Harmonic Arris Windswept Mackenzie-Jones in all her white-girl glory, wearing a black t-shirt emblazoned with the logo of The EAST. She winked at me.

"And how do we know that the hostages are still alive, Miss Williams?"

I kept staring at Harmony.

"Miss Williams?" Calderón said.

Without a word, I turned around in the chair and glanced over my shoulder toward the truck. On command, the fifty-gallon black trash bag rose from the rear bed, weaved past the seven brothers and sisters, and drifted across the barren field in my direction—drooping heavily, as though filled halfway with gravel—until it came to rest gently at my feet.

"The hostages are fine," I said. "Other than what I took from them."

I leaned down and spread open the mouth of the bag, folding down its edges so that the contents were fully visible.

Calderón covered her mouth with both hands, rearing back in her chair.

There were hundreds of severed fingers inside.

Five hundred forty-eight of them, to be exact.

I had taken both index fingers from every police officer in the pit. Trigger fingers. One from each hand, just to be safe.

• • •

The Baraza were beyond pissed.

To a person, the council viewed my actions over the previous twenty-four hours as one continuous series of colossal fuckups. I had held an unauthorized interview with the press, during which I had presented an unauthorized plan for the town of Fort Mose, alongside a bag full of cop fingers that no one had authorized me to remove. ("Fingers?" Dare said. "What the fuck's wrong with you, Sis?") In the eyes of the Baraza, I had gone completely off-script, had overstepped my bounds by a mile, and had further jeopardized the future of the town and the lives of those living within it. There was no doubt in my mind that they would have removed me from the council immediately if it weren't for a few inconvenient facts: (a.) they needed me, (b.) they knew they couldn't force me to do a damn thing, so it was better to keep me close than to push me away, and (c.) the things I had done— the public press conference, my description of our town, shit, even the whole "finger incident"—seemed to be working in our collective favor, at least for the time being.

In the weeks following the interview, applications for membership skyrocketed by roughly a factor of ten. Yes, I had turned off an enormous cross-section of Black folks with my posturing, bad attitude, foul mouth, unchecked power, and apparent propensity for barbarism—critiques that were lobbed at me via social media every minute of every day—but there were plenty of other folks who understood the reasons why I had made the choices I'd made. These people could see my heart, could relate to my anger, and could support the goals of a place like Fort Mose (if not the particular tactics I used to preserve it). Sisters and brothers who believed in our mission came to us in droves, from all over the country; in fact, so many people applied for membership that we had difficulty expanding our infrastructure to match the overwhelming influx. I found myself working almost around the clock to keep up with demand. Eventually, we had to create a waiting list; that was how fast we were growing.

Donations from the outside poured in as well.

As it turned out, even among Black folks who would never dream of joining us in the new frontier of Mose, there was a large number who were willing to contribute their hard-earned cash to the cause. Small amounts, mostly—usually five to ten dollars—but when those amounts were multiplied by the hundreds of thousands? Let's just say they made an immediate impact. We received in-kind donations as well: food, water, shelter, and even services like plumbing and light construction work. The outpouring of generosity from the outside was moving, even to the most hardened among us.

Donations from non-Black folks rolled in, too—from people of all races and ethnicities. There were those who supported the idea of a Black-owned space as a symbol of Black empowerment, and there were those who simply wanted as many negroes as possible to leave their cities and settle someplace else. For the latter group of donors, this was as close to Go Back to Africa as they were ever going to get, which was fine with us. We were willing to take whatever money we were sent, regardless of the source, as long as the paper it was printed on was green.

Thankfully, as our population grew and Mose began to flourish, we received outside help with our appeal for legal status as well. At first, only a handful of academic scholars contacted us to offer their help, but because of their early support, we were soon approached by well-known intellectuals like Toni Morrison and Cornel West (neither of whom I had ever heard of), and while none of these academics expressly endorsed our community's philosophy or its practices, every one of them argued passionately—and publicly—in favor of our existence. At the same time, a number of famous recording artists, athletes, and actors joined the growing chorus of voices calling for Fort Mose to be embraced by the Union, and before long, we had the ACLU, the Southern Poverty Law Center, and the NAACP Legal Defense Fund working on our behalf, which was when the tides really began to shift. While the voices of scholars and artists had helped us win hearts and minds, the legal lobbyists were the ones with the expertise to help Fort Mose win what mattered most—actual votes.

Here is why votes mattered.

Under national law, a new U.S. territory can be created under two relatively simple conditions: the consent of the legislature of the state involved, and the consent of Congress. Neither of which would be easy to come by.

So, it was the job of our legal team to secure enough Yes votes in Florida and Washington, D.C.to carry the motion. And how did they do this? By offering the right kinds of concessions. Releasing hostages, first and foremost. Making public apologies for our misdeeds. Denouncing violence. Creating a fund to reimburse those we had harmed. These concessions allowed lawmakers to present themselves as modern-day heroes to their constituents (look at what I brought home for you!)—or at least provided them with enough political cover to vote in favor of Mose and still keep their jobs. (Lucky for us, it wasn't an election year.)

There was still a mountain of opposition, of course—from white supremacists, environmental groups (led by EAST), and everyday Americans of all backgrounds who couldn't stomach the idea of what amounted to modern-day secession, who deplored our tactics and values, and who believed we deserved to be punished rather than rewarded with legal standing. But in spite of everything, it was looking more and more like Fort Mose would eventually become a sanctioned American territory—with everything that status entailed, both good and bad.

• • •

I woke up on my seventeenth birthday to a sound from outside.

A deep rumble, like thunder rolling in the distance, followed by the sound of screams. A moment later, the windows of the outpost rattled lightly, like car windows when the stereo volume is high.

I rushed outside into the town square.

It was dusk. Our version of streetlights—stand-up LED lanterns spaced at regular intervals along the sidewalks and roadways—made the town look almost city-like; it was jarring for a moment, seeing how dramatically Fort Mose had changed, and how quickly.

The square was alive with activity.

Sisters and brothers were rushing to get themselves indoors, scanning their surroundings like sentries as they jogged across the cobblestone plaza. At the far end of the square, I saw a column of smoke. Firelight. A low-burning blaze, orange and quavering, as if on the verge of flickering out. At first I thought I was seeing the dregs of the community bonfire, but when I looked more closely I saw that it was something else. A vehicle. The remains of the redneck truck, its chassis reduced to a twisted metal hulk.

At least three heavily burned bodies lay motionless on the ground nearby.

I made my way to the Baraza House and found half of the council gathered there.

Lying at the center of the table, tied up with what looked like a length of common clothesline, a light-skinned brother was staring up at me, his face bloodied and swollen. He looked like the man I'd seen running across the plaza carrying something unknown in his arms, but I couldn't be sure.

"You need to shut your mouth," Allen said, glaring down at him.

The brother shook his head slowly side to side. "It wasn't supposed to be like that," he murmured, slurring his words. The swelling made it difficult to tell, but it looked like there were tears building in his eyes. "This wasn't what we wanted. I swear it wasn't."

"Hand to God, bruh," Allen said. "On my fucking life. I will kill you if you don't shut your mouth."

"What happened?" I asked.

Allen looked at me. "This mulatto-looking motherfucker right here? This coward thought he would try and send the people of Fort Mose a message about 'Save the Trees' and 'Earth first' and shit. So he bombed us. Motherfucker right here." Allen made a fist and brought it down hard on the brother's face, spattering the tabletop with blood. "Motherfucker right here thought he would sneak up into Mose like a little bitch. Do his dirty work without getting caught, right? Well you got caught, didn't you, bruh? You undercover brother motherfucker. You got caught." Allen reared back and hit him again.

"Stop," I said. "Allen. That's enough."

Allen didn't stop.

He hit him again, sending the brother's skull ricocheting off the surface of the table like a rubber ball.

"Allen. I said stop."

Allen froze with his fist cocked back, staring at me with what looked like pure, unvarnished hatred.

"You want to help this pretender?" Allen asked. "Motherfucker acts like he's one of us so he can murder our people in front of us, and now he's supposed to get mercy?"

"No," I replied. "Not mercy. I just want to talk to him first."

• • •

Robert was the light-skinned brother's name; I'd pulled it from the driver's license in his wallet.

Robert Holloway, Jr. from Tallahassee, Florida.

Five-foot-ten, one hundred eighty pounds. Clean-cut hair, nice-looking face (before the beating). Twenty-six years old.

I brought Robert back to the ranger's outpost, laid his body down on one of the extra cots, and untied his restraints. He was fading in and out of consciousness, murmuring incoherently. Every once in a while, he reached out clumsily and swatted at the air above him as though trying to put out an invisible fire. I sat down on the cot next to his and put a hand on his shoulder.

"Robert," I said. "I need you to stay awake, now. I'm serious. Stay awake."

His eyes opened—they looked like thin black lines scrawled onto the surfaces of two purple balloons.

"Can you hear me?" I asked.

He nodded his head almost imperceptibly.

"Good. You don't have to speak, Robert. Just nod your head for yes. And for no, you can just stay still. Does that sound okay?"

Robert nodded his head.

"Good," I said. "First question. Did you actually do what they say you did? Did you put some kind of explosive in one of our vehicles? It's okay to tell me, Robert—I just want to know the truth."

He nodded, then tried to open his mouth.

"Shh. It's okay," I said. "Don't try to talk. I know you didn't mean to hurt anyone. Is that what you want to tell me? That you weren't trying to hurt anyone?"

Robert nodded.

"I understand—and I believe you. The bomb was meant to be a message, that's all. No one was supposed to get injured. But something went wrong, and I understand that. So let's move past it, okay?"

He nodded.

"Good," I said. "Now, I need to know more about the plan, Robert. I need to know if you did this on your own or if you had help. And I need to know whose idea it was. If it was yours or someone else's. So let's start there—was this your idea, Robert? To send us a message?"

He didn't move.

I waited, giving him time to respond. But he stayed completely still.

"So the answer is no?" I asked.

Robert nodded.

"Was it someone from EAST?"

His eyes slowly drifted closed.

"Robert," I said, shaking his shoulder gently. "Stay awake. Did someone from EAST tell you to do this, yes or no?"

He opened his eyes and nodded.

"Good. Good job, Robert. You're almost there," I said. "I'm

going to get you some water now, and when I come back, I'll ask one more question and then you'll be done. Does water sound good to you right now?"

Robert nodded.

"Okay. I'll be right back."

I went to the refrigerator in the kitchen and pulled out a bottle of water, twisted off the cap and took a long drink, holding the water in my mouth as I stared at the broken man lying on the cot. His ruined face, his battered body. Closing my eyes, I asked God to forgive me for what I was about to do, and as I prayed for my forgiveness I wondered, as I always had: does feeling remorse beforehand mean anything at all if it doesn't stop you from committing the sin?

I opened my eyes, set the half-empty bottle down on a nearby countertop, went back into the fridge, and pulled out one of the glass vials of fentanyl citrate from a shelf in the door. *Injection, USP*, the label read. *Warning: May be habit-forming.* I broke the seal on the vial and paused, thinking about the implications of what I was planning—to dose a human being with enough horse tranquilizer to put him to sleep for good. For me, it wasn't a question of whether he deserved it. He did, at least in my mind. The question was: should I?

Should I be the one to take this deserving man's life?

The answer wasn't clear to me.

I had to think about it for a while before coming to a decision.

I took the vial and emptied the clear liquid into the open water bottle, then brought the mixture back to the cot, swirling the bottle gently.

Robert tried to sit up.

"Don't. It's okay," I said. "Let me help you."

Cradling his head in the crook of one arm, I brought the bottle to his lips and helped him drink. Only the smallest sip, though, nothing more than that. Not yet.

"Okay, Robert. Last question, and then you can have the rest of it."

He nodded. I could hear the sound of his breath wheezing in

and out of his lungs.

"I need to know if there are more of you," I said quietly. "Hiding in Mose, I mean. Did EAST send other people like you? To hurt the town somehow?"

Robert nodded faintly.

"And can you tell me their names? What they look like? Anything about them?"

He didn't move.

"Robert. I need you to tell me something about them. At least tell me how many there are. Do you know how many people they sent?"

Robert was motionless, staring toward the ceiling. If it weren't for the slow rise and fall of his chest, I would have thought that he'd passed on.

The truth was that he didn't have any answers. For some reason, I believed that. Which meant that I would need to find the answers to my questions somewhere else.

"Okay, Robert," I said, nodding. "Okay. I believe you."

I brought the water bottle to his lips.

"It's over now, okay? Just drink. You did good, Robert. Thank you."

I tilted the bottle upward, watching as the liquid shifted and slid toward the opening.

But then I stopped myself.

I lowered the bottle before he had a chance to drink.

• • •

I brought Robert back to the Baraza House and handed him over to Dare and Tressie. Without a word of explanation, I left Mose and sped toward the boundary zone.

Night had fallen, but I knew that I'd find members of EAST camped out just outside the exclusion area—most of them seemed to stay there around the clock. The only question in my mind was whether I could find the right member: the one who could tell me who the infiltrators were, how I could find them, or at the very least, what they planned to do next.

As I approached the boundary zone, I scanned the ground from the air, but I couldn't make out much detail. The entire area—from one end of the trampled-down, trash-strewn lot to the other—was dark and desolate. Over the past few months, most of the equipment had been packed up, the floodlights had been taken down, and the crowds had dwindled. Journalists, law enforcement officers, rubberneckers—every group had largely faded away with one notable exception. The protestors.

The number of protestors had grown over time. Dramatically. Ever since the idea of Fort Mose (and its controversial spokesperson, yours truly) had begun to go mainstream, the ranks of white supremacists and environmental activists in the boundary zone had swelled.

Each group viewed Mose as a threat for its own particular reason: white supremacists saw the emergence of a permanent, legalized, Black-owned territory deep in the heart of the South; while environmentalists saw the permanent loss of formerly protected lands, a bitter end to their hopes that the forest might return one day, given enough time. (The fact that a bunch of uppity negroes had been responsible for the damage didn't seem to help.) The two groups of protestors had converged into a (perhaps) unlikely alliance, not based on ideology necessarily, but based on their agreed-upon end goal. The eradication of Fort Mose. It was no secret. Both groups openly discussed the idea of destroying the town on social media almost daily.

Wrapped in Bel, I made my descent and touched down onto the soil on the other side of a group of soldiers in camouflage uniforms. National Guardsmen. Young men, probably not much older than I was. The police had refused to provide security at the perimeter of the exclusion zone (citing my treatment of our former hostages as the reason why); instead, members of the Guard had been posted at regular intervals along the imaginary line where the dome used to stand. This particular group didn't look to be guarding anything, though; they were seated on a tarp, immersed in a heated card game, arguing over whether a particular player had tossed the right ante amount into the pot.

Just past the guards, the largest group of protestors had set up camp. Hundreds of men and women scattered across countless makeshift sites. Talking amongst themselves, staring at their phones. Sleeping, using drugs, drinking beer. Typing on laptop computers, playing music on guitars. Fucking each other like animals in plain sight or inside nylon tents (you could hear them *and* see the tents moving). It didn't take long to pick out members of EAST—the coordinated outfits helped a lot—but I didn't see Elijah or Harmony among them. Just a jumble of dirty, hippie-looking white people in matching black t-shirts. I considered giving up the search and choosing an EAST member at random for questioning (all of them were complicit, as far as I was concerned), but I decided against it. I kept on looking for the head of the snake. Elijah and Harmony were the ones most likely to have the information I needed, and they were also the ones I wanted to punish most for what had happened back at Fort Mose.

I walked through the camp, searching. Studying face after face in the darkness. But after a while it became clear that my strategy wasn't working.

Eventually, I decided that I needed to ditch the subtle approach.

"Harmony," I shouted. "Harmonic Arris Windswept Mackenzie-Fucking-Jones."

The people around me nearly jumped out of their skin, searching in vain for the owner of the voice they'd just heard coming from the ether.

I waited, continuing to scan the crowd.

Before long, I saw her.

She was at the far end of the campground. Topless, crawling out of a red tent, her blonde hair loose around her shoulders. If I hadn't known better, I would have said the bitch was smiling, as though she was genuinely looking forward to seeing me again.

I didn't hesitate.

Shedding Bel like a snakeskin, I hurled myself in the direction of the tent, taking flight, my arms spread wide and my mouth wide open.

• • •

"I was worried we'd never be together again," Harmony said, smiling. "Especially not in a tent like this."

She was lying face-up on a foam bedroll, unable to move from the neck down. Covered by a blanket, hands pinned to her sides. I had chased some buck-naked, dirty-ass white boy out of there earlier, so now we were alone, the two of us.

I sat in the corner of the tent nearest to her head, knees to my chest. I hadn't spoken a word since I'd shouted her name outside.

"Tally," she said. "You don't have to hold me down. I'm not going anywhere."

I didn't respond.

Now that I had found her, I wasn't sure what to do next.

"Look, Tallah," she said. She sounded drunk. "You and me? We've got some issues—I know that. You fucked things up. I fucked things up. We all fucked things up. But that doesn't mean we can't work things out."

"I fucked up? And how did I do that, exactly?"

Harmony's brow furrowed. "Um. Maybe that part where you ran away and ripped out a national forest? Mass murder of plant life? Those don't seem like big wins to me."

"They aren't. But you don't understand why I did those things."

"I don't give a shit why," Harmony said. "I only care that you fix it."

"Fix it? How am I supposed to do that?"

"With your—whatever it is. Your black voodoo magic. Make

things how they were before."

"It doesn't work like that, Harmony," I said. "I can't grant wishes."

"Well, you better start granting them."

I stared at her.

This bitch seriously must have lost her mind.

"I swear, Harm. On my mom. You need to watch who the fuck you're trying to threaten with all that 'you better' shit. You don't get to tell me what I better or better not do."

"Sorry. I'm just saying. You need to figure it out."

"And I told you—I can't. And even if I could put everything back the way it was, I wouldn't."

Harmony didn't respond. Her expression reminded me of a child who'd just learned that her parents were divorcing.

"Tell me about EAST," I said. "And none of your stupid nonsense, either, Harmony. I want the truth."

"It's just a group. That's all. 'Leaderless resistance on behalf of the environment'—that's what we call it. We all believe in the same kinds of things. It's like a family."

"And how about the drug dealing? Is that family too?"

Harmony hesitated.

"What," I said, "you didn't think I remembered your weed-dipped-in-formaldehyde game?"

"Selling drugs is only to bring in money that goes to pay for EAST business. It's not the point."

"So what is the point, exactly?" I asked.

"What do you mean?"

"I mean what do you assholes actually do?"

"I don't know," she said. "Whatever we have to, I guess."

"Like hurting people?"

"What? No. Hell, no."

"I don't believe you."

"Well, I don't give a fuck what you believe," Harmony said. "You need to let me go. Seriously, Tallah. Let go of me. It's claustrophobic."

"I will. Once you tell me who else you sent into Mose. Besides Robert Holloway. Who else did you send?"

Harmony started struggling against her invisible bonds, thrashing her head from side to side.

"Harmony," I said sharply. "Tell me who else you've got hiding in Mose."

"I don't know what the hell you're talking about, Tallah."

"I don't believe you."

"Well fuck you, then, bitch. That's all I have to say."

My anger flared up; it was like a gas burner igniting.

"No. That's not all," I said. "You're going to talk until I tell you to stop."

I closed my eyes.

"Tallah. Please don't," Harmony said. Her voice was quiet, but piercingly clear—she didn't sound intoxicated anymore.

I ignored her.

Focusing my energy, I envisioned the bones resting beneath her pale skin. Not all of them—I chose the bones of her feet for some reason. The human foot contains twenty-six bones, thirty-three joints, and more than a hundred tendons, ligaments, and muscles. I made the decision to target the phalanges—the bones of her toes.

I slowly separated the bones from one another, drawing them apart a millimeter at a time. Not enough to injure her. Just enough to make her feel it.

I steadied her tongue and clamped her mouth closed before she had a chance to scream.

I worked on Harmony for a long time.

Asking a question—delivering a dose of pain. Asking the same question again, in a different way—delivering another dose of pain, in the same way. Repeating the cycle over and over.

She never told me a single useful thing.

Eventually I'd had enough; I left her in the tent, sobbing and curled in the fetal position, trembling. I didn't care. I needed to get back to Fort Mose and root out the infiltrators on my own before it was too late.

• • •

By the time I made it back to Mose, something had broken in me.

I had lost all connection. My mind had been reduced to a closed circuit, a looping path along which only one thought, one emotion, flowed.

I went on a rampage.

Anyone I'd ever suspected of a misdeed, anyone I'd ever profiled, anyone I'd ever spied on—I scoured the town until I found every single brother and sister I'd ever distrusted and, one by one, I interrogated them like a group of enemy combatants. Torturing each one without mercy, same as I had with Harmony. Throughout the night, I swept through the town like a wildfire, snatching people from the streets, from their homes, from their beds, and burning their psyches to the ground, reducing their spirits to little more than ash. Driven by unbridled rage and a fear of the unknown, I began abducting people I had never seen before, random strangers I came across in town who struck me as untrustworthy or treacherous for any reason whatsoever, dragging them into pitch-black alleyways between buildings and subjecting them to ruthless, bone-shifting torment. Demanding information, and disbelieving absolutely everything I was told.

I learned nothing.

No one confessed to anything that felt truthful, no one could tell me a single thing about The EAST that I hadn't already known (most had never even heard of the group), and no one was willing or able to point the finger at anyone else in town who might know something of interest. By the time I was through, I was no closer to finding the phantom infiltrators than I had been when I'd started. All that I had accomplished was to turn myself into a savage. A living, breathing devil.

• • •

"Lil Sis?"

I looked up.

It was Dare, standing in the doorway to the ranger's outpost. The glasses were gone, and someone had braided his hair into zigzagging cornrows like a beautiful storm of lightning strikes. I almost hadn't recognized him.

"Hey," I said.

I was sitting on the floor in the far corner near the bathroom door. I'd been drinking something—a mint-flavored liquor—straight from the bottle for the past hour and a half.

"All right if I come in?" Dare asked.

I shrugged by way of a response.

He closed the door, walked over to the fridge, and browsed for a minute before pulling out a can of soda.

"Okay if we talk?" he asked.

I nodded.

Dare popped open the soda can and took a long pull, grimacing when he was through. "I need to quit these, you know? My teeth, my skin, my gut." He rubbed his stomach. "Getting too old for this, man. I'm telling you."

"What do you want, Dare?"

He hesitated. Keeping his eyes on the floor, he took another pull from the can.

"Dare," I said. "Come on. Tell me whatever you need to tell me."

"I just need to talk to you, Lil Sis. All right? About everything. So, how about we start with that man Allen beat half to death on the table. Robert Holiday."

"Holloway."

"Right. Holloway," Dare said. "So while you were gone, we figured out who he is. Who he works for."

"I already know who he works for."

"No, Sis. You don't know. That's what I'm trying to tell you." Dare paused, drank from the can, and sighed, scratching his chin through the thick beard growth. "You brought Holloway back to the Baraza House, right? Well, once we got him back on the table, he started getting talkative and shit—I mean, this fool was running his mouth like he'd lost his mind. So he's going on and on, talking about how he's a federal agent, and how sorry we're all gonna be for holding him prisoner, and what his partners on the force have got planned for us. Just going off, right? It was like he was drunk off his ass or high as a kite or something. So at first we're all dismissive, thinking it's just chatter, but then Tressie decides to look into it, calls a few contacts, and sure enough: this asshole is telling the truth. Holloway doesn't give a shit about the forests and trees and animals and all that. He's not with any protest movement. He's undercover law enforcement. A straight-up cop that they planted in here to eat us like cancer from the inside out."

I stared at him. I couldn't believe what I was hearing.

Robert was a cop?

"That's bullshit," I said. "He told us himself that he was an activist."

"Yeah, he did—he told us a lot of shit. But he was lying."

"How do you know that?"

"Don't worry about it," Dare said. "It's not your problem anymore."

"No, Dare. Tell me how you know."

He sighed and took another sip. "Like I said: he was volunteering all this shit. You understand? Telling us all kinds of details—personal details. Things about a man's life that nobody would want anybody else to know. It was like something in this fool's brain had snapped. Real talk."

"What about others?" I asked.

Dare looked at me. "Others?"

"Others. Other cops. He can't be in Mose all by himself, right?"

"Look. Holloway told us he was working alone, and we believe him. But it doesn't matter now, Sis—you don't need to worry about it anymore."

"But what are we going to do with him?"

"I said don't worry."

"What the hell, Dare? Why not?"

"Because we got this. Okay? We'll take care of it, Sis. Mose is in good hands now. You need to take a break from everything. Go somewhere. Relax."

I stared at him.

"So now you're trying to tell me to leave?"

"No. You need to take a break. That's all."

"But you're saying I have to go. To take my break someplace else."

Dare shrugged. "I'm sorry. Look, everybody here understands that Fort Mose couldn't have started without you, but you also need to understand something—you can't do the kind of things you did tonight and be a part of what we're building here. You just can't. And it wasn't just about tonight, either. People are legit scared of what you're all about, Sis. I'm just being real with you right now. We've been watching you turn into everything we're trying to get away from."

doing for myself

I left Fort Mose behind.

No one could have forced me to go, but I had far too much pride to stay in a place where I wasn't wanted. So I packed up what little I owned and disappeared, headed back to Tallahassee. I didn't even say goodbye to anyone. On my way out, I stopped by Jabari's grave, kissed my fingertips, and tapped the stone. That was it—I was all the way gone after that.

For a while, I stayed in The Alhambra on the south side, the same motel where we'd stayed the last time. Maybe I was looking for familiarity, maybe I was hoping against hope that I would run into Harmony, or maybe both. It didn't matter either way, though; I never saw a single sign of her, and the familiarity of the room didn't make it any less solitary. But the place was safe, less filthy than most, and the manager left me alone (I wore shades and a hoodie so he wouldn't recognize me at check-in). All in all, the place worked fine.

In the beginning I spent almost all of my time alone, lying on the bed, watching TV and ruminating over the mistakes I'd made during my time in Mose, especially at the end. I had inflicted pain on innocent sisters and brothers with abandon. Shamelessly. And for no good reason—I had been wrong about absolutely everything, making accusations against the wrong people, trying to extract information that hadn't even existed.

And Harmony.

I had done the same to her.

• • •

I went back to living my life as a ghost.

Before I set foot outside the motel room, I wrapped myself in Bel and became invisible. Stalking the streets like a wraith somewhere in Purgatory. Slipping into stores and stealing products from the shelves; jumping the counter and snatching bills out of the cash drawer at a bank branch; following strangers into their homes and watching them live actual lives with real relationships, normal routines, and simple problems like faulty plumbing, stock options that haven't vested yet, sons who never come home on time, and a Check Engine warning light on the dashboard that won't turn off.

• • •

A few months before my nineteenth birthday, I came down with something. A flu virus, maybe. Something really hard to shake.

It took me a long time, but when I finally started feeling well again, I remember trying to use my abilities for something simple— summoning Bel from a pocket in my jeans, hanging over the back of a chair—and being unable to do it. My powers had left me, seemingly overnight.

Panicked, I tried everything. Herbal remedies to aid potency, veganism, exercise, bed rest. Red meat. Meditation, visualization. More time indoors, more time outdoors. Anything I could think of. I even called a sports psychologist and booked a month's worth of phone sessions, posing as a collegiate athlete who'd somehow lost her edge, her spark, her ability to concentrate. But nothing I did helped— it was like I was irreparably broken.

Over time, my abilities gradually returned, seemingly on their own. But they were never the same as they used to be. My power became diluted, weakened, like the sunlight during winter—pale and faded. I still shined, but my shine had become oblique and indirect. It didn't blaze eternal anymore.

From that point on, I had to be mindful, to budget my power. To use it sparingly, conscientiously, and to allow myself recovery time afterward. Always making sure that I kept something extra in reserves, for a rainy day. Gone were the carefree days when I would use my abilities for everything imaginable—for traveling by air, for filling a glass of tap water, for killing time by making cockroaches march in formation, for making myself permanently invisible to the world. I had to be more cautious now. I had to become him.

• • •

I gradually rejoined the rest of humanity.

As part of the process, I began experimenting with new identities, using gravity to change my facial features until I no longer recognized myself in a mirror. Doing the same as my father had done.

During this period, Gabriela "Gabby" Wyse was born. Prettier than I was (her features were higher and smoother), slightly taller than I was (her spine was stretched like an astronaut's), thinner than I was (her waist was cinched up), and kinder than I was (her tolerance for people's bullshit was higher). Everything about her was fraudulent as hell, but it was still liberating somehow. Like faking your own death and starting over under an assumed name. Using a contact I'd met during my time living in Fort Mose, I managed to purchase a set of passable identification documents: a driver's license, birth certificate, and Social Security card. With my new identity in place, I practiced being human again: running to the corner store for bread, politely chatting with strangers at bus stops, and going on simple walks through the neighborhood surrounding the motel, letting the light fall on my skin.

• • •

When I was twenty, I earned my GED certificate.

I had always considered myself reasonably smart, but I hadn't realized until I'd gotten older that I actually cared about getting a piece of paper that showed it. The certificate didn't really prove shit, of course; I wasn't any different afterward. All it demonstrated was that I had achieved General Educational Development (which hardly sounded like something to crow about). And on top of that, it wasn't even in my name—little miss Gabby had earned it. But it still mattered to the real me.

GED in hand, I enrolled at Tallahassee Community College in the Journalism department, and after two years' worth of classes, I transferred to Florida State for another two years' worth. During that time, I never lived on campus, preferring to live alone in a one-room studio apartment on the southeast end of the city, and I didn't make any lasting friends to speak of, but still, those years were some of the best I'd ever had. I loved going to class, my job as a copy editor at the *Tallahassee Democrat* newspaper, and the fact that I didn't have to use my abilities in order to feel safe in the world. In fact, as a student, I barely used my powers for anything at all.

• • •

In the years that followed, I kept up with the progress of Fort Mose online.

My own newspaper, the *Democrat*, reported on it from time to time—*Emancipation or Extortion: The Fight Over the Future of North Florida and the Nation* was the running headline. Our editorial board had even taken an official position on the impending vote. They were encouraging the State Legislature and United States Congress to vote No on Mose. To do otherwise would set too dangerous a precedent for the rest of the country, they argued.

In the meantime, as the debate raged on, Fort Mose was busy transforming itself into a proper city, completely funded by private donations from individuals and corporations sympathetic to the cause (or eager to profit from the outcome). With a constant infusion of outside capital, Mose adapted and evolved at a frenetic pace, adding improvements seemingly by the hour, as though preparing for a looming storm or an imminent invasion. Almost overnight, Mose had built asphalt roads, concrete sidewalks, freestanding buildings, municipal-level utilities. Its own business district. Its own internal transit program with a fleet of shuttle vans. Its own community policing service, fire department, and burgeoning school system. Satellite medical clinics. Churches. Universal internet via high-altitude balloons hovering in the stratosphere.

Residents had gradually returned to work, finding jobs either inside or outside the city limits. Jobs as construction foremen, physicians, postal workers, scientists, pilots, hair dressers, store owners—whatever they did before coming to live in the wilderness. Seemingly every day, farmland was being converted to apartment-style housing in order to accommodate a steady flow of new arrivals. A parcel of twenty thousand acres had been turned over to the Apalachee Nation, the original inhabitants of the area; otherwise, the city continued to expand its reach into every corner of the land I'd cleared years earlier.

As the city's infrastructure had matured, the government of Mose had formalized in parallel. Tressie had been elected to the office of mayor, responsible for overseeing day-to-day operations, while Cory Booker, former United States Senator from New Jersey, agreed to serve as governor ex officio, negotiating with members of the federal government on Mose's behalf, hammering out the details of a potential treaty agreement behind the scenes.

When the referendum was finally called and the votes were cast and tallied, the result was clear. Far from unanimous, but unequivocal. The motion passed in both legislatures, state and federal.

Fort Mose was free.

• • •

I didn't set foot in the city again until I was thirty.

When I finally returned, it wasn't under the guise of Gabby; I returned as myself—with my own face and my own body, flaws and all. You weren't going to catch me walking down Tallah K. Williams Drive as anybody else.

As far as I could tell, no one recognized me.

I walked through the city completely anonymously, overwhelmed by the soul-stirring sight of thousands upon thousands of brothers and sisters simply going about their daily business unhindered. Unafraid. Driving cars, walking the sidewalks, coming and going from shops. Creating things. Playing. These ordinary activities were made extraordinary by the fact that they were being done by a people rarely afforded the opportunity to be ordinary, to simply exist without apology or explanation or defense. Eventually, the sights and sounds were too much for me to take in all at once; I had to sit down. I went into a coffee shop, sat at a round pub-style table near the window, and stared out at the streets like a first-time visitor to a foreign nation, someplace vibrant and still developing in fits and starts, leaps and bounds. The view was breathtaking. I had never seen so many sisters and brothers in one place, at one time, in all my life.

I went to the old town square—now known as the Fort Mose City Center Plaza. What was once a field of tamped-down soil with a fire ring at its center had been transformed into an expansive, modernized community space. Twin concrete arches crossing the common; a long, rectangular reflecting pool with a surface so perfectly still that it looked like smoked glass; a wide expanse of patterned brickwork underfoot. At the center of the square was a modest park with black mangroves, cypress, and palms. It was early afternoon on a Saturday, and the plaza was filled with brothers and sisters and their families—walking leisurely through the square; seated on park benches made of wrought iron and stone; jogging or biking on a winding footpath; taking pictures of various markers and monuments that commemorated the history of the still-young city.

To my surprise, one of those monuments—situated at the far

end of the square—was the ranger's outpost. My former residence. Its trailer attachment had been removed, but the main structure looked almost the same as it had over a decade ago: the black solar panels on the metal roof, the oversized plastic water tank, the grey Yamaha generator, and the green woodcut sign above the door that read Ranger Outpost Area A-12. It looked far cleaner than it had ever looked when I'd lived there, but otherwise it was almost like coming home again.

The outpost had been placed on a raised dais and moved to a patch of grass next to Jabari's gravesite, which had been preserved as well.

A marble lectern rose out of the ground between them.

On the face of the lectern was a bronze plaque with an embossed relief. The finish was immaculate—no sign of the greenish patina that would eventually develop from exposure to the elements.

Dedicated to Our Founders, the plaque read.

I was kneeling in front of Jabari's headstone when I heard someone approaching from behind.

"Excuse me," a man's voice said.

I turned around, shielding my eyes from the sun.

I saw a dark-skinned brother with close-cropped hair and thick fashion frames covering his eyes. He looked older than I'd remembered (and the beard was gone), but there was no doubt in my mind: it was Dare. I could tell by his doe-eyes and his warm smile.

"Darius," I said, grinning.

"Damn. I thought that was you. I saw you walking, and it hit me right away. *Bam.* I was like, 'That's Lil Sis right there.' I swear to God."

I got to my feet. "You were right."

"I can't believe it's you," he said. "Tallah K. Williams, back in Mose. You look good."

"Thanks. You too."

He stared at me for a few beats, shaking his head, seemingly in disbelief. "Man, where the hell you been, girl?"

"I've been around. Here and there, you know? Working, going back to school, trying to hold it together."

"School for what?"

"Journalism. I finished up at FSU."

"Nice," Dare said, nodding. "We could use a few more journalists out there working. Real ones, you know? Getting the right story told the right way at the right time."

"I try to."

"I'll bet you succeed at it, knowing you," he said. "I'll bet you do things the right way."

"Thanks," I said.

There was a long silence.

It was strange, running into someone who I hadn't seen since I was a child—I suddenly felt as though I hadn't really grown up at all, as though everyone else had been allowed to mature and evolve while I'd stayed stuck in time as the same hardheaded brat I'd been in the past. And maybe I had. Maybe I wasn't as different from the old me as I thought I was.

"Look, Sis," Dare said. "I'm sorry about how things went down at the end."

I shook my head. "That was my fault. It was wrong what I did. I don't know—it was like I lost my mind for a while."

"You were a kid."

"That's not an excuse, though," I said. "It's just not. I could have stopped myself. I didn't."

Dare shrugged. "It was a crazy time, Sis—it's still crazy, matter of fact, just a different flavor of crazy. But we're all a little bit older and wiser now. A little greyer. So we got to move forward, right?"

I didn't respond.

There was another long silence.

Eventually Dare smiled.

"Tallah K. Williams," he said, shaking his head. "I still can't believe you're really here, you know? The legend in the flesh. History in the making. I sure as hell hope this means you're staying with us for a while."

"No. Just visiting."

"Oh, hell no you're not. Just visiting? Please. You need to get your stubborn self back here and stay with us. We need you."

"Thanks, Dare—really. But I'm good. I've got a place in the city."

"Bullshit," he said. "I got an apartment in Mose with your name on it. For free. I'm talking no rent, no light bill, no nothing. Who else can offer you a deal like that?"

I shrugged, grinning.

"Exactly," he said. "Look here. Seriously. Let us take care of Miss Tallah Williams for a little while. At least come with me to see everybody again, yeah? Trust me—these fools about to lose their damn minds when they see you again. They aren't gonna let you leave."

I thought about it for a little while.

"Yeah. Okay," I said.

The handle of the knife is beautiful in a way.

A warm, yellowish wood with a spiraling grain, like a fingerprint. Clean and smooth and polished. Gleaming metal insets along its length. At the top, nearest to the hilt, there is an etching of a black stag's skull with antlers branching to either side like wings. In my imagination, all of the gilding was completed by hand, by an accomplished artist in a workshop dedicated to this purpose.

On instinct, I wrap my fingers around the handle and start to pull. But then I remember—the bleeding. If I remove the blade from its home inside my abdomen, it will be like removing a dam from a river. Without the steel in place, my life will flood out of me in a matter of moments.

Still holding the handle, I collapse onto the pavement. My back pressed against a brick building.

Struggling to catch my breath, I try calling out for help, but I've lost the ability to form words. My arms and legs have gone numb; I can't move them. Across the street, on the opposite sidewalk, people are entering and exiting stores, talking amongst themselves, but no one seems to notice me.

My eyes gradually close. My head falls back against the brick.

• • •

It's raining lightly. More of a misting than a proper storm, like spray from an aerosol can.

I open my eyes. A grey, overcast sky stretches across my vision, end to end. No buildings, no trees, no movement. Just the heavens above me, as drab and impervious as a span of cement.

I'm lying on my back somewhere in a field. The grass underneath me is bristly like a bed of reeds, and I feel something—tiny beetles, I think—crawling between my fingers. Weaving over and under. I try to sit up, but I feel a sharp pain in my belly; it's so intense that I cry out. Looking down at my body with tears in my eyes, I see the handle of the knife protruding from my stomach, pointing straight up like a marker in the ground, like a claim over recently discovered territory.

I have no idea where I am or how I got here.

The only thing I know is that this isn't Fort Mose. It's not even the state of Florida. I can tell by the chill in the air and the leaden sky, more unforgiving than any I've ever seen or felt in the Sunshine State; I've been moved somewhere else. Either that, or I've passed on.

Something flies into my field of view. A dark shape, like a black bumblebee, the kind I used to be afraid of as a child, or maybe a small hummingbird.

It hovers directly over my face, turns a few tight circles, shakes off a shower of tiny droplets, and alights on my nose.

It's Bel.

Only I'm not in control of her movements; I'm not in control of anything right now. As far as I can tell, she is acting on her own, making decisions for herself.

Bel takes off into the air and flitters over my torso, pauses for a moment, and sends out a threadlike stream of dust from her body that coils and snakes its way toward me like the tendril of a strange vine. I watch, transfixed, as the stream of dust curls its way around the handle of the knife.

"No," I say weakly. "Bel. Don't."

She seems to hesitate.

"I'll die," I murmur. "If you take it out, I'll bleed even more."

The tendril continues snaking around the handle, winding around and around until the wood is completely obscured.

"Please," I whisper.

Bel begins to reel in the thread like a length of fishing line.

I hear a wet sucking sound and the knife comes loose. Blood pours from the open wound in gouts like water from a broken pipe.

The knife falls into the grass. Bel's tendril suddenly breaks loose from her body, disperses into a fine powder, and—as I watch in horror—wheels in circles like a swarm of bees and dives directly into the opening in my stomach. Forcing its way into my flesh. Almost immediately, I can feel Bel's presence inside of me as she disperses to every broken vessel, every ruptured membrane, and simultaneously seals them off. Binding to the damaged areas at what feels like a cellular level. Creating a new barrier between my blood and the outside world.

The pain slowly subsides.

I drag my blood-soaked shirt up to my ribcage and look down at my bare stomach—I see what looks like a two-inch, jet-black scar to the left of my bellybutton.

"Bel?" I whisper. The word comes out raw and cracked.

I try clearing my throat, but it sends me into a coughing jag. "Bel?"

All I can see is a blank sky stretched out above me; Bel is nowhere to be found.

Too weak to stand, I stay down on my back in the wet grass and try to slow my breathing down, to gather my strength for whatever's coming next.

Over time, the rainfall slows and eventually stops.

I can feel myself nodding off. My eyes drift closed.

Without warning, my body is lifted gently off the ground—only now I don't think it's my body anymore. I think it could be my soul. My soul leaving. Yes. I've lost too much blood, and the sensation I'm feeling at the moment is my soul's departure, its ascension. I'm almost certain that this is true, that I'm moving on to a better place, until something changes. I stop rising. Instead, I feel myself being pulled upright into a vertical position.

I open my eyes.

Bel is spread out directly in front of me, hovering at eye level like the diaphanous bell of a dark jellyfish. Billowing gently as though pulled by an unseen current. If I didn't know her—and for some inexplicable reason, I feel as though I do—I might be afraid.

"Hello, Bel," I say quietly.

It feels absurd, talking to her out loud like this, but it also feels right for some reason.

Bel continues to float silently; I'm not sure exactly what I was expecting, but nothing seems to change.

I look around and see that I'm in a field full of tall, reed-like grasses and low-slung rock formations covered in pale lichens—a broad bluff—overlooking the ocean. From here, I can see waves cresting and breaking against the black sea cliffs of the headlands offshore.

It feels familiar. Not this particular view exactly, but the complexion of the landscape.

I turn around.

I see a long, rust-red suspension bridge extending across a vast rocky inlet.

The Golden Gate Bridge.

I stare at Bel—she looks almost like a hole in the grey sky. "How did we get here?" I ask.

Nothing happens, which shouldn't be a surprise—what exactly was I expecting? A verbal reply?

"Can you understand me, Bel?" I ask gently. "Do my words mean anything to you?"

Bel continues to undulate slowly for a moment—completely mute and nearly motionless—before something changes: the entire surface of her body lightens and then darkens again in a flash, like a set of window blinds opening and closing in quick succession.

It happened so fast that I can't be sure it was even real.

"Was that a yes?" I ask. "Can you understand what I'm saying, Bel?"

It happens again—Bel blinks.

I can't believe it.

A side of me is ready to weep with gratitude—my friend, my Bel, has seemingly come to life—but another side is inexplicably hurt: how could this goddamn dust pile have kept something so important from me for all this time?

"How long, Bel?" I ask. "How long have you been able to do this? Acting on your own, I mean."

Bel doesn't move. The surface of her body stays the same: a monochromatic, dusky grey.

"Have you always been able to? The whole time?"

There's no response. Looking at her is like staring at an endlessly looping video clip.

"*Most* of the time?" I ask.

She blinks.

"So you've been able to do this for most of the time we've been together?"

She blinks again.

Unbelievable.

I desperately want to know why—why she didn't reveal herself sooner, why she waited until now—but I manage to stop myself from asking. Even if there were a way to pry the information out of her, there's no time to dwell on the past; I need to move forward.

"You brought me all the way here to San Francisco. Didn't you."

Bel blinks.

"But I don't understand, Bel—how did you know? I've never said a word about this, not to anyone. So how could you have possibly known I wanted to come here?"

There's no response. She just sits there like a stubborn stain.

I shake my head at my own foolishness. Look at me. Trying to coax an explanation from a floating cloud of dirt. I need to simplify my approach, to ask straightforward questions—only those that can be answered with a simple yes or no.

I consider it for a moment.

"Bel. Do you know what I'm thinking?" I point to my temple. "Are you able to understand my thoughts somehow?"

I stare at her, waiting.

She blinks.

• • •

Bel envelops me. Encasing my body in folds of dust. The process feels much different than it did in the past, back when I had control (or thought that I did). Covering myself with Bel used to feel as basic as putting on clothes or applying lotion to my skin, but now it feels like I'm being swallowed whole by another living thing. It feels almost aggressive.

Bel lifts me from the field and carries me across the bay—past Sausalito, past Tiburon, past Corte Madera—eventually descending toward a high cliff overlooking a peninsula full of drab buildings surrounded by chain-link and razor wire. San Quentin State Prison. The home of the largest death row block in the Western Hemisphere, with over seven hundred inmates awaiting lethal injection (I read it online)—including one inmate in particular, set to be executed around five hours from now.

Anthony Ray Jellison.

Barely over eighteen years old, Jellison was a young black man convicted of murder and sentenced to death for the fatal shootings of two Oakland police officers a couple of years ago, in spite of overwhelming evidence of his innocence. Witnesses recanted their testimonies, forensic evidence was inconclusive, and he had a compelling alibi—none of it made any difference. Not only was he found guilty, but they even decided to fast-track his execution (it was election season at the time). His case made national headlines—I heard about it all the way over in Florida—but it wasn't until yesterday that I saw a picture of Jellison's face for the first time.

He looked familiar.

I couldn't place his face in the moment, but he looked familiar enough that I took the time to check out his backstory—born in San Jose, lost his mother when he was just a toddler, father nowhere to be found—and that was when I realized.

It was Anthony. Leti Sanders' son. The last time I saw him, he was still a baby in her arms.

Bel sets me down on a rock outcropping, peels away from my body as though drawn off by a vacuum, and coalesces into a cloud that wafts and wavers in front of me. Rippling like a pond's surface. Rising and falling to an unknowable rhythm.

I peer over the cliff's edge at the prison complex below us. It's still hours away from midnight, but I can already see a cluster of media vans, camera crews, and demonstrators (both for and against the execution) gathered around the front entrance gates.

It's getting late.

If I'm going to do this, I need to act soon. But I also need to think.

Once I've made some semblance of a plan, I turn to Bel, drifting above my shoulder.

It's dark enough on top of the cliff that I'm having a difficult time making out her exact shape, locating her boundaries. She looks almost like a rippling patch of the dusk sky itself.

"Will you help me?" I ask.

Bel blinks. Even in the darkness, I can see her color shift.

"Thank you, Bel. There are two things I need from you. And I'm not sure if you need me to tell you what they are, or if you just know somehow, but I'm going to tell you anyway, just to be sure. I need you to make me invisible, and I need you to carry me down there. I'll have to figure out the rest on my own. Can you do that?"

She doesn't respond.

I wait for a bit. Maybe she needs time?

"Bel?"

Nothing—no response.

"Bel. I need you to make me invisible. Then I need you to drop us inside the front gates and keep me invisible while I figure out the rest. Can you do all of that for me?"

I study her surface, searching for any indication that she heard my request, but there's no obvious sign. It almost seems as though she's become even more monochromatic, if that's possible. By all appearances, Bel is flat-out refusing to do what I've asked.

I'm about to try again when I notice her moving, and at first I think it's her surface features changing, fashioning themselves into a new kind of signal for me to interpret, but then I realize—Bel is moving away from me. Leaving me behind. She passes over the cliff's edge and begins drifting downward toward the bluish lights of the prison complex below us.

"Bel," I hiss. "What are you doing?"

I try using my abilities to call her back, but nothing I do has any effect. She's beyond my control.

• • •

I wait, huddled against a black rock face at the top of the cliff in the darkness, shivering. Arms wrapped around my shins.

I've given myself a deadline—if I don't see Bel within the span of an hour, I'm going down there to collect Anthony myself. I trust Bel, but I can't risk running out of time.

After around forty-five minutes, I hear the deep drone of an alarm, almost like the air-raid siren from an old war movie, followed by a chorus of shouting. The sound of gunshots. A loudspeaker comes to life, and I hear a booming voice announcing that a lockdown is now in effect, ordering all inmates to get down on the ground and hold in place until told to do otherwise. I scramble to the edge of the cliff and peer over.

I see prison guards in dark blue uniforms barreling across the grounds with military-style rifles in their hands, entering and exiting buildings, rounding up a handful of inmates in orange jumpsuits, ushering civilians to safety. The demonstrators have scattered, fleeing in the direction of the parking lot, while three or four camera crews are busy jockeying for the best position to film the bedlam unfolding on the other side of the fence.

Soon I hear an isolated voice rising above the noise. A man's voice. It's not from the loudspeaker; it's coming from somewhere else.

The man is cursing, hurling profanity in long, sermon-like rants—it sounds like he's in the middle of dressing somebody down, cutting them to size. I hear him barking out orders, making vividly descriptive threats of physical violence, calling down the wrath of a higher power on someone, on everyone. Whoever this man is (Anthony?), he's not a part of the chaos below. He's much closer to me than that. In fact, the man's voice has grown so loud and so clear that I would swear he was directly in front of me, if it weren't for the fact that I can't see a thing—there's no sign of anyone. As far as I can tell, I'm completely alone.

I back away from the cliff's edge, keeping my guard up, standing at the ready.

Suddenly I'm not alone anymore.

As if birthed by the night itself, a man in a beige jumpsuit materializes out of thin air and falls heavily to the ground in front of me. Cursing, he scrambles to his feet and looks around wildly, his fists clenched and chest heaving. Thin as a greyhound. His long hair twisted into two thick braids. Bel appears nearby, a haze of dust—she immediately condenses into a perfect, chippy sphere, flits to my shoulder and hovers there, bobbing up and down almost expectantly.

Eventually the man's eyes settle on me.

"The fuck is this, bitch?" he says. "Why am I here?"

"Anthony, right?"

"Who's asking?"

"Is your name Anthony Ray Jellison or not?" I'm already starting to lose my patience.

"I don't know. Who the fuck are you?"

"Well, to start off—and you need to get this clear—I'm nobody's bitch, Anthony."

"Not yet, maybe."

"Not ever, Anthony."

I pause, taking a few deep breaths. So far, this isn't going at all how I imagined it would.

"I'm here to take you home," I say calmly. "If you want me to. Otherwise, you can go on back to where you came from."

Anthony turns toward the edge of the cliff, looks down, and spits. "Nah. I'm good. I ain't going back there."

"Then come with me. With us." I gesture toward Bel.

Anthony doesn't respond. He seems to be considering his options, which—as far as I can tell—couldn't possibly be more limited.

"Listen," I say. "I knew your mom for a little while. Back in San Jose, when you were just a baby. She was good to me."

"So?"

"So I'm here to help you, if you want it."

"I don't."

"You don't?"

"Bitch, you heard me," he says.

I can't believe this little hardheaded fool.

"You want to die, Anthony?" I ask.

He shrugs. "What be, will be."

"Well, *what be is about to be* if you don't come with us. Look around you."

"You need to mind your business."

"Anthony. I want you to listen to me. Just listen. I'm offering to take you out of state, to Florida. To Fort Mose. You've heard of it before—I know you have. You won't owe anybody anything if you decide to accept the offer. There's no debt to be paid. It's a chance for you to start a new life. That's all it is."

"You fucking deaf? I said no."

I stare at him in disbelief.

"Did you do what they say you did, Anthony?" I ask. "I want to know. Did you do it?"

Anthony shrugged. "What if I did?"

"Answer the fucking question. Did you or didn't you?"

"No," he says, almost spitting the word. "No. I didn't kill nobody—especially not cops. If I did, then I would say I did." He pauses, rubbing his face. When he drops his hands, I can see that his eyes are glistening wet. "I've done wrong, though, I'm not gonna lie about that. Over and over, I did shit that I'm not proud of. I'm not innocent."

"I'm not saying you are."

"Then what do you want with me?" he asks.

"I told you. Come with us. That's all I want."

"I can't."

"You can," I tell him. "There's no reason not to. Just come and see Mose for yourself."

He doesn't respond.

I watch as he rubs his face and stares at the sky for a while.

"Anthony?"

He looks at me. "Is Mose really how they say it is?" he asks. "Black owned, black run? Fists up, Black power and shit? All in one place?"

I smile. "Come and see."

Anthony nods. He glances up at the sky again, closes his eyes, and makes the sign of the cross—forehead, belly, shoulder, shoulder. He kisses his fingertips.

Before I have a chance to react, he turns around, sprints toward the edge of the cliff, and casts his body over.

Bel brings me back to Fort Mose.

Wearing the same blood-covered t-shirt with a hole in the belly, I stagger into my apartment, collapse onto the mattress, and stay there for the next week of my life—sleeping or sobbing uncontrollably or staring out the window at the sky, irrespective of the time of day. Dwelling on the past, troubled by an unknown, unwanted future.

I think about Anthony a lot as I lie there: the things he said, the things I said, and whether our conversation could have ended any differently. I think about his face. The image of him going over the cliff's edge. And how he used to be a small boy sitting on a carpet in a quiet room pulling socks out of a drawer.

Bel stays by my side the entire time, compressed into an even tighter sphere than usual, hovering over me and bustling around like a mother bird. Alternating between perching patiently on the bedpost and dancing across my field of view (presumably) as a distraction from my woes.

Nothing seems to help.

The truth is that Anthony was a total stranger to me; I know that. He was never mine to save. I had ignored his basic humanity and turned him into a symbol of something else, something too large for any single individual to embody—our ability as a people to succeed, even while holding the weight of someone else's crimes on our backs. Our capacity to build and rebuild in the face of crushing odds. I had conflated Anthony with the hopes and dreams of every sister and brother who has ever lived on the continent over the past four hundred years. And so, by failing him, I feel as though I've failed us all.

• • •

Over time, I force myself to leave the apartment and walk the streets of Mose during the daylight hours. But I do it as an apparition—invisible and soundless, slathered in a layer of greyish dust skimmed from the atmosphere. As for Bel, she refuses to participate. Tough love, I think. She wants me to be seen by the world, to shine through—she wants no part in serving as a mask, not anymore. Instead, she sets off on her own, traveling throughout the city.

I try to follow her sometimes.

Every once in a while, I catch a glimpse of her—circling a building near the plaza, hovering near a group of sisters chatting around a patio table in a sidewalk cafe, sweeping over the last remaining farmsteads in the northernmost part of Mose. Her destinations never seem accidental, but they have no obvious meaning either, as far as I can tell. All I know is that she has her own agenda, and she is busy carrying it out.

• • •

One morning I wake up and find Bel suspended above my face, like a spider at the end of a long web.

I check the clock.

Ten thirty-seven.

That's still early, at least for me.

"Go away," I murmur, waving my hand feebly.

I yawn, stretch, and pull the blankets up to my shoulders, settling back in.

Something doesn't feel right.

I open my eyes.

Bel is still there, frozen in place. She's like an extremely irritating cat waiting to be fed.

"What, Bel?" I stare at her. "What?"

She continues to hang there, motionless.

"Fine," I say, throwing off the blankets. "Fine. I'm up."

From the moment I'm on my feet, Bel is buzzing around and around my body like a tiny satellite, getting tangled in my clothes as I try to get dressed, knocking into my elbow while I'm brushing my teeth, blocking my view of the screen while I read the news.

"Seriously, Bel. Dang. I get it. You want to go somewhere, right?"

She blinks.

"So go, then." I point to the open window. "Nobody's stopping you. You don't need anybody's permission."

Bel suddenly stops moving and hangs in front of my eyes. Utterly motionless. It feels like I've been challenged to a staring contest.

"Okay, fine. You want me to come with you. Is that it?"

Bel begins to blink, rapid-fire—hundreds of blinks in a matter of seconds. She looks like a fucking strobe light at a dance hall.

"Damn, Bel. Okay. I don't need you to give me a seizure, thank you."

I try to finish getting ready, but halfway through breakfast Bel seems to run out of patience. She plants herself firmly in the small of my back and starts shoving me in the direction of the door.

With Bel snapping at my heels the entire way, I walk to the city center plaza. It's a Sunday. The vendors at the farmer's market have cordoned off most of the square, and the weather is clear and warm, so the plaza is humming. Brothers and sisters, young and old, all body types, everywhere.

I look at Bel.

"The plaza? This is where you wanted to go so bad?"

She doesn't respond.

"I'm sorry—it's fine, okay? I'm not mad. I'm just wondering why we're here. Did you need something?"

Bel ignores me.

It's strange; she seems different all of a sudden. Hanging listlessly in the air. No pep, no buoyancy. It's as though she's lost her energy, her edge—her budding sense of self—and become a lifeless object again. A collection of dust particles held together by gravity and nothing else.

"Bel?"

Without warning, she begins to rise slowly. Ascending, drifting with the air currents like a dropped balloon. Climbing past the kiosks of the farmer's market, past the summits of the concrete arches, past the rooftops of city buildings that surround us.

As she ascends, she breaks apart. Transforming into a diffuse cloud. The dust of her body spreads out across the sky above the plaza like a pall of smoke.

I stare, transfixed. Out of the corner of my eye, I see that every man, woman, and child on the plaza is doing the same, gawking at the heavens like witnesses to an alien invasion.

In the distance, seven dark tendrils rise from the farmlands in the north, black funnels of debris, snaking their way like twisters across the sky until they reach the centerpoint of the plaza, where they begin to weave together and merge into a single dark sphere—an orb made of the earth we once worked with our hands—spinning above our heads. It's like watching the accretion of a strange new planet.

The orb suddenly bursts without a sound.

There is a blinding flash of light.

When I open my eyes, I see that the entire sky is filled, from one horizon to the next, with countless drops of dust—smaller even than my Bel—descending slowly toward the ground below like a dark snowfall. Like fallout from a cataclysmic blast, drifting with the air currents.

As the tiny orbs approach the plaza their movements begin to change. They show signs of life. The orbs begin to flit and flutter. Vibrating like bees. They begin to choose direction and speed.

They begin to choose people.

Alighting on shoulders, nestling in outstretched palms. Gently coaxing the unwilling. Orbiting around bodies like protective wards.

about the author

Jonathan R. Miller lives in the Bay Area of California with his wife and daughter.

www.JonathanRMiller.com

Made in the USA
Coppell, TX
02 September 2020